Magelord
The Time of
Madness

Thomas K. Martin

ACE BOOKS, NEW YORK

This book is an Ace original edition,
and has never been previously published.

MAGELORD: THE TIME OF MADNESS

An Ace Book / published by arrangement with
the author

PRINTING HISTORY
Ace edition / June 1998

The Penguin Putnam Inc. World Wide Web site address is
http://www.penguinputnam.com

Check out the Ace Science Fiction/Fantasy
newsletter, and much more, at club PPI!

ISBN: 0-441-00533-0

ACE®
Ace Books are published by The Berkley Publishing Group,
a member of Penguin Putnam Inc.,
200 Madison Avenue, New York, NY 10016.
ACE and the "A" design are trademarks
belonging to Charter Communications, Inc.

PRINTED IN THE UNITED STATES OF AMERICA

10 9 8 7 6 5 4 3 2

THE MADNESS IS SPREADING LIKE FIRE . . .

The letter said *Mage and ungifted alike are being burned by the dozens in the Hunt. I have sent my son on this quest to establish a line of safe houses through the Wastes to you, Bjorn. If you are reading this, he has succeeded.*

That was impressive, Bjorn thought.

Soon, Ivanel added, *you will see the first groups of those who flee the Hunt arrive at your location. In all likelihood, they are already on their way to you. I hate to burden you with this duty, but their lives are now in your hands. I know of no other who can aid them better than you. My son Ian does not realize it, but in a way, you have already received your first refugee. I have enclosed another letter for him, instructing him to re-main with you until such a time as I send for him. I will not have this madness claim my only son. Please keep him safe for me.*

The fate of our people now lies in your capable hands. Until we meet again. Ivanel.

Bjorn set the letter aside, and wondered how many were on their way. Certainly more than he could ab-sorb . . . but he could not turn them away either . . .

Ace Books by Thomas K. Martin

A TWO-EDGED SWORD
A MATTER OF HONOR
A CALL TO ARMS
MAGELORD: THE AWAKENING
MAGELORD: THE TIME OF MADNESS

This book is dedicated to my wife and children and to all of those for whom the words ''Never again'' have special meaning.

Be sure to visit my official web page at:
http://ourworld.compuserve.com/homepages/tkmartin

Magelord
The Time of
Madness

CHAPTER

------- O͏ne ------------

"MOMMY!" HER DAUGHTER screamed as the wood of the door cracked beneath the heavy blows. She wrapped her free arm around her daughter, clutching her son of three summers in the other. Her older son, eight summers, cowered behind the fireplace, wielding the bronze poker like a sword. He was trying to be brave, but tears of fear streamed down his cheeks.

Gods, she thought, *please don't let them hurt my babies!*

Life had not been easy since her husband had passed away two winters ago. Still, her friends from the Circle had helped her, and her skill with a needle had kept food on their poor table. But now the Hunt had come for her.

The heavy wood of the door shattered on the next blow. Her scream echoed those of her two younger children. Angry men kicked away the remains of the door and stepped inside.

Her older son stepped out and swung his poker at the first of them. The man caught the pitiful weapon and ripped it out of the boy's grasp. He raised it overhead to smash the boy's skull. The boy cowered, frozen with fear.

"Nooo!" she screamed, releasing her youngest. With a speed she didn't know she possessed, she got between her son and his attacker, ramming the dagger from her belt into his stomach.

Rough hands grabbed her by the arms as the man she had just killed doubled over her knife. In horror, she recognized him as the man who had tried to rape her last spring. Now she knew who had turned the Hunt on her!

Someone bent her right arm back, forcing her to release

1

the dagger. She cried in pain as she felt the bones of her wrist snap. The dagger fell from her suddenly limp fingers.

Her crying daughter grabbed at her skirts as the townsmen carried her out. One of them struck the girl away before scooping her up to carry her outside as well.

"No!" the woman screamed. "Leave her alone! Please, she is only a child!"

The townsmen threw her face down into the muddy street. She struggled to her knees and looked up at the man before her. He was clad in bronze armor covered by a white tunic emblazoned with the symbol of Hrothgar. Her breath caught in her throat. Then she clutched at the man's tunic in desperation.

"My lord!" she cried. "Please, lord, I am innocent! I have done no . . ."

The back of a gauntleted hand smashed across her face. Blood flew from her lips as she was knocked back down into the mud.

"Lying whore!" the man spat. "The stench of your crime is an affront to the nostrils of pious men everywhere! Strip her!"

The woman shrieked as the townsmen lifted her from the mud and tore her clothing from her body. They carried her up a mound of wood and tied her to a stake in the center. Her screams subsided to bitter sobs.

With the woman's screams gone, the cries of her children filled Mathen's ears. He watched as the townsmen brought three children from the home. Two were boys, one about eight summers old, the other less than three. The one girl looked to be about six summers.

"My babies!" the woman shrieked anew. "In the name of Hrothgar, not my babies! Please—they have done nothing! They're just babies!"

"Lord Mathen?" one of the townsmen asked.

"The children of a mage are mages also," he replied. "Still, they need not suffer the flames alive. Cut their throats and throw them on the pyre at her feet."

"*Noooo!*" the woman screamed. "*Noooo!*"

Her screams continued as the bodies of the children were laid at her feet. Mathen took a torch from a nearby townsman and stepped forward to thrust it into the pyre.

The flames licked out from the torch, swiftly catching the wood of the pyre. Mathen stepped back as the flames engulfed the dead children and climbed toward the magess.

"Damn you!" she screamed at him. "Damn you to Hell, you monster!"

Then her curses turned to screams of agony as the flames reached her. Mathen watched until her screams fell silent and her body slumped against the ropes. One could not be too careful with a magess, after all.

"Burn the house," he ordered.

"But, lord," one of the townsmen objected, "there is much . . ."

"Burn it!" he shouted. "Trust me, you want no part of a mage's possessions. Or do you want the Hunt to come to you?"

"N-no, lord," the townsman replied.

"Then burn it."

Mathen watched as the townsmen put their torches to the woman's house. Soon the flames were licking high up into the sky, sending a column of smoke toward the heavens.

Ivanel glared at the man who stood next to him at the foot of Gavin's throne. He wore no beard, and his black hair was close cut in the manner of a priest in penance.

And penance was due, Ivanel felt. Mathen was responsible for the deaths of almost a score of Gavin's subjects accused of practicing the Forbidden Arts. The sad fact was that all of those accusations had been true. The man seemed to have an almost inhuman talent for sniffing out the magi.

"What evidence have you that this woman was a mage?" Ivanel demanded. "*What?*"

"I have the testimony of her neighbors . . ." Mathen began.

"Oh, I *see*," Ivanel interrupted. His voice was heavy with sarcasm. "So," he continued, "we now resort to burning seamstresses and slitting the throats of infants based on the word of ignorant *peasants*!"

"Uncle, calm yourself," Gavin said.

"*Calm* myself?" Ivanel replied. "Majesty, this man cut the throat of a boy less than three summers old and laid him at the feet of his mother before burning her alive!"

"What was this testimony, Mathen?" Gavin asked.

"The woman was observed departing her home late at night on evenings with no moon or on the evenings of the full moon," Mathen said.

"According to her fine, upstanding neighbors," Ivanel quipped.

"Uncle!" Gavin said in rebuke. "Allow the First Knight to present his evidence."

"She would leave roughly two hours before midnight and return a few hours before dawn," Mathen added. "These patterns are consistent with gatherings of the magi."

"Do you have the names of your so-called witnesses, priest?" Ivanel asked.

"I can produce such a list if you desire," Mathen replied.

"No need," Ivanel assured him. "I already have that list. Did you investigate these men?"

"No," Mathen replied, a trace of confusion in his voice. "They were not under suspicion."

"How unfortunate," Ivanel said. "Had you done so, four innocent lives might have been spared."

"What do you mean, uncle?" Gavin asked.

"The first man that Mathen questioned was Joren Karlson," Ivanel replied. "Last spring he was accused of attempting to force himself on the woman in question. There was insufficient evidence to hang him, so he merely spent the spring and summer in your majesty's dungeon."

Gavin glanced toward Mathen and then back to Ivanel. Ivanel was happy to note that the king's expression was not a pleasant one. Perhaps he was finally getting through to his nephew. *Gods, please let it be so!* he thought.

"All of the other men who testified against the seamstress," Ivanel continued, "were friends of his. Most of them have labored for your majesty under less than voluntary conditions at one time or another. Of course, I highly doubt that such fine, upstanding citizens would lie to a priest!"

"I presume you have records to support this," Gavin said.

"Yes, majesty," Ivanel said, handing a sheaf of parchment to the king. Gavin perused the documents.

"Mathen, how do you answer this?" Gavin asked.

"Majesty," Mathen replied, spreading his hands before him, "I do not base my investigations on testimony alone. I personally followed the woman after she was accused. On the next night of the full moon she departed and travelled secretly to a mage's circle. Sadly, my approach was detected and the vermin fled before my men could surround them."

"You saw this?" Gavin asked.

"Yes, majesty," Mathen confirmed. "I am familiar with how these infidels operate. The woman cloaked herself as soon as she believed herself alone. She was passed by the Guardians of the Circle when she arrived. All were cloaked. All fled at our approach."

"I have heard enough," Gavin said. "Have you any leads on her accomplices?"

"Not at this time," Mathen replied. "However, my investigations continue."

"Did you have to kill the children?" Ivanel asked. "Could they not have been taken as wards of the temple?"

"Your compassion does you credit, Lord Ivanel," Mathen said. "But blood will tell. Had we taken them into the temple, they would only corrupt the temple as well. If one leaves the roots of the weeds in the ground, they will sprout anew. I did spare them the fire. And I thank you for pointing out my oversight in not investigating my witnesses as well. Rest assured, I shall do so in the future."

"Thank you, Mathen," Gavin said. "You may depart us."

"Your majesty," Mathen replied, bowing before he left. The guards closed the gilded doors of the palace behind him.

"Pompous ass," Ivanel growled.

"He is necessary, uncle," Gavin replied.

"No, he is not!" Ivanel said. "Gavin, you and I know more about these people than anyone else. Those three children would not have grown to be mages if they were raised by the temple. We have become murderers of children."

"They *are* mages, uncle!" Gavin said. "They are born with the Power, and if we leave but one alive, we risk the return of the MageLords!"

"And how many innocents will die?"

"No innocents died here!" Gavin countered. "Mathen was sufficiently thorough despite the dubious nature of his witnesses."

"Majesty, panic is spreading throughout the kingdom!" Ivanel objected. "Most of the so-called mages being put to the fire are never investigated by the priests. Their own friends and neighbors put them to the stake. *Majesty, these are your people!* You are *sworn* to defend them!"

"I will hear no more of this!" Gavin said. "We must hunt these mages out!"

"I pray to Hrothgar that my brother will forgive you for what you have done to his kingdom," Ivanel said quietly. Gavin winced at his uncle's words. Ivanel knelt at the foot of the throne.

"I beg your leave, majesty," he said. "I must depart for Smithton soon."

"Uncle . . ." Gavin began. Ivanel waited, silently.

"You . . . may depart us," Gavin finally said.

Ivanel rose and turned to leave. It was apparent that Gavin was not willing to listen to reason. Ivanel had exhausted his last hope of that. It was time to seek other solutions.

Gavin stood staring out the window of his chambers onto the courtyard below. His uncle's parting words still burned in his heart. The worst part was that Ivanel was right—to an extent.

Panic *was* spreading throughout the kingdom. Gavin had little doubt that many who died truly were innocent—slain out of fear and superstition or, as Ivanel had suspected in the case of the seamstress, out of revenge under false charges. He could not allow these crimes to go unpunished any more than he could allow the temple to stop their search for the mages.

As Gavin watched, the workers below labored to repair the remaining damage from Valerian's battle with the great dragon, Arcalion. He was determined that no MageLord would ever again threaten his lands. The Sacred Hunt was the only means by which he had any hope of succeeding. He dared not stop it.

But it was not the Hunt to which his uncle objected, Gavin realized. It was the spreading panic. *That* he might be able to do something about.

"Guard!" he called. A guard opened the door to his chamber and stepped in.

"Yes, majesty?"

"Send me a scribe," Gavin ordered.

"Yes, majesty," the guard replied.

"Noo!" the woman screamed as the huge man beat her. Mathen clutched at the man, trying to pull him away. But he was just a child—the man was too big.

"Mommy!" he shrieked.

"No, Mathen," the woman screamed. "Run away!"

"Mommy!" he cried again. Again he tried to pull the man away. The man turned and struck him away effortlessly and then turned back to beating the woman.

"Stinking magess!" he shouted. "What have you done with my wife? Answer me!"

Little Mathen capped his hands over his ears but that wasn't enough to block the woman's screams or the sound of heavy fists slamming into flesh. He cowered back against the wall, pressing his hands over his ears as tightly as he could and screaming.

Finally, the woman's screams stopped and the man stepped away from her. Mathen opened his eyes and saw the woman's broken, bloody face.

"Mommy!" Mathen shouted, sitting up on his cot. For a moment, he looked around in panic, disoriented from the nightmare. The bedclothes of his cot were soaked with his own perspiration.

Shaking, he got up from the bed and knelt at the small prayer stand. The dream was always the same. The night his father had beaten his mother to death in front of him.

Only it had not been his mother, his father had explained when Mathen was older. Rather, it had been a magess who had killed his mother and used her foul art to take her form and her place.

Mathen's father, thinking his wife had taken a lover, had followed the magess to where she gathered with her foul kind beneath the full moon. There he had learned that the truth was even more terrible than that. His wife had been replaced with some foul creature of the Forbidden Arts.

He had returned home, grief-stricken. After several hours the magess had returned and Mathen's father had snapped. He beat the impostor to death with his bare hands. Mathen had been too young to understand that the woman his father had killed was not his mother, but he understood in time.

Even so, when the dream came, all memory of that understanding was gone. He was the child all over again, watching his mother die. Shakily, Mathen signed himself and bowed his head.

"Thank you, mighty Hrothgar," he began in prayer, "for sending this vision to remind me of my holy cause . . ."

Chapter

------- Two ------------

IVANEL RODE UP to the gates of Smithton just before sunset. It had been a hard two days' ride from Reykvid. With the spring rains it should have taken three, but Ivanel had pushed himself and his men mercilessly. Time was a precious commodity at the moment.

I'm getting too old for this, he thought. Forced marches in the rain made his entire body ache.

The guards at the city gate passed them with only a cursory challenge. Soon the hooves of their horses were clacking on rain-soaked cobblestones.

Like Reykvid, the city of Smithton still showed much damage from last year's war with Chief Valther. Throughout the city, the burned-out husks of buildings loomed at them from the darkening rain.

Reykvid had not fared well in that war. Ironically, had it not been for the MageLord Valerian, they would have lost. Of course, if not for Valerian there would have been no war in the first place.

The guards at the castle were more thorough, challenging them as they rode up and only allowing one rider, Ivanel, to approach.

"Your pardon, my lord," the captain said. "You may pass."

"Thank you, Wiegel," Ivanel replied. He and his escort rode through the outer wall into the courtyard.

The damage to the castle was almost completely repaired. New gates had been hung on the keep. Only a few feet missing from one section of the outer wall remained of the breach Valther's engines had made.

It was unfortunate that souls were not so easily mended. This fear of the MageLords that now gripped Gavin had spread throughout the land. Now, none were safe—gifted and ungifted alike.

Ivanel dismounted and allowed the pages to take his horse.

"Have a bath and dry clothing prepared for me," Ivanel ordered as he entered his hall.

"Yes, m'lord," Eva replied as she took his sodden cloak. "Have ye eaten, m'lord?"

"No, but I want my bath first."

"I'll have dinner waitin' for ye, m'lord," Eva replied.

"In my chambers," Ivanel added. "And have Ian join me at dinner."

"Yes, m'lord," Eva acknowledged.

Both dinner and his son were waiting for him when Ivanel finished his bath. It felt good to be warm and in dry clothes again. He was getting old.

"How was your journey, father?" Ian asked. Ivanel sat at the small table across from his son. Ian's hair was as red as Ivanel's had once been, but he had his mother's ice-blue eyes.

"Wet," Ivanel replied. "And disheartening."

"Disheartening?"

"The burnings continue," Ivanel explained.

"Oh," Ian replied.

Ivanel lifted a spoonful of stew to his mouth. Eva was an excellent cook. This stew had more than likely been cobbled together from the remains of the hall's dinner, but one could not tell that.

"The king will do nothing to stop them," Ivanel added, tearing a piece of bread from the steaming loaf between them. "In fact, if anything, he is encouraging them."

"Why?" Ian asked. Ivanel glanced up at his son as he chewed a mouthful of bread. Had Ivanel himself ever been so innocent? He shrugged.

"Why have the ungifted always killed us?" Ivanel

asked. "Fear. His experience with Valerian has filled him with terror. He is convinced that one of us will discover the Power of the MageLords."

"That's impossible," Ian stated.

"*Nothing* is impossible," Ivanel corrected. "But I agree, it is extremely unlikely."

"Yes, father," Ian replied. They ate in silence for a little while. Ian was more subdued after Ivanel's news. Finally, Ivanel set his spoon in his empty bowl and sat back. He felt almost human again now that he had a meal in him.

"There is something else I wanted to speak of with you," Ivanel told his son.

"What, father?"

"You have passed fifteen summers now," Ivanel said. "Soon it will be time for your Rite of Manhood." Ian smiled. Ivanel smiled in return—he remembered his own Rite.

"Unfortunately, no one here is qualified to perform it," Ivanel added.

"What about Eva?" Ian asked.

"She has the ability," Ivanel agreed, "but your Rite should be overseen by a man. I am without the Gift."

"I wish it could be you," Ian said.

"As do I, son. I am going to send you north, into the Wastes, to someone I know. You will also carry important letters for me."

"The Wastes!" Ian exclaimed. His eyes shone with a mixture of fear and excitement.

"Yes," Ivanel confirmed. "You will travel to Nalur's Ridge. Then you will continue your journey to Hunter's Glen and from there you will travel north and search for a lodge."

"A lodge?" Ian asked.

"Yes," Ivanel replied. "Once there you will ask to see Bjorn Rolfson."

"Bjorn!" Ian exclaimed again. "The one who defeated the MageLord?" Ivanel nodded.

"With whom shall I travel?" Ian asked.

"No one," Ivanel replied. "This journey is your test of manhood. You shall be equipped as a warrior and given a steed. This is your time of errantry—when you become a man."

"You will be carrying three sealed letters for me," Ivanel continued. "One you are to give to the Circle in Nalur's Ridge. The second you will give to the Circle in Hunter's Glen. The third is for Bjorn. This is your quest."

Ian swallowed. He had not expected this.

"I know the journey is long," Ivanel said. "And not without danger. But you are the only messenger I dare send. The only one of the Circle who will not be missed for such a long journey."

"Yes, father," Ian agreed. It was not unusual for a young warrior to be gone for a year or more during his errantry.

"Your time of errantry will be announced on the morrow," Ivanel said. "You will depart the next morning."

"Yes, father."

"Short of outright cowardice, there is only one way you can disappoint me, son," Ivanel added.

"How?"

"By not coming back alive," Ivanel replied.

Ian found it difficult to sleep that night. He had known this day would come—it came to every young warrior as he became a man. But to have it thrust upon him so suddenly had taken him unawares.

No doubt that was the case with most men, he supposed. One spent one's life anticipating this moment, and then it arrived when it was least expected.

The suddenness of it was not all that weighed on his mind, however. This message his father was sending with him to Bjorn almost certainly had bearing on the recent burnings. No doubts his father was asking for Bjorn's help. The fate of the magi was being placed in Ian's hands.

Part of him wanted to scream, "But I'm just a boy!" After tomorrow that would no longer be true. He could not remain a boy forever. This was the duty of a man.

Ian could only pray that he was worthy of his father's trust.

With difficulty, Ivanel penned the final words of his long letter to Bjorn. Sending his son away for the time of errantry was often the most difficult task a father ever performed. Sending him away possibly forever was worse.

Ivanel sealed the letter to Bjorn with a shorter letter to Ian within. Ian could not remain in Smithton or anywhere else in the kingdom during these times. Ivanel's own Power was nonexistent. Through some trick of fate, however, Ian had been blessed with more than any other of their tiny Circle.

Ian needed to complete his teachings in the ways of the Circle, but Ivanel would not risk him by having that training take place under the eye of the Hunt. He hoped that Bjorn would honor his request to keep Ian until this . . . madness had passed.

He was not overly concerned. Bjorn's sense of duty was stronger than that of many of the warriors and lords whom Ivanel knew. He would keep Ian and teach him, and he would find a way to help Ivanel save others from the burning.

If there was a way.

Mathen knelt before the prayer stand in his room. It was nine days before the next new moon. The delay gnawed at him—he was anxious to resume his search for the seamstress's accomplices.

They had gone to ground, however. A thorough search of the meeting site had turned up no evidence as to who might have been there.

Mathen had his suspects, however. Even now, he had agents watching the woman's known friends. No doubt some among them, if not all, were members of this foul coven. So far, none had done anything suspicious and none bore the Mark.

If only he could seize and question his chief suspects!

Mathen had no doubt that a few hours of torture would reveal the mages among them. Unfortunately, that would never be allowed. There would doubtless be some innocents among them as well and Gavin, upon Ivanel's insistence, would never tolerate that.

The king's recent edict, banning all executions by those outside the church and the nobility, demonstrated that. The pronouncement had been made the morning after Mathen's confrontation with Ivanel in the king's chambers. The penalty for disobeying the edict was death in the same manner as the victim. If Mathen seized and tortured suspects without proof, he had no doubt that Gavin would act against him.

Besides, such an action would only serve to alert the remaining mages to their danger. They would flee the area, and even Mathen would be hard pressed to track them down again. No, it was much better to wait and bring them all to justice.

"Hrothgar, grant me the patience to complete this holy quest," he prayed.

Ian sat at the warrior's table in his new armor. Breastplate, bracers and greaves of bronze over heavy leather. The sword that hung at his side was not a practice weapon, and neither was the dagger that accompanied it.

His lance, shield, helm and crossbow waited with the steed that had been presented to him before the feast. It was a fine chestnut mare. Ian had ridden her many times in training. Now she was his.

On the morrow he would depart for Reykvid. After he was presented to the king, he would embark on his time of errantry. Ian still could not believe it. Two days ago he had been a boy. Today he would be declared a man and would be sent away for at least a year with a man's duty laid on his shoulders. Ian lifted his goblet and took another drink. The wine calmed his nerves a little.

The tales that the other warriors related to him about their own times of errantry did nothing to calm those nerves, however. True, they were exciting. However, the thought of facing alone the dangers they described was a sobering one.

Another slab of beef was set before him. Ian's father had slaughtered three cows for tonight's feast. Twice that many kegs of wine had been tapped, and Ian was starting to feel a little giddy.

"Silence!" Ivanel's voice said over the din of the hall. After a moment all fell silent.

"It is with a father's pride, and a father's anxiousness, that I send my son forth on his time of errantry," Ivanel announced. "So, I offer a toast—to Sir Ian. May his courage and his sword see him through what lies ahead."

"To Sir Ian!" the hall echoed, rising to lift their goblets. Ian struggled to his feet, although his legs did not want to hold him. He had definitely had too much wine.

The rest of the warriors drained their goblets. Ian joined them—it would be unseemly to refuse his own toast. But this goblet would be his last tonight.

He set the empty goblet on the table, not noticing that it did not remain upright, or even on the table.

"Sir Ian, step forward!" Ivanel commanded.

Ian made his way unsteadily to the high table. Some few hands reached out to steady him on his way, and he heard a few muted chuckles as he passed. Ian felt his face flush— he was making a fool of himself! His father would be *furious*!

He looked nervously up to where his father stood waiting at the high table. Thank the gods, he did not see any anger there!

Ian did his best to stand upright before his father. He felt himself sway slightly.

"Kneel, Sir Ian," Ivanel commanded. Ian dropped to one knee—and kept going.

Ivanel looked down where his son lay before him and smiled. He drew his sword and touched his son's shoulder.

"In the name of Hrothgar I grant you the right to bear

arms and mete justice in all the lands of the Sword clan,''
he said. Ian did not stir.

"Tomorrow," he added. Laughter broke out through the
hall.

"It seems that Sir Ian has had enough feasting for one
night!'' he announced. There were a few chuckles.

"Let us hope he holds his sword better than he holds his
wine!'' There was more laughter.

"Sir Evan, Sir Alhric," Ivanel said once the laughter had
subsided, "see our young warrior to his chambers and rejoin us.''

"Yes, lord,'' the men replied. Smiling, they stepped forward and lifted young Ian by his arms, carrying him between them.

"Let the feast continue!'' Ivanel announced.

A hundred men with hammers were beating on the inside
of Ian's skull. He groaned and rolled away from the light
that burned through his eyelids.

"Good morning,'' his father's voice said. Ian opened his
eyes. That had been a mistake—the dimly lit room burned
his eyes and swayed eerily, making his stomach churn. He
closed them again and groaned.

" 'Twill pass,'' his father assured him.

"Have you been here all night?'' Ian asked, daring to
open his eyes again. The room swam less.

"No,'' Ivanel replied, "just since breakfast.'' At the
mention of food, Ian's stomach rebelled again. He groaned
and closed his eyes again.

"You were quite a sight last night,'' Ivanel added.

Last night? Ian thought. Then memory returned.

"Gods above!'' he shouted, sitting up. His head exploded and he fell back to the bed.

Oh, gods, he had made a fool of himself! Worse than
that, he had made a fool of his father. He would be fortunate if he were ever allowed to return to Smithton after
this!

"Father,'' he croaked, "I'm sorry . . .''

"It happens," Ivanel assured him. Ian was surprised to hear amusement rather than the stern anger he had expected. Surprised and relieved.

"Now you have learned the dangers of drink," Ivanel added.

Actually, Ian was still learning them. The men with the hammers were hard at work teaching them to him.

"What . . . happened?" he said.

"You passed out at my feet before I could knight you," Ivanel replied.

"Oh, gods."

"As I said, it happens."

"I have made a fool of myself!" Ian wailed. The men with the hammers struck harder.

"It could have been worse," Ivanel assured him.

"How?" Ian moaned. No doubt the entire castle was laughing at him by now. No wonder the errants stayed away so long. They were too embarrassed to return before at least a year had passed!

"You could have done what *I* did to my father," Ivanel replied. *His* father? Curiosity got the better of Ian. He sat up and opened his eyes.

"What?" he asked.

"I did *not* pass out," Ivanel explained.

"How is that worse?"

"When I knelt for my knighting, I vomited all over my father's feet. That is why I wore my old boots last night."

"Did they laugh at you?"

"They still do," Ivanel said. "In fact, I was reminded of that occurrence by several people shortly after you left us last night."

"How did you stand it?"

"Because it was funny," Ivanel explained. "You must learn to laugh at yourself, Ian. It is important for a chieftain. Of course, my father did make me wash his boots afterwards."

Ian laughed.

"See, I told you it was funny," Ivanel said. Ian laughed

harder, despite the increased pounding in his head.

"You should have seen me knighting you while you were lying unconscious at my feet last night," Ivanel said.

"You knighted me while I was . . ." Ian began.

". . . dead to the world," Ivanel finished. Ian fell back on the bed, laughing hysterically. Then he grabbed his head.

"Oh, gods, my head," he said, still laughing.

"Come on. Let us get you something for that before you go," Ivanel said.

It was almost midday by the time Ian left for Reykvid. He had managed to keep down a sizeable meal before he had left. It had been the last time he would taste Eva's cooking for some time.

Ian turned in the saddle and looked back. Smithton was almost lost in the distance. Part of him wanted to turn and ride back as hard as he could.

He turned away and gently nudged Maiden, his mare, in the ribs. There was a tug as the pack mule's reins pulled at his saddle before the stupid beast began following. Loud-mouth, as he had named the mule, was carrying extra lance heads and sleeves as well as a moon's ration of food.

Fortunately, the weather had cleared in the last two days. This trip would not be near so pleasant in the rain. Of course, it would almost certainly rain, if not snow, before his journey was complete. An oilcloth cloak and several tarpaulins had been packed on the mule for such weather.

The sound of barking drew his attention. Ian smiled. Hunter had found something in the tall grass beside the road. For the large hound, this was all nothing more than a lark—a chance to explore and flush out small game.

"Come on, Hunter!" Ian called. The dog looked up and then back down at whatever he had flushed. His black coat and brown muzzle made him easy to spot in the tall grass beside the road. Hunter barked twice more and then ran to catch up with Ian.

"Stay close, boy," he said. "I don't want to lose you before we get to Northguard."

Hunter smiled pantingly at him and immediately bounded away back into the tall grass. Ian laughed. That had done a lot of good. He could command the dog to follow at his side, but there was no need.

He looked back again. Smithton was now lost in the rolling hills. Something twinged inside his chest. He turned away and rode on, ignoring it.

CHAPTER
------- THREE ------------

IAN REINED HIS horse to a stop outside Reykvid at his first
sight of the palace. For a long time he sat astride his mount
and stared up at the palace. The keep alone was fully as
large as his father's entire castle, courtyards and outer wall
included.

Two concentric walls surrounded that immense keep. Ian
could see why Valther had raised an army twenty thousand
strong to assault that fortress. Nothing less would serve.
Even with all the damage caused by the battle not yet repaired, Reykvid was still the most formidable fortress he
had ever seen.

Most impressive, however, was the head of Arcalion
mounted over the main gate. The royal huntmaster had
done marvelous work in preserving it. The huge, smoked
glass eyes almost seemed to glow in the afternoon sun. The
black scales scintillated with myriad colors. Even in death
an aura of Power clung to the dragon's head.

Ian took a deep breath and exhaled it, releasing the
Power as he did so. His father had given him explicit instructions. He was to answer no Sign passed to him, and
he was to shed the Power so that his aura did not invite
the Sign. The dragon's aura faded from sight as his own
Power was released.

Reykvid was deep in the grip of the Hunt. During his
brief stay in the castle, Ian was to be as head-blind as the
rest of them.

Once he had finished releasing the Power, Ian roused his
courage and rode on toward the castle. For some reason,
he felt very alone.

• • •

"Your majesty," the guard announced as Gavin sat at court. "A young knight errant wishes to present himself to you before embarking on his quest."

"By all means!" Gavin replied. Anything for a reprieve from Sigmund's report on the castle stores. This would be a welcome break in the monotony.

"Show him in," King Gavin urged the guard.

"At once, majesty," the guard replied. He turned and opened the door to the throne room, stepping aside. A youth in bronze armor entered the throne room. Gavin rose to his feet in surprise at the identity of the errant. Murmurs of surprise followed Ian through the throne room.

"We greet our cousin, Ian Urqhart," Gavin said. Ian advanced to the foot of the throne and knelt on one knee. He drew his sword and proffered it, hilt first, to Gavin.

"Your majesty," he said. "I offer my sword in your service."

Gavin descended the steps of the throne and took the sword from Ian.

"We accept, cousin," he said. He touched Ian's shoulders, first the right and then the left.

"We grant you the right to bear arms and mete justice in all the lands we command," Gavin pronounced. "We charge you to settle disputes, defend our borders and protect our citizens."

A duty you yourself have forsaken, Ian thought bitterly.

"Arise, Sir Ian," Gavin finished. Ian rose, and Gavin reversed his sword and proffered its hilt back to him.

"Take up your sword and always wield it in our service," Gavin charged.

"I shall, your majesty," Ian swore. He rose, took his sword and resheathed it.

"We shall recess," Gavin informed the assembled court. "The royal court shall meet again after noon. Come, cousin. We have much to talk about."

• • • •

Gavin's temporary chambers were in a windowless room immediately off the throne room. Even here, one could not escape the unending sound of the workers repairing the castle walls.

The room was pleasantly furnished with tapestries and tables and comfortable chairs. Numerous oil lamps battled the gloom with only partial success. There was no fireplace.

A steward filled a goblet with wine and set it on the table to Ian's right. Then, bowing first to the king and then to Ian, he departed.

"How long has it been?" Gavin asked once the steward had left them. He sipped at his wine.

"A long time, majesty," Ian replied.

"There is no need to be formal," Gavin said. "We are alone here."

"Yes . . . Gavin," Ian replied.

"As I recall," Gavin noted, returning to the original subject, "you were still playing with wooden swords when I last saw you."

"And *you* were the errant," Ian added.

"That would have been four years ago," Gavin said. A sudden wave of melancholy overtook him.

"It has been a long four years," he said quietly. How could he have changed from the carefree youth he had been then into what he was today so quickly? There was an uncomfortable silence for a moment.

"Do you still have that god-awful pup?" Gavin suddenly asked. Ian startled at the sudden break in the silence and then laughed.

"Aye," he replied. "But Hunter is no pup any longer."

"Did he grow into those huge feet of his?"

"And then some," Ian confirmed. "His back reaches almost to my waist."

"Did you bring him with you?" Gavin asked.

"Yes," Ian replied. "He is in your kennels."

"My dogs may never be the same," Gavin said in mock horror, "by the time that brute gets through with them." Ian laughed.

"Seriously, he will be a good companion on your journey," Gavin added.

"Yes," Ian agreed. "That is what father said."

"How . . . is your father?" Gavin asked.

"Father is well," Ian replied, curiosity in his voice. "You saw him yourself but a few days ago, majesty."

"We parted . . . unpleasantly," Gavin said.

"Oh," Ian said. "I . . . am sorry."

"Did he speak of it?" Gavin asked.

"No," Ian lied. "Father is a private man." Gavin smiled.

"That he is," Gavin agreed. "And far wiser than I, I fear." There was another uncomfortable silence. Finally, the king broke the silence.

"Listen to me!" he said. "I sound like an old man mourning over his younger years! We will have a feast tonight to celebrate your new status."

"Your majesty is too kind," Ian replied.

"Nonsense!" Gavin said. " 'Tis not every day my cousin becomes a man. I will have Sigmund assign you quarters for the night. Unfortunately, they will be in one of the outer buildings. Space in the palace is extremely limited."

"So I have noticed," Ian said. "How are the repairs coming?"

"We had hoped to repair the roof over the second floor by winter," Gavin replied. "At this point, it does not look as though we are going to accomplish that."

"I could stay in town," Ian offered.

"Not while *I* am king!" Gavin said. "You shall sleep here before you depart tomorrow. Have you considered where you will travel?"

"Not really," Ian lied. "I was thinking about travelling toward the Wastes for a time."

"The Wastes can be a dangerous place, Ian," Gavin cautioned. "Take care."

"Yes, majesty," Ian replied.

"I must return to court and finish listening to Sigmund's

interminable report on the castle stores,'' Gavin said. ''Feel free to enjoy the garden and explore the palace. Just don't get in the way of the workmen.''

"Thank you, cousin," Ian said, grateful for the dismissal. He knelt before his king before rising to leave.

Ian stayed the wine steward with his hand. He had imbibed enough for one night. It would not do to repeat his performance of three nights ago—not among enemies.

It was distressing to think that. This was his king! And his cousin. He had sworn an oath to this man.

And he would keep it—including those portions that Gavin would not have him keep. He would protect *all* the citizens of the kingdom—magi and ungifted alike.

"Is the wine not to your liking, cousin?" Gavin asked.

"It is excellent, majesty," Ian replied. "But I must depart early on the morrow. I do not wish to drink overmuch."

"Such restraint is admirable," Mathen said in Ian's praise. "Especially in one so young." Ian glanced over to the First Knight, trying not to glare.

"Thank you," he said.

How many of my people have you burned alive, you monster? he thought. *How many of our children have left their blood on your hands?*

The priest wore his black hair close cut in a bowl, and his dark eyes pierced Ian like those of a hawk gazing at a mouse. He wore the garb of penance—poor cloth tied with a coarse rope. No amount of penance could ever erase this monster's crimes.

"I think 'tis time," Gavin said to the royal huntmaster.

"Yes, majesty," the man said, rising from his place at the table.

"Time?" Ian asked.

"You shall see," Gavin replied. Ian's eyes followed the huntmaster from the room. What was about?

Gavin rose from his seat and lifted a hand. Soon the din of the great hall gave way to silence.

"Today," the king said, "our cousin is a man. On the morrow he shall depart on his time of errantry. He has told us that it is his intention to travel into the Wastes to seek his adventure."

A few mutters of awe greeted this announcement. Were the Wastes truly that bad?

"Yes," Gavin said, as if answering Ian's unspoken question. "That is a noble, and dangerous, quest. We have prepared a gift to help see him safely home. Jorlas?"

"Here, majesty," the huntmaster replied, coming back into the hall. He carried something large and round, covered with a white cloth. A shield, perhaps? Gavin bent and took the item from the huntmaster, letting the cloth fall.

Ian's gasp of surprise echoed those of everyone else in the hall. It was indeed a round shield, fully a third of Ian's height in size. The center boss was polished steel—very rare.

Not so rare, however, as the glittering black scales that covered the remainder of the shield, radiating out in an overlapping pattern from the boss.

"As Arcalion defended us against the MageLord Valerian," Gavin said, "so shall this shield ward you in battle. No sword can pierce it—no flame can harm it. Take it, in our service."

Ian reached for the shield.

"'Ware, young lord," Jorlas warned quietly. "The edges are more keen than any sword."

Ian nodded, swallowing. He carefully took the shield from Gavin. The back of the shield was some type of leather, yet was harder than wood. If Ian's magesight were not banished as thoroughly as his Power, he had no doubt that this shield would have an aura of its own.

"Dragonhide," Gavin explained. Ian met the king's gaze without speaking.

"You may close your mouth now," Gavin told him, smiling.

"Majesty!" Ian exclaimed. He dropped to his knee and bowed his head. The hall behind him erupted into cheers.

Never had such a gift been given a young errant. Truly a gift worthy of a king.

"Rise, Sir Ian," Gavin said. "We take it that you are pleased with our gift?" Ian obediently rose to his feet.

"Majesty, how could I not be?" Ian asked. "Never in my wildest dreams could I have imagined it."

"I ordered this fashioned for your father," Gavin explained. "I believe he can wait another fortnight for his own, however."

"Of course, I am certain his majesty has one as well," Ian mused.

"I have armor of it," Gavin replied. " 'Tis very light."

It was. The dragon shield was less than half the weight of Ian's bronze-covered shield. Ian retook his seat on trembling legs. Such a shield was, itself, the stuff of legend.

Ian motioned to the wine steward. He needed another goblet.

Ian sat in the garden, allowing the night air to clear his head. From the garden, one could see more of the damage to the palace. To the west and north, the second floor was exposed and the third floor was simply not there. The sound of stonework continued, even though the sun had long set. Flickering torches lit the work areas.

A couple of the castle ladies had wandered by and flirted with him briefly before passing on. They had said nothing . . . improper, yet his ears had burned furiously. Perhaps that had just been the wine.

Ian examined the shield by his side. Never in his wildest dreams had he imagined that he would receive such a gift from the king.

"Good evening, Sir Ian," a soft-spoken voice said to him. Ian looked up in surprise at Mathen. The priest still wore his garb of penance.

"Good evening," Ian replied, standing.

"I had hoped for an opportunity to speak with you in some privacy," Mathen told him. "Apparently Hrothgar has seen fit to bless me with one. Are you enjoying the garden?''

''Yes,'' Ian replied coolly. ''It was quiet.''

''Before I disturbed you,'' Mathen added. ''Please accept my apologies.''

When Hell thaws, Ian thought.

''Why did you wish to speak with me?'' Ian asked.

'' 'Tis about your father, young Ian,'' Mathen replied. ''My last meeting with him was less than pleasant, and I was hoping you could give me some insight on how to gain his confidence.''

You could die, Ian thought.

''I regret that I cannot help you,'' Ian replied. ''My father is very much his own man.''

''As is his son, I can see,'' Mathen said. ''It just concerns me that one of his station would use his position to impede my efforts against those who practice the Forbidden Arts.''

''What are you saying?'' Ian asked coldly.

''Just that I do not understand why a loyal baron would . . .''

''As the First Knight of the Sacred Hunt, you are a knight as well as a priest, are you not?'' Ian asked, interrupting Mathen's reply.

''Ah . . . yes,'' Mathen replied. ''Yes, I am, Sir Ian.''

''If you question my father's loyalty again, *Sir* Mathen,'' Ian said, his voice lowering in anger, ''you had best be prepared to defend that accusation with your sword!''

Anger flared very briefly in the First Knight's eyes. It was quickly replaced by the priest's normally blank expression.

''I . . . apologize, Sir Ian,'' Mathen said. ''I did not mean to question your father's loyalty. I regret if it seemed thus. I was merely attempting to gain a deeper understanding of the man.''

''Then speak with *him*,'' Ian replied. ''If you will excuse me, I am very tired and I must depart early tomorrow.''

''Of course,'' Mathen replied. ''Hrothgar watch over you, and rest well.''

Ian cringed inwardly at the priest's blessing.

"Thank you," he said. Ian turned and strode angrily away.

Mathen watched as Ivanel's son walked away. He had not expected such overt hostility from the baron's son. Something was not right here—secrets were being protected.

Mathen smiled—a cold, predatory thing. Uncovering secrets was his best talent.

Ian rode out onto the plains outside the castle. Below, at the bottom of the fjord, lay the city. He glanced down at the longships sailing into and out of the harbor.

He turned and looked back at the castle. Arcalion's maw loomed above him. The dragon's fangs were longer than his forearm.

What was it like to ride such a beast? Ian wondered. A shudder passed over him. Compared to Bjorn's trials, his own mission seemed trivial. He only hoped that he proved worthy of the trust his father had bestowed upon him.

Ian's gaze travelled up to the battlements. A figure among several waved to him from one of the inner towers. Gavin.

Ian drew his sword and saluted the king before turning to ride away. It felt good to be away from the palace and the city. He took a deep breath, allowing his Power to flow back into him.

With his magesight restored, Ian looked at the new shield on his arm. As he had suspected, a faint aura clung to it.

Ian spared the city below a final glance. His travel would be easier if he booked passage on one of the longships to Nalur's Ridge. If he did that, however, everyone would know his destination. Ian did not like the thought of that. Not when matters of the Circle were concerned. He would simply have to follow the river on horseback.

The river ran almost due west to the sea. Ian knew that, further east, the river turned to flow from the north and east. Eventually, it would lead him straight to Nalur's

Ridge. From there, he would have to ask directions to Hunter's Glen.

Ian sighed. It would take him almost a moon to ride to Nalur's Ridge. In many ways it was going to be a long journey.

CHAPTER
-------- FOUR ------------

"LORD IVANEL," A guard announced, "the messenger has returned from Reykvid."

"Thank you, Wiegel," Ivanel replied. "Send him in." With a sigh, Ivanel set aside the papers before him. He had a feeling this was not going to be good news.

"My lord," Arik said, kneeling before Ivanel.

"Greetings, Arik," Ivanel replied. "How was your trip?" Arik rose and seated himself in the chair opposite the small table from his lord.

"Fruitless, my lord," he replied.

"How so?"

"If any of the Circle remain in Reykvid, they are not to be found," Arik explained.

"You searched?"

"For five days, my lord," Arik assured him. "I made my aura quite visible, and I shudder to think how many people I passed the Sign to."

"Hopefully, you did not attract . . . other attention," Ivanel said.

"Hopefully," Arik agreed. "There is little risk of that, however. So long as I do not return to Reykvid anytime soon."

"Yes," Ivanel agreed.

"I passed your son on the road on my way home," Arik mentioned.

"Indeed?"

"Yes. He did not see me."

Ivanel smiled. If Arik did not wish to be seen, a flying

hawk would not have been able to pick him out of an empty meadow.

"He looked quite the warrior," Arik added. "You should be proud."

"I am," Ivanel replied. "I have several letters for you to deliver."

"Yes, my lord," Arik said.

"The first is to the Circle in Star Lake," Ivanel said. "There is another for the Circle in Star Hall. The last is for the Circle in Ravenhall. Assuming, of course, they can all be found."

"Yes, my lord."

"Deliver them in that order," Ivanel added. "Do not deliver the others if you cannot deliver the first. Do not deliver the third if you cannot deliver the second. I do not have to tell you how vital it is that you succeed."

"No, my lord."

"I have one other task for you," Ivanel added.

"Yes, my lord?"

"While you are in Star Lake," Ivanel said, "I need you to find me a reputable moneychanger."

"A moneychanger?" Arik asked.

"Yes, one who is known for his discretion," Ivanel added. "And, preferably, one who is *not* Circle."

"Yes, my lord," Arik said.

"Take a meal and your rest," Ivanel said. "And then be off."

"Yes, my lord."

"And may Bairn ride with you."

"Let us instead hope that he rides with young Ian," Arik replied.

"How long will you be away, brother?" the temple father asked.

"I am not certain," Mathen replied as he tossed his saddlebags over the back of his horse. "Most likely several days."

"Would it not be best to leave in the morning?"

"No, brother," Mathen replied. "If I am seen leaving, it may spook my quarry. I would prefer to follow them by night."

"Hrothgar ride with you," the father wished.

"He always does," Mathen replied, lifting himself into the saddle. He kicked the horse firmly in the ribs and rode away from the temple.

Mathen had told the temple father that he was leaving in pursuit of a family he strongly suspected of practicing the Forbidden Arts. He disliked having to deceive one of the brethren, but it would not do to tell the temple father that he was in pursuit of the king's cousin.

As Ian had ridden away from the palace, Mathen had seen the Mark rise about Ivanel's son. This could explain much—very much, indeed.

Mathen would follow Ian until the young errant left Gavin's lands. Then it would be a simple matter to extract whatever knowledge the boy possessed. If Ian's body was ever found, the unfortunate incident could then be blamed on bandits. After all, it was not unusual for a young warrior to meet an unfortunate end during his errantry.

By midday of his second day of travel, Ian passed from the lands directly controlled by Reykvid into the lands of the Star clan. Here the river flowed from the northeast.

Ian glanced heavenward. The gray sky had threatened rain all morning. He was tempted to journey to Star Hall for a day. Although not of the Circle, Chief Balder and Ian's father were close friends.

Still, that would cost him two days—three if he were asked to stay. Ian did not know what his father's letters concerned, but he did know they were crucial to the fate of the magi. It was best to press on. Gods willing, he would visit Star Hall on his return from the Wastes.

A small hill rose beside the river, covered in trees. One tree in particular rose above the others.

If I climb that tree I might be able to see a village from here, Ian thought. The thought of spending the night in an inn, or even the loft of some farmer's barn, seemed a whole lot better than making camp in the rain.

Ian dismounted and led his horse up the hill. The mule followed. Ian tethered both to the tree and began to climb.

He finally climbed as high as he could reach, panting for breath. The frail limbs above would never hold him. He scanned the treetops to the northeast, searching for some sign of habitation. Nothing. Only the river lazily snaking through the hilltops.

It was a beautiful sight. The trees were just beginning to blossom with the bright colors of spring, and the clear, blue river snaked in and out of them. For a moment, Ian just sat and enjoyed the view.

He scanned around once more, searching for any sign of habitation. There was nothing—no rooftops, no chimney smoke, nothing.

A flash of white amid the greenery caught Ian's eye. It was to the southwest, back along the river. He looked carefully where he thought he had seen it.

There it was again! Just a flash of white, disappearing back into the greenery. What was it?

Ian stilled his breathing, gathering the Power. He had never been very good at this, unfortunately. He concentrated, attempting to direct the Power into his sight.

Slowly his perception of the forest ahead of him sharpened. Around him, sounds and sensations faded as he forced his eyes to see more than they would normally reveal to him.

An armored man riding a tan horse briefly emerged into a small clearing. It was his white cloak that Ian had seen flashing amid the brush. Unfortunately, at this distance, he could tell nothing more.

Ian released the Power, and his vision slowly returned to normal. The rider was less than half a day behind him. On a trail that saw little traffic.

Was he following Ian? That seemed much more likely than mere coincidence. Unlike Ian, a legitimate traveller would keep to the roads unless he just happened to be travelling to Nalur's Ridge and knew no other route. It was an unsettling thought.

Ian made his way back down the tree, carefully but quickly. He needed time to think, and it was best to do that on horseback while he was putting distance between himself and his pursuer.

Who could it be? One of his father's men, surreptitiously watching over him?

No. Father would have sent Arik, and Ian would not have known he was about unless the scout had tapped him on the shoulder.

Neither was it likely to be one of Gavin's men. Gavin's colors were purple, not white. And his scouts, like Arik, wore forest green in the spring and summer. Ian would no more have spotted them than he would Arik.

Ian jumped from the lowest branch to the ground and quickly untethered his horse. He lifted himself into the saddle and carefully guided the mare down the hillside.

Who, then? Bandits? No, there appeared to be only one of them. The Hunt? White *was* the color of the Temple, after all.

Ian's blood chilled at that thought. But that was almost as unlikely as one of his father's men. He had done *nothing* to arouse the suspicions of the Hunt. Even his threats toward Mathen in the garden would have been taken as nothing more than a headstrong, and half-drunken, son defending his father's honor.

Who, then?

Ian clutched the oilcloth cloak around him. The rain had lasted for a full day with only a few short breaks. He had spent the night in a wet camp, his only shelter the oilcloth stretched over him like an awning. He had not slept well for more reasons than simply the weather.

Ian had not caught sight of his pursuer since the rain had begun. The man was still back there, though. Now that Ian knew to look, his Art gave him vital clues. The reaction of small game to the man's passing, even the feel of his horse's mind.

The pursuer had narrowed his distance to less than two hours' ride. That was not surprising. Unburdened by a pack animal, the man should have overtaken him by now—even with the rain. The only explanation was that he was, as Ian had suspected, following him.

To what end? Was it the Hunt, hoping that Ian would lead them to other mages? Or was it simply a rogue, waiting for an opportunity to rob him?

The last was probably the most likely. If that were the case, Ian's pursuer would most likely make his move once they had left Gavin's lands. That would happen sometime tomorrow. Ian's free hand strayed to the hilt of his sword.

Ian reached up and tightened the neck of his cloak against the rain, then looked longingly at the river. A longship had passed heading northward early this morning. If Ian had booked passage from Reykvid, he would now be dry.

More important, he would not now be alone.

On the young warrior's heels, as Mathen was, the rain did not obscure the trail. Rather, it made it easier to follow, for the horse's hooves sank deeply into the softened earth.

There was little doubt now. Ian was apparently headed for the town of Star Lake—would have already arrived there if not for the weather.

This put Mathen in a difficult position. Once he was in town, it would be difficult to track the young warrior. In his armor and vestments, Mathen would be far too noticeable. On the other hand, if he changed into his priest's robe, Ian would still recognize him.

Were they not still within Gavin's lands, Mathen could have used the brethren of Star Lake to watch Ian. That would be far too dangerous here, where loyalties to the king were strong.

Likewise, capturing Ian before they reached the town would be equally risky. Ian bore the crest of one of the noble houses of Reykvid. Any assistance would likely come to his aid, not Mathen's. Any witnesses would indict the First Knight, not the young errant.

No, Mathen would have to rely on other, less reliable means and trust that Hrothgar would see to it that he prevailed.

The next day dawned bright and clear. Ian crawled out from beneath his oilcloth cloak. He was only slightly less soaked than he would have been without it. Hunter got to his feet and shook, spraying water around himself in a cloud. Then he proceeded to chase a butterfly into the brush.

"Hunter!" Ian commanded. "Attend!"

Obediently, the hound abandoned his pursuit and came to sit next to his master's feet. Ian slowed his breathing and gathered the Power. Where was his pursuer?

He cast back along his trail, searching for the mind of the man's horse. He found nothing. Puzzled, Ian widened his search.

There! Another horse—about a quarter day ahead of him. But . . . this did not seem to be the same horse he had touched before. Ian fought to concentrate.

He could feel the horse straining against the harness it wore. Ian struggled to join with the animal's mind. A whip cracked on the animal's flank, and the horse put more effort into it. It wanted to stop, but the man behind it would not allow that.

Ian opened his eyes. He could not determine what task the horse was performing, but he knew that it was not the warhorse of the man who had been following him. Of that animal, and its rider, there was no sign. Apparently there were other people up ahead, however.

By mid-morning, Ian found the first human habitation—a farm. The farmer was out plowing one of his fields in preparation for a late planting. He stopped his work as Ian rode up. He watched the young warrior suspiciously.

"Good day, sir," Ian said once he was within earshot.

"Good day, m'lord," the man replied. He was dark-haired with a full beard and dark eyes. His face and hands had a weathered look.

"Is there a village of size near here?" Ian asked.

"You jest, m'lord," the man said.

"No," Ian said. "I do not."

"M'lord is just outside Star Lake," the farmer told him. " 'Tis no mere village, m'lord."

Star Lake! Ian realized. *Of course!* Ian felt his face flush. Fortunately, his helmet hid that from the farmer. He should have *known* that—Ian had heard of Star Lake before.

"Oh" was all he could think of to say.

"You should reach town by midday, m'lord," the farmer assured him. "Just follow the river roads."

"Thank you," Ian said.

"Yes, m'lord," the farmer replied.

He was about to ride off when a thought occurred to him. He turned his mount back to face the farmer.

"Has another man passed through here today?" Ian asked.

"Another, m'lord?"

"Yes," Ian said. "A man in armor with a white cloak, riding a roan horse."

"Not that I've seen, m'lord."

"Thank you," Ian said again.

"Yes, m'lord," the farmer replied. Ian turned and rode away along the river. What had become of his pursuer? Perhaps the man had not been following him, after all. Perhaps he had been on his way to Star Lake and had pressed on once they got close rather than make a wet camp.

Soon, as the farmer had said, Ian found a road not far from the river. Ian led his horse and mule onto the packed road. This would take him into Star Lake.

Ian, you idiot! he thought. If only he had remembered Star Lake, he could have taken the roads this far. Or gone ahead and booked passage from Reykvid. That would not

have betrayed his ultimate destination. Either way would
have saved a day or two from his journey.

He started down the road toward Star Lake. He would
feel a lot better if he knew where the person behind him
had gone.

CHAPTER

------- FÍVE ------------

IAN LOOKED DOWN at the town of Star Lake from a nearby hilltop. The town, about a quarter the size of Reykvid and about half the size of Smithton, sat on the shore of Star Lake itself. The town sported a modest wall, about twelve feet high and perhaps three thick. Just past the town, the river flowed out of the lake toward Reykvid.

Across the lake, near the lake's inlet, sat another town about half the size of Star Lake. Ian could not remember the name, but he knew that it sat in the lands of the Ram clan. Ian could ferry across the lake here and continue his journey on the correct side of the river to reach Nalur's Ridge—tomorrow.

Today, Ian would rest in Star Lake and clean and dry his clothing. At the moment he looked more like a bandit than a knight of the realm.

Ian turned back toward the road to rejoin the traffic into Star Lake. The traffic into town was surprisingly heavy. Of course, a lot of trade was carried into Star Lake by the river. The town market was almost legendary. Ian smiled. Maybe he could buy a tent while he was here.

The traffic choked the southern gate. Ian debated riding around to another gate, but they were probably all this busy.

Of course, he didn't *have* to wait. He could ride around the wagons and enter immediately. His station afforded him that.

Ian debated with that thought for a moment. His quest *was* urgent, and he had to have time to tend to his business and still leave town early on the morrow.

Satisfied with his reasoning, Ian turned his horse out of

the press and rode toward the gate. Before he had ridden ten paces, he stopped in surprise.

A leper sat by the gate, far enough from the traffic to satisfy the law, but no further. That in itself was not surprising. Lepers, and other beggars, would often sit by town gates hoping that people would take sympathy on them and offer them a few coppers.

What was surprising was that this leper was a mage. His aura was clearly visible to Ian. Ian nudged his horse forward.

The man was not Circle. Even if he had been at one time, he would have been barred once his disease had manifested itself, although the Circle would still donate generously to his cup.

Ian stopped a respectful distance away and dismounted. He approached the beggar on foot, leading his horse. Once Ian was closer than the distance that the leper was required to maintain from people by the law, the poor creature began ringing its bell.

"Unclean," the man croaked, bowing his head.

"I know, friend," Ian replied. "Your cup?"

"Yes, lord," the leper croaked in reply. He held out his cup toward Ian. Ian fished a coin out of his pouch and dropped it into the cup.

"Hrothgar . . . bless you, m'lord," the leper croaked.

"Good day to you, friend," Ian replied. He led his horse a few steps away before remounting.

Mathen looked into his cup. A single Reykvid gold sovereign lay among the few coppers. Once the young errant had ridden away, Mathen breathed a sigh of relief.

He had thought that Ian had spotted him for certain. Most people kept the required distance, or further, from the lepers. Ian had walked up close enough to touch him. Only Mathen's hood had kept the young warrior from recognizing him.

Mathen rose to his feet. He would apparently need a less conspicuous disguise within the city.

• • •

"Where is the First Knight?" Gavin asked.

"He is away, majesty," Temple Father Olaf replied. The temple father was an elderly man, portly and balding with an iron-gray beard.

"Away?" Gavin asked.

"Yes, majesty," Father Olaf said again. "He was pursuing some friends of the magess he discovered. They left town in . . . suspicious haste."

"I see," Gavin observed. "And in his absence you have uncovered these?" Gavin returned his attention to the elderly couple before him. The man and woman were securely chained and gagged.

"Yes, majesty," Olaf said.

"Have they any children?" Gavin asked. The fear in the couple's eyes grew. Gavin had to look away.

"Yes, majesty," Olaf replied. "They have two sons and a daughter, all of age. We are investigating them as well."

"Present your evidence," Gavin commanded.

"Yes, majesty," Olaf said. Gavin listened as the priest presented his evidence.

The couple were known friends of the magess whom Mathen had discovered. They had been watched since that discovery and, for many days, had done nothing untoward.

Then, last night, the husband had travelled, cloaked and hooded, to the very site where Mathen had followed the seamstress.

"We lost track of him during his journey, majesty," Olaf said. "However, when he slipped us, we were near the place where we had caught the magess. We found him there."

"And you apprehended him there?" Gavin asked.

"Not immediately, majesty," Olaf replied. "We watched for a time. He performed some odd ritual at the site—marking trees and . . . well, he appeared to be praying. We apprehended him when he attempted to leave the grove."

"Marking trees?" Gavin asked.

"Yes, majesty. He carved this mark into the bases of the trees." Olaf handed Gavin a sheet of parchment. On it was a simple mark—two nearly horizontal lines rising up toward each other with a gap between them.

"Have you questioned him?"

"Not under torture, majesty," Olaf replied. "Not without your leave."

"Very well," Gavin said. "Place them in the dungeon until the First Knight returns. Upon his return, we shall question these mages under torture at his direction. After the questioning is complete, they will be executed."

"Thank you, majesty," Olaf said.

"Thank you, Father Olaf, for bringing this matter for *us* to decide," Gavin replied.

"Of course, majesty."

Gavin watched as the guards led the couple away. The woman was weeping.

I hope my brother can forgive you for what you have done to his kingdom, Ivanel had said. Gavin hoped so as well.

Ian checked the animals over one last time. He had only managed half a day's travel after taking the ferry across Star Lake to Ramshead. Then it had taken him well over an hour to set up camp with the tent he had bought before leaving. Hopefully, it would take less time as he got used to it.

"Hunter!" Ian called. The black hound came running in from the nearby trees.

"Guard!" Ian commanded. Hunter lay down out of the horses' reach. Ian knelt and patted him on the head.

"Good boy," he said.

Ian went into his new tent and carefully laced up the flap with a slip knot that would undo quickly. He was in nearly lawless lands now and was glad to have Hunter to stand watch for him. He was still unsettled over the man who had seemed to be following him. Ian had felt no trace of him all day, but the experience had unnerved him.

He unrolled his bedroll onto the canvas cot he had purchased in Star Lake. The small tent and the cot had set him back almost two sovereigns. As Ian crawled into his bedroll, though, he decided it had been worth it. For the first time in many days, he fell asleep in moments.

Arik rode through the town gate into Star Lake. He had ridden hard and had made the trip here in three days. Once he completed his mission here, another day's travel would see him in Star Hall.

Arik rode down the main street. He would find an inn at which to spend the night and stable his mount. Then he would begin his efforts to locate the Circle here.

A largish, well-built inn seemed best suited for the task. It looked reputable. The sign out front depicted a star falling from the sky above a longship in the water. The Star Ship Inn?

"Boy!" Arik called to the lad out front.

"Aye, m'lord?" the boy replied.

"Do you work here?"

"Not hard enough, if ye ask my father," the boy replied. Arik smiled.

"Then stable my horse," he said, dismounting and handing the reins to the boy. "Is your father the innkeeper?"

"Aye, m'lord."

"See that she's brushed and that her hooves are tended," Arik ordered, handing the boy a copper. " 'Twill make your father happy."

"Aye, m'lord!" the boy said.

A few patrons glanced at Arik as he walked into the inn, but the conversation did not falter. Star Lake was used to travellers. Ivanel's chief scout was a very ordinary-looking man—a good quality in a scout. His plain features were framed with equally nondescript dark hair and beard.

Arik walked up to the bar. A large man was leaning on the counter, talking pleasantly with one of his patrons. He stood up as Arik approached.

"Good evenin', m'lord," the man said. "May I help ye?"

"Yes," Arik replied, placing his hands flat on the bar. He crossed the middle finger of his right hand over the index finger in the Sign. "I'm looking for a few days' lodging."

"Well, ye've come to the right place, m'lord," the man replied, smiling and taking no notice of the Sign. "The Ship's Star has the best rooms in town. Do ye have a horse?"

"Your boy is taking care of it," Arik replied.

"Then for you and your horse, 'twill be one crown a night."

"One crown!" Arik said.

"That includes one meal a day for ye *and* feed for yer horse, m'lord," the innkeeper explained.

"Even so . . ." Arik began.

"Ye can stay elsewhere," the innkeeper said, shrugging. "If ye don' mind pickin' fleas out of yer clothes."

"No, that will do," Arik said. Obviously, the innkeeper did not haggle over the price of his rooms.

"Very good, m'lord," the innkeeper said. "Shall I fetch ye a bowl of stew, some bread and a mug of ale?"

"Yes, that sounds good."

"Comin' right up, m'lord."

The innkeeper returned shortly, bringing the promised items along with a key. He set these down on the table Arik had selected.

"One crown, m'lord," the innkeeper said.

"You can just call me Sven," Arik told him, handing him the small silver coin. Again, Arik passed the Sign to the innkeeper.

"Johann," the innkeeper added, again ignoring the Sign. He pulled out a chair and sat down across from Arik.

"Where are ye bound?" the innkeeper asked.

"Reykvid, eventually," Arik replied. He placed a spoonful of stew in his mouth. He was surprised—there was actually beef in the stew.

"This is very good," he told the innkeeper.

"Now ye know why it cost ye a crown," Johann said, smiling. "If ye're bound for Reykvid, ye'll be wantin' to book passage."

"I'd rather travel overland," Arik said. "Boats and I don't get along."

"Ah."

"Will the market be open this late?" Arik asked.

"No, m'lord," Johann replied. "Most of the merchants pack up an hour or so before sunset. They'll be back with the sun, though."

"Johann!" someone called. The innkeeper looked up to see someone waving an empty mug at him.

"Ye'll excuse me, m'lord?" Johann asked.

"Of course," Arik replied. "Thank you."

"Anytime," Johann replied.

Arik turned the key in the lock. Not that it was much of a lock—any key in the inn would probably open it. However, inside there was probably a bolt. It seemed to be a good inn, although the wall lamp nearest his room had apparently run out of oil.

Arik had spent several hours, and several crowns, in the common room to no avail. He had not seen one aura, nor had one person acknowledged the Sign. He would try his luck at the market tomorrow.

The room was dark. Arik stepped in to let his eyes adjust to the feeble light coming in from the hall. Someone closed the door behind him.

Arik spun around, drawing his sword as he did. The expected attack did not come.

"Calm yourself," a voice said from behind him.

How many of them are in here? he thought.

"Odd advice from voices in the dark," he replied, turning and taking a step back so that both of the known intruders were to his front.

"It was you who sought us out," a woman's voice said from directly behind him.

"Was it?" Arik asked. He did not move. If she had wanted him dead, there would already be a dagger in his back.

"Aye, Sven," a more familiar voice said from in front of him.

"Johann?"

Lights appeared in the darkened room. Ghostly outlines of people that gave no true light. They grew from dim, almost imagined things into steady beacons of Power. Arik sheathed his sword.

"So we meet," he said.

"So we meet," the first male voice acknowledged. At least now he could associate the voice with an aura, if not a face.

"Do you think we might get some real light in here?" Arik asked.

"I think it's better if we do not," the unknown man replied. "What you do not see, you cannot reveal under . . . persuasion."

"So, the panic has spread here as well?"

"As have the burnings," the man replied. Arik sighed.

"Look, is there somewhere I can sit?"

"Can you find the door?" Johann asked.

"Yes." Arik stepped to the door. He was a little irritated at having been caught unawares. The unlit lamps outside his room should have warned him. There was probably still oil in them—if only he had bothered to check!

Johann directed him from the door to the bed, and Arik reached out with his right hand and found the foot of the bed. He took another step and sat on the bed.

"Thank you," he said.

"Why have you sought us out?" the unknown man asked.

"May I assume that you are the Guardian?" Arik asked.

"You may assume what you like," the voice replied.

"I have a letter for the High Magus from my lord," Arik replied.

"Your lord is of the Circle?"

"Yes," Arik replied.

"What is in this letter?" the woman asked.

"I do not know," Arik replied. "My lord is a powerful and influential man. All I know is that he is seeking a way to end the burnings, but that he needs the help of your Circle and others to accomplish this."

"Are you to wait for a response?"

"Yes," Arik replied.

"You may leave the letter with Johann," the man said. "Rest assured that it will be delivered to the High Magus unopened."

"I would prefer to deliver it myself."

"Unfortunately, in these sad times, that is not possible."

"Your High Magus was discovered, wasn't he?" Arik said. The ensuing silence told Arik that he was correct.

"He died under the temple's tender care," the man finally replied. "We do not know what he revealed ere he died."

"If anything," the woman added.

"Very well," Arik said. "I shall leave the letter with Johann."

"Good. We shall depart now. Johann is going to cover your head until we leave."

"So we part," Arik said.

"Until we meet again," the others replied.

"A safe journey to you, Sven," the leader added.

One of the auras moved toward him. Arik sat quietly as a rough sack was placed over his head.

"All right," Johann said. Arik heard the door open and three sets of footsteps depart. Then the door closed again. Johann removed the sack.

"Can we get some light in here now?" Arik asked. "I *know* you."

"Sorry about all that," Johann said, lighting a lamp near the bed. Arik blinked in the sudden brightness.

"These are troubled times," Johann apologized.

"That they are," Arik agreed. "I'll get the letter."

Once Johann had left, Arik threw the bolt on the door and adjusted the wick until the lamp flame was but a dull glow. He would leave for Star Hall as soon as he was given the Circle's response.

CHAPTER
------- Six ------------

WHEN IAN AWOKE, sunlight was streaming through the canvas walls of the tent. Startled, he sat up quickly. What time was it? Ian pulled open the lacing on the flap and peered outside. The sun had been up for a good hour at least. *Gods!*

He hastily dressed in the undertunic and leggings for the armor and began carrying the supplies out to the pack mule. He would put on his armor once camp was broken. He could work faster without it.

In spite of his haste, Ian carefully checked the packing on the mule. It would cost him even more time if everything fell off a mile down the trail. The mule brayed its displeasure at being awakened so rudely, but Ian ignored it.

Thank the gods, the tent went down more quickly than it came up. Ian carefully folded it and loaded it onto the mule. From now on, he would only use the tent in poor weather. Had he slept under the stars, the sun would have woken him at dawn. Fortunately, his father had not been here to witness Ian's sloth in the face of his quest!

With camp packed up and loaded onto the mule, he could finish dressing. Over the padded undergarments went heavy leather. Over that, Ian placed his bronze breastplate, his greaves and bracers. Lastly, he donned his leather coif and his helmet.

His cloak, with the emblem of the Fire Sword clan, was dry and clean. He looked like a warrior again, instead of a bandit. Of course, it also made him an easy target. Nevertheless, a warrior was supposed to display his clan proudly.

If he did not, Ian might be taken for a rogue or a bandit.

That reminded him—he had not checked for pursuit. Ian sat down on a stone near his long-dead campfire and concentrated.

He could feel the life of the forest around him. Plenty of small game, rabbits and squirrels, as well as a few deer. Ian's mind even touched a pack of wild boars several miles to the west. Perhaps Ian should think of hunting soon. A few stone of venison or boar would go a long way toward stretching his supplies.

A horse! Ian's mind touched that of a horse nearby. He concentrated—focusing on the mind of the horse. Was it . . . yes! It felt like the same horse he had sensed before. His pursuer had returned!

Ian opened his eyes. How had the man eluded his detection at Star Lake? No sooner had the question formed in his mind than the answer came with it.

The man must have waited for him in the town itself. With so many other horses about, it would have been impossible for Ian to pick out a specific animal. In fact, he had not even tried for that very reason. When Ian had crossed the lake and continued on his journey, the stranger had resumed his pursuit.

Ian had felt the horse less than half a day's ride from here. This had gone on long enough. Ian would wait for this man at the first clearing he could find. After all, he was a warrior of the Fire Sword clan. He would not run from this person as though he were a frightened child.

No matter how much he felt like one.

Ian waited about twenty feet into the forest surrounding the clearing. The mule was tethered another twenty feet back with Hunter standing guard. The pennant of the Fire Sword clan fluttered from his lance.

At least I look *like a warrior,* he thought. The knot of fear in his stomach did not make him *feel* much like a warrior, however.

Ian's pursuer should arrive any moment. The horse felt

very near. Ian released the Power, focusing on the here and now. He waited.

Eventually, a flash of white rewarded his patience. Soon a man on horseback emerged into the clearing. Ian gasped in surprise. *Mathen!*

The First Knight wore bronze armor beneath a white tunic. The leggings beneath his greaves were also white, although soiled from the road. Over this he wore a white cloak, and his shield bore the hammer symbol of Hrothgar.

None of this was the source of Ian's surprise, however. Part of him had realized that it could very well be the Hunt, meaning Mathen. What surprised him was Mathen's aura. Mathen *himself* was one of the gifted!

Ian had even seen this particular aura before, around a leper at the gate of Star Lake. He had put a sovereign in the man's cup, by the gods! Mathen dismounted and knelt to check Ian's trail.

Ian clenched his jaw and spurred his horse forward into the clearing. Mathen looked up at the sound of Ian's horse. He quickly remounted.

"Greetings, Sir Ian!" Mathen called across the clearing.

"Mathen," Ian said disgustedly. "Why are you following me?"

"I suspect that we both know the answer to that question, *mage*," Mathen replied. He hurled the final word at Ian like an insult.

"You are mistaken," Ian said. "And mad."

"I think not," Mathen disagreed. "The Mark surrounding you is clear proof of your guilt. Most cannot see it, but Hrothgar has granted me that boon that I might serve his holy cause."

Gods! Ian thought. *He can see my aura!* That *is how he ferrets us out so easily!*

"You are still mad!" Ian said. "You are as much a mage as I—your aura is as clear to me as mine is to you."

"Your foul lies shall not avail you, mage," Mathen said.

"The lie is within your own mind, madman," Ian said.

"Even so, what action do you think you can take against one of the royal line without proof?"

"We are far outside Gavin's lands," Mathen explained. "If you never return, it will be thought that you did not survive your time of errantry. No one knows that I am here."

"So, you mean to kill me," Ian said.

"Actually, I had hoped to capture you alive," Mathen said. "But it appears that I shall have to settle for your death. Perhaps I will find the evidence I need against your father on your lifeless corpse."

"My body shall not be the one lying in this clearing when we are done!" Ian shouted. "Prepare yourself, villain! Today I avenge the blood of my people!"

"You have me at a disadvantage, Sir Ian," Mathen said. "I have no lance."

"You also have no honor," Ian said. "Defend yourself!"

Ian spurred his mount forward into a charge. Mathen did not move. Instead, he raised a crossbow that had been hidden behind his shield. Ian raised his own shield, just barely peering out from behind it.

The aim of Ian's lance was true. Once he had made it halfway across the clearing, Mathen fired. Ian ducked behind his shield. There was no lethal target that the First Knight could hit. Ian might take a minor leg wound, but Mathen would be dead.

Maiden's scream was almost human as the quarrel buried itself in her chest. Mathen had not fired at Ian at all, but at his horse!

The horse's front legs crumpled beneath it. Ian threw his lance to the side just before he was thrown forward from the saddle. Fortunately, Ian's shoulder struck the ground first rather than his head.

The breath was knocked from his lungs as he rolled across the ground. His shield caught the ground, wrenching his left shoulder. Ian did not have the breath to cry out in pain.

Ian stopped rolling and fell onto his back. For a few seconds his vision was black, filled with spinning stars. He lay there, gasping for air. His shoulder throbbed with pain.

He heard the sounds of Mathen's horse moving toward him. Ian rolled to one knee, ignoring the pains throughout his entire body. Mathen charged past him and aimed a vicious side-swing at Ian's head with his sword.

Ian blocked the blow with his shield.

"Aaaagh!" he cried as fire exploded from his shoulder. The force of the blow knocked him onto his back again.

Mathen rode past and wheeled his horse around for another charge. Ian staggered to his feet and lurched toward the lance he had thrown. As Mathen began to charge toward him again, Ian lifted the lance, planting the butt like a pike. Mathen reined his mount to a halt and sheathed his sword.

Mathen dismounted and drew his sword. Ian waited until the First Knight had stepped several paces from his mount before dropping the lance and drawing his own.

"So, it seems we settle this face to face, after all," Mathen said.

"So it seems," Ian agreed. He did not feel as brave as he was trying to sound. He could barely hold his shield up with his injured shoulder.

Mathen opened with a thrust that Ian easily caught on his shield. However, pain flared from his wrenched shoulder at the blow.

Ian swung overhead, aiming a crushing blow at Mathen's head. The priest raised his own shield over his head to block. Ian arrested the swing as he had planned and snapped the sword around to the side, aiming for the leather covering Mathen's thigh.

Mathen stepped back and brought his own sword across to block the blow. Almost too fast for Ian to catch, he responded with a thrust toward Ian's throat.

Ian's shoulder protested as he snapped his shield upward and then again as Mathen's sword struck the shield. Ian stepped back, but Mathen pressed him. His countering side-stroke rang off Ian's helm.

"You are not my equal, boy!" Mathen said. Ian blocked an overhead blow with his shield.

Ian cried out as his shoulder burst with pain. Even so, he aimed a thrust below Mathen's breastplate. The First Knight of the Hunt blocked it easily with his shield, returning with a thrust of his own.

Ian ducked behind his shield and stepped back, letting his sword arm drop behind him. He brought the sword up and around from behind him with all the strength of his anger, screaming in rage. Mathen blocked the blow with his shield. Wood and bronze split as the force of the blow drove the sword deep into the shield.

Mathen wrenched his shield away, and the sword was torn from Ian's grasp. Contemptuously, Mathen hurled the shield, Ian's sword still trapped within, to the side. He seized the hilt of his sword with both hands over his head and slammed it down.

Ian threw his shield arm up to block the blow and cried aloud as intense pain flooded from his shoulder. He staggered back as Mathen hurled blow after blow at him. He cried in pain again as, at one point, the edge of his own shield caught him in the leg, drawing blood.

'Ware, young lord. The edges are more keen than any sword. Had Mathen noticed?

Ian blocked the next overhead blow from Mathen. Ignoring the searing pain in his shoulder, Ian slammed his shield down into Mathen's abdomen, below the breastplate.

He felt the edge of the shield bite through the leather and felt wet warmth soak his arm. Mathen did not cry out. He merely stepped back and then fell to his knees. Then the First Knight toppled over onto his side.

Ian knelt there for a moment, panting in agony. His shoulder felt as if several strong horses had tried to rip his arm from his body. He looked down at Mathen's dying form and then at the shield on his arm.

"Thank you, cousin," he whispered. Ian staggered to his feet.

His horse was dead. Ian took his saddlebags and his tack

off her. Loading the tack onto Mathen's horse was painful, but it would not look right if he rode a horse bearing the livery of the temple. Pulling his sword from Mathen's shield proved even more painful.

He took Mathen's horse by the reins and led her from the clearing. At the edge of the clearing he turned and looked back at Mathen's body.

"Good riddance, monster," he said. Then he turned and limped toward where Hunter and the pack mule waited for him.

Ian gave the animals minimal attention that night. After several hours of travel, his shoulder had become too stiff to move. They would sleep in their tack tonight. He sat cross-legged on the ground and tried to summon the Power.

It was slow in coming. Ian could not concentrate easily because of the pain from his shoulder. That was his first target—the pain. Ian used the Power against the pain in his shoulder, numbing the throbbing agony that robbed him of his focus.

As the pain subsided, his control of the Power improved. Now he directed that Power into the torn and bruised muscles of his shoulder.

He had won. He had faced his first battle as a man and won—against an opponent far superior to himself. A torn shoulder was small price to pay for his life. Father would have been proud of him.

With the pain eased, and what little healing he was able to manage, Ian could move his arm again. He wrapped his belt around it as a sling and leaned back against a tree.

Then he focused all his Power into one thought.
Sleep.

Ian awoke to the sunlight. During the night his arm had stiffened again. He could barely move it, and any attempt to do so resulted in excruciating pain. He sat back against the tree and raised the Power once again.

As soon as he could move the arm without too much

pain, he rose. He would have to tend to the animals. They had spent the entire night in their tack. Hunter jumped up, now that his master was awake.

"Good morning, Hunter," Ian said, patting the dog on top of the head. "Why don't you go play for a little while? Go play!"

Hunter barked once and ran off into the nearby trees, sniffing the ground. Ian smiled and turned his attention to Mathen's horse. He unbuckled the saddle strap and lifted the saddle from her back. His injured arm was almost no help at all.

"So, what's your name, girl?" he asked. The horse did not reply, of course.

"Ooh, this does not look good," Ian said. The saddle had galled the horse.

"Looks like I walk today," he noted. "And maybe tomorrow. We need to clean this and let it air. Good thing it's a dry day."

He carried the mare's tack to the side and set it down. He patted the mare's neck when he returned.

"I'll be back," he promised. "But I have to get Loudmouth out of his tack, too." Ian walked over and began unfastening the mule's pack harness.

"EEYAWW!" Loudmouth objected, living up to his name.

"I'll have it off in a minute," Ian grumbled.

Loudmouth was in much better shape than the horse. His pack had not galled him much at all. A good brushing and a few hours rest ought to do him a world of good. Ian turned back to tend to the horse.

"EEYAWW!" Loudmouth cried.

"I'll be back!" Ian said. "I know you're hungry."

"EEYAWW! EEYAWW!"

"Stupid mule," Ian grumbled. The galling underneath the warhorse's saddle was not quite as severe as it had first appeared. That was good.

"So," Ian said, as he combed her mane, "if we're going

to be travailing together, I'm going to have to come up with a name for you.

"You're the right color for me to call you Buttercup," he added, "but that doesn't sound like a good name for a warhorse." The horse snorted.

"Yeah, I didn't think you'd like that. How about . . . Brazen? Yeah, I think Brazen sounds good."

The horse snorted and tossed her head.

"Brazen it is, then," Ian decided. "Let me see your hooves, Brazen." The horse's hooves were in fine shape. Ian cleaned out a few small rocks and patted her on the flank.

"Let me brush out Loudmouth," Ian said, "and I'll get you both some breakfast." Ian brushed out Loudmouth's mane and coat and then filled the two feed buckets with meal.

With the horses tended and fed, Ian sat down and rubbed his shoulder. The exertion had made it even more sore, but it seemed able to move more freely. He steadied his breathing and summoned the Power yet again. Once the pain had subsided, he would build a fire and see about fixing his own midday meal.

Chapter

------- Seven ------------

"*DEAD*?" GAVIN SHOUTED, throwing back his bedclothes. "By Hrothgar, someone will pay for this!"

"Majesty!" the guardsman pleaded. "No one has entered their cells. Your seal is still unbroken on the locks!"

"Show me!" Gavin ordered. He followed the guard from his chambers. Curious eyes followed them as people hurried to clear their path. The sight of the king walking the palace in his nightrobe was not a common one. Gavin did not notice the stares.

Even if his seal was unbroken, the mages could still have been murdered. Their food could have been poisoned, or any number of other methods could have been used.

Could one of his guards be a mage? Was it possible that they had been killed to prevent them from revealing the secrets of the magi?

They crossed the throne room to the northeast tower. The guard led him down the stone steps to the dungeons. His steps echoed sharply from the tower walls. After about ten feet, the stonework was replaced by carved bedrock. Much of the original stone for the palace had come from these subterranean chambers.

After another twenty feet, they reached the hallways of the dungeon. Gavin's escort claimed a lantern from a hook on the wall and led him into the dungeons.

They stopped at the door to one of the cells, and Gavin inspected the bulky lock. It was still cased in lead with his seal stamped into the metal. Gavin stepped to the next cell and inspected its lock. It, likewise, was still sealed.

"Break them," Gavin ordered.

"Aye, majesty," the guard replied. The guard cut through the lead seal with his knife and pried the soft metal away from the lock, exposing the keyhole.

Inside the room, the smell left no doubt. The old man was dead—had been for at least a day. Part of his face had been chewed away by rats. The guard looked as ill as Gavin felt.

"The next," Gavin ordered.

"Aye . . . majesty," the guard replied.

The picture in the second cell was as the first. The old woman had been dead for at least a day, and the rats had been at work on her body as well. Her last meal still lay on the cell floor, partially eaten, although whether by her or by the rats Gavin could not tell.

"Summon the crypt keepers," Gavin ordered. "Have the bodies shrouded and removed for burning."

"Aye, majesty," the guard replied.

"And summon the physician," Gavin ordered. "I want this food checked for poison. And summon Temple Father Olaf at once."

"Aye, majesty."

The Hunt would learn nothing more from these two. Someone would pay for that.

Nearly an hour later Gavin was dressed and in the council chambers with his physician and Temple Father Olaf. His mood had improved little since his unseemly awakening this morning.

"I can find no sign of poison, majesty," the royal physician told him. "I fed the food to several rats I was able to trap in the dungeons. They have suffered no ill effects."

"Then what killed them?" Gavin asked.

"They were old, majesty," the physician offered. "It may simply be that their hearts failed them from fear. They knew what fate awaited them."

"I think not," Olaf said.

"What do you mean, Father Olaf?" Gavin asked.

"We have had this problem with mages before, maj-

esty,'' Olaf explained. "Many times, if one does not deal
with them quickly, they simply . . . die.''

"Why did you not tell us this before?'' Gavin demanded.

"Would you have believed me, majesty?'' Olaf asked.
"Or would you have thought me a superstitious old man?''

"We . . . understand,'' Gavin replied. "How is your in-
vestigation proceeding?''

"Slowly, majesty,'' the temple father replied.

"What of their children?'' Gavin asked. "The children
of a mage are mages also, are they not?''

"Most certainly, majesty,'' Olaf agreed.

"Seize them,'' Gavin ordered. "Question them under
torture immediately and then put them to the fire.''

"It will be done, majesty!''

Gavin watched as the priests left. Olaf had accepted his
charge almost with glee. Somehow, that left him uneasy.

"Is such . . . severity warranted, majesty?'' Sigmund
asked. Gavin looked to his castellan.

"We must remove this festering sore, Sigmund,'' he replied. "Or have you forgotten the damage that Valerian
wrought upon us?''

"No, majesty,'' Sigmund said, bowing his head. "I have
not.''

"You may go,'' Gavin said.

"As you wish, majesty.''

Gavin sat for a time in the throne room, alone. He almost
wished that Ivanel were here. Gavin looked up toward the
ceiling.

"Forgive me, father,'' he whispered to the empty room.

Gavin was having his midday meal in the gardens in an
attempt to lighten his mood. A page came up and conferred
briefly with one of the guards. The guard dismissed the
page and stepped forward toward the king.

"Majesty,'' he said, "Temple Father Olaf wishes to see
you.''

"Have him brought to council in a few moments,''

Gavin replied, rising from his half-eaten meal. It was just as well. He found that he had little appetite.

The council room would be more private than the throne room and less personal than his chambers. Gavin took his seat at the head of the long table. Soon afterward, Father Olaf was admitted into the room with a temple page.

"Do you have them?" Gavin asked.

"Alas, no, majesty," Olaf replied. "They are gone."

"Gone?" Gavin said, hardly believing his ears. "How could they be *gone*?"

"They simply . . . are, majesty," Olaf said. "When we went to seize the mage's children, they and their families had fled."

"I *thought* you were *watching* them!" Gavin said. His voice was rising close to a shout.

"Th-they took nothing, majesty," Olaf explained. "Even their neighbors did not realize they had left."

"How long ago?"

"Not since before this morning, majesty," Olaf said. "That is when they were last seen."

"You have people who would recognize these mages?" Gavin asked.

"Yes, majesty," Olaf assured him. "Several."

"How many?"

"Six," Olaf replied. "One of two brethren watched each of the three families at all times."

"Guard!" Gavin shouted. The door was quickly opened. Six priests would enable him to form six parties to search for these mages. Gavin would be damned before he allowed these vermin to escape his grasp.

"Yes, majesty?" the guard asked, scanning the room as he did so.

"Summon the captain of the cavalry and the captain of the scouts," Gavin said. "I want them here *immediately*!"

"Yes, majesty!" the guard replied. He left the room hurriedly. Gavin turned back to Father Olaf.

"I want those six priests here, *now*," Gavin said.

Olaf gestured to the temple boy who was with him. The lad ran off.

"They will be here shortly, majesty," Olaf assured him.

"Mathen picked an inopportune time to deprive us of his services," Gavin grumbled. "Where *is* he?"

"I . . . do not know, majesty," Olaf replied, spreading his hands before him. "He has never been gone this long before now."

"Well, Brazen," Ian said, "I think you're ready to be ridden again." With a little Power, Brazen's galling had healed quite nicely. The same could be said for his shoulder, although that was a slower process. It would be several more days before Ian's arm was free of pain.

"Let me pack Loudmouth and then we'll get you saddled up," Ian added. "How does that sound?" Brazen snorted and stamped as Ian left.

It would be good to ride again. Ian's feet had gotten sore over the last two days. Loudmouth brayed his displeasure at the load that Ian tied onto his back, as usual.

"It'll be good not to have to drag your lazy tail around with nothing but my own weight, too," Ian told the mule. "I'll be hitching your lead to Brazen's saddle today."

"EEYAWW!"

"Tough," Ian said. "It's about time you started pulling your *own* weight around here again. We've got a long trip ahead of us to Nalur's Ridge."

If Ian was correct, he would pass out of the lands of the Boar clan today and into the Wastes. Whereas the greater clans, even the Boars, imposed a certain amount of law within their bounds, the Wastes were free of such . . . restraints.

Save for a few relatively safe areas patrolled by the lesser chiefs and villages, the Wastes were rumored to be the haven of bandits. Some claimed the Wastes even harbored a few monsters left over from the Time of Madness.

Once he had packed the mule, Ian returned to the horse and got her tack in order. Then he gathered up Loudmouth's lead and put his foot in the stirrup and lifted himself into the saddle. He slipped Loudmouth's lead over a heavy hook on the back of the saddle and clicked his tongue at Brazen as he gently nudged her in the ribs.

"Come on, Hunter!" he called. Hunter bounded alongside him, and then off into the nearby woods.

"Hunter!" Ian called. "Attend!"

Hunter obediently returned and fell into step alongside Ian's horse. The land they entered was no longer safe enough for Ian to allow the dog to explore at his leisure.

"We have found no sure sign of them, majesty," Captain Heinrich reported.

"No *sure* sign?" Gavin asked.

"We came across something unusual," Heinrich replied. "A farmer on the road to Smithton hailed one of our patrols this morning. It seems that his four team horses had been stolen during the night, and four other horses left in their place. The four that were left had been driven hard during the night."

"That must be them," Gavin said.

"That was my thought as well, majesty."

"They must be in a wagon—probably together," Gavin mused. "But why Smithton?"

"'Tis a large city," Olaf suggested. "They are not known there—'twould be easier for them to hide. They may have accomplices there, as well."

"What action have you taken?" Gavin asked, turning back to Heinrich.

"I ordered two of the patrols to combine and head on to Northguard," Heinrich replied. "I sent written orders with them that they be provided with fresh horses at Northguard."

"Excellent!" Gavin said. "With any luck, we'll overtake them on the road to Smithton!"

"The patrol has been ordered to stop all wagons and search them," Heinrich added.

"They'll not be able to steal any more horses during the day," Olaf pointed out.

"We all but have them," Gavin agreed. "Send word to my uncle by pigeon. If they *do* reach Smithton, he can have men waiting for them."

"Yes, majesty," Heinrich replied.

Baron Ivanel looked up at the knock on the door to his chambers. He quickly rolled up the maps he had been studying and set them aside.

"Enter," he called. A guard opened the door.

"My lord," he said. "A letter has arrived by pigeon from Reykvid." The guard handed a tiny leather tube to Ivanel.

"Thank you," Ivanel replied.

"My lord," the guard replied, leaving and closing the door.

Ivanel examined the tube, briefly. Its wax seal was unbroken. Of course, the tube was too small to impress the seal. However, Ivanel had no reason to suspect that it had been tampered with.

He broke the wax and removed the small roll of parchment from within.

Mages fled Reykvid. Three families in wagons to Smithton. Capture.

Ivanel tossed the note into the fire and sat back in his chair. This was . . . unfortunate. If Ivanel did not comply, he would be guilty of treason. If he did comply, he would still be a traitor—to his people.

Of course, there was compliance and there was compliance. He walked over to his desk and took out a small slip of parchment.

Will comply. Ivanel.

He rolled the parchment and slipped it into the leather tube before sealing it with a drop of wax. He walked over and opened the door to his chambers.

"My lord?" the guard said.

"Have the pigeon keeper send this to Reykvid," Ivanel ordered, handing the tube to the guard.

"At once, my lord," the guard replied, hurrying to leave.

"Summon Eva," he told the other guard. "Have her bring me my dinner."

"Yes, my lord." Ian closed the door and returned to his chair.

Thank Bairn they came here! he thought.

Arik sat in the common room of the inn. He had spent all day passing the Sign in the marketplace to absolutely no avail. He sipped at a mug of spiced cider, observing all those who came into and out of the inn—searching for even the faintest glimmer of an aura.

There was nothing. Not even the slightest . . .

A flicker across the room caught his eye. The flicker quickly grew into an easily discernible aura surrounding a young man with dark hair and eyes. Arik cupped his chin in his hand, laying his middle finger across his index finger.

The young man returned the Sign. Finally! Arik nodded to the young man and got up from his table. Arik walked up the stairs to his room. He waited outside the door.

Eventually, the young man emerged from the stairs into the hallway. Arik opened the door to his room and stepped inside. Soon, the door opened behind him.

"So we meet," Arik said.

"So we meet," the man replied. "You have certainly made yourself obvious. Who are you?"

"You can call me Sven," Arik replied, using the name he had used in Star Lake. "And you are Guardian."

"As are you," the young man noted. "I am called Molin. Why have you sought us out?"

"I have a letter for your High Magus from my lord," Arik replied. The young man held out his hand. Arik took the letter from his pack and handed it to Molin. Molin broke it open.

"That is for . . ." Arik began.

"I am Guardian," Molin interrupted. Arik fell silent as Molin read the letter.

"Do you know what this contains?" he finally asked Arik.

"I do not," Arik replied.

"Hm" was all Molin said. " 'Tis an interesting proposition. I shall take it to the High Magus. You shall have our response on the morrow."

"Thank you."

"So we part," Molin said.

"Until we meet again," Arik replied.

Arik awoke. Bright sunlight gleamed between the cracks of the shutters. He had slept late. With a light groan, he slid his legs off the edge of the bed and sat up.

Something near the door caught his eye. On the floor, as if it had been slid under the crack of the door, lay a folded piece of parchment. Arik rose from the bed and walked over to pick it up.

The letter was sealed with a plain wax seal. On the outside was scribed a single word—Sven. This was the reply from the Circle.

"Hell of a thing to leave lying around," he muttered. Arik placed the letter in his saddlebags. He would pack up and eat breakfast downstairs before leaving for Ravenhall.

CHAPTER

------- EiGHT -----------

IVANEL LOOKED UP as the guard admitted Hervis into the room.

"My lord," Hervis said, kneeling before Ivanel.

"Please, sit," Ivanel said. "That will be all, Hans."

"Yes, lord," the guard replied, leaving the room.

"I presume you got to them," Ivanel said once the guard had gone.

"Barely, m'lord," the young Guardian replied, slouching in the chair. Hervis was the Guardian of the South for the Circle. His blond hair and blue eyes fit the role well, as did his skill with a sword.

"They're safely hidden in Heinrich's old farm, as you ordered," Hervis added.

"Excellent," Ivanel said, relaxing. It had been a near thing. Gavin's men had arrived last night—practically on the heels of the fleeing mages. It was fortunate that Ivanel had not yet granted the deceased Heinrich's farm to anyone.

"And the wagons?" Ivanel asked.

"Wagon," Hervis corrected. "There was only one. I drove it here. 'Tis in your bailey with your other wagons, and the horses are even now being groomed in your stables. No one will think aught of it."

"Good," Ivanel said. Hervis was right. Gavin's men would scour the countryside for the wagon and never realize that it was right under their noses.

"However, they are far from safe," Ivanel noted.

"That's the truth," Hervis agreed. "An abandonded farm is the *first* place the Hunt would search."

"Then we cannot leave it abandoned," Ivanel said, going to his desk and removing a sheet of parchment. He sat down and began to write.

"Hervis, you are about to become a farmer," he said.

"Me, lord?" Hervis asked, sitting up straighter in his chair. "But I know nothing of farming."

" 'Tis not difficult," Ivanel replied. "Here is your grant to the farm."

"Aye, m'lord," Hervis reluctantly agreed, taking the document from Ivanel.

"I have a task for your new tenants while they're hiding in the barn," Ivanel added.

"M'lord?"

"Have them dig a secret cellar beneath the barn," Ivanel explained. "Take care that they do not dig too close to the walls. If they've the skill, we shall wall and floor it as well."

"What is the purpose of this cellar?" Hervis asked.

"To hide them," Ivanel replied. "And others like them who come to us in the future. You should go now. Your new farm is waiting for you."

"As you wish, lord," Hervis replied. Ivanel watched as the Guardian left.

Once he had left, Ivanel cradled his brow in his hand. Thank the gods that Hervis had gotten to them in time!

He was getting too old for this.

There was no hint of a road. Ian was forced to make his way along the river by way of game trails. Many times he was forced to dismount and lead Brazen through the tangled underbrush.

This was going to make for slow travel. He had to find a road, or a cart track or something. Surely there was something!

For now, he travelled along the riverbank itself. The underbrush near the river was thick, and progress was slow. He was certain not to lose his way in this manner, but it would also at least double his travel time to Nalur's Ridge.

Perhaps there might be a road further in, he thought. It

was certainly worth a try. Ian led his mount back into the forest. He threaded his way through the trees and dense underbrush for almost an hour without finding any sign of a trail.

The problem with roads, he thought, *is that they have to have someplace to go.* Apparently there just wasn't anyplace for a road to go to in this area. That explained why all of the traffic from Nalur's Ridge came down the river.

Suddenly, Ian broke through the underbrush onto a narrow trail. The trail was barely wide enough for the horses. Still, it was a trail, and it ran in the general direction that Ian wanted to go. Ian mounted and turned to the right to follow the trail.

Eventually, the narrow game trail crossed a slightly wider road. Although wide enough for one or possibly two horses, the road, if such it was, was not wide enough for a wagon.

Again Ian turned to the right, for the trail he had been following had been curving left for some time. The afternoon sun sank to his left as he rode northward. He would have to find some place to make camp within the next few hours. That did not seem promising in this tangled forest. He might have to camp on the road itself. Not a pleasant prospect if there were bandits about.

An hour's ride did not take him past any more suitable prospects, although the road had widened a bit. In another hour, Ian would be forced to make camp wherever he could.

Then he came upon the farm. Ian stopped to look the place over. Some farmer had managed to carve a few acres out of the forest. A small pen was filled with sheep—a little over a score. A small shack served as the farmer's home. There was another, slightly larger building that might be a barn.

The remaining few acres were devoted to crops—apparently turnips and potatoes. The smell of sheep pervaded the entire farm.

"Hello!" Ian called. There was no reply save for the

bleating of the sheep. Ian nudged his horse forward along the edge of the pen toward the house.

There was no smoke from the crude stone chimney. That was odd. The farmer, or his wife if he had one, should either be out working or inside fixing his evening meal.

"Hello!" Ian called. "I mean you no harm! I am merely seeking shelter for the night! Is anybody here?"

Again there was no response. Ian dismounted and wrapped Brazen's reins around one of the posts of the sheep pen.

"Hello!" he called again, as he walked up to the shack. There was no response.

The door was not barred. Ian opened the door and looked into the little one-room shack. A cot sat against the far wall. Against the wall to the right was the fireplace, and the wall to the east was filled with crude cabinets. A rickety-looking table sat in the middle of the room with a crude but sturdy-looking stool.

Apparently, only one person lived here. Ian closed the door and walked over to the barn. It wasn't much of a barn. Rather, it appeared to be a storehouse and shearing shed. Bundles of raw wool sat next to a carding table and a spinning wheel. There was another cot here and a small fireplace in the back. Did someone live in here as well?

Well, however many people lived here, there were none here now. Ian closed the door to the shearing shed and looked the farm over again.

Everything seemed normal. The sheep looked well tended, as did the crops. Perhaps there was a town nearby and the farmer had gone there for some reason. If so, he would either return soon or not at all tonight.

The sun was sinking toward the horizon. Ian would wait and see if the farmer returned. In the meantime, perhaps he could help earn his keep. He had noticed that the sheep's watering trough was empty.

The farmer had not returned by nightfall, and Ian had done everything he could find to do. He had filled the sheep trough with water and had even found some meal in the shed, which he had fed to them. The sheep had attacked it with relish—almost as if they had not eaten recently.

Once the sheep had been tended, Ian had set to hoeing the fields. While at first glance they appeared well tended, it was obvious that they had gone at least two days without attention. The soil had been dry, and weeds had begun to sprout among the crops. It had been necessary for Ian to carry more water from the creek to irrigate the crops.

Wherever the farmer was, it was now certain that Ian would be spending the night here. He freed Brazen and Loudmouth from their tack and tended to them. He was tired—it had been a hard afternoon. Scratching out a living in the Wastes was apparently not an easy task.

Satisfied with their condition, he returned to the shed and eyed the cot with suspicion. It, and the shed, were probably both filled with mites from the wool.

Ian could sleep on the porch of the farmhouse. His own bedroll was free of pests. He could not vouch for anything else here. He returned to get his bedroll from the packs.

"Hunter, guard," he commanded. His dog obediently lay down a respectful distance from Brazen and Loudmouth. Ian gathered up his bedroll and walked over to the porch. The slight overhang of the roof would serve to keep him dry if it rained—or, at least, less wet.

Ian spread out the bedroll and crawled into it. Tomorrow, if the farmer had not returned, he would be on his way. As he lay down, he summoned the Power and fashioned it into a ward about him. If someone crossed it during the night, he would wake.

Comfortable and exhausted, Ian fell asleep quickly.

The farmer had still not returned by the next morning. Ian did some minor chores around the farm before getting ready to leave. He filled the sheep's trough with water again and made certain that all of the farmer's tools were back in the shed.

Ian smiled as he mounted Brazen. The farm had made a

pleasant camp, and the farmer would be completely mystified at the work that had been done while he was away.

Ian rode away, and soon the farm was lost in the forest behind him. The road had led him to the farm. Now Ian would find where it led *from* the farm. There must be a town or a village nearby. Somewhere for the farmer to take his crops to trade.

Suddenly, Hunter stopped in the road and began to bark loudly. Ian reined back on the horse.

"What is it, boy?" he asked. Ian lifted his crossbow from the hook and fitted a quarrel into it. Just as he did so, a woman broke from the brush alongside the road. She froze when she saw him.

"Hunter, heel!" Ian commanded. The dog had started to charge forward. He continued to growl as Ian stared at the woman.

She was beautiful, although dirty and slightly bloodied. Her poor clothing had been torn by the underbrush of the forest, revealing the pale skin beneath. Her blonde hair was tangled and filled with leaves. She ran toward him and Hunter jumped up, barking viciously.

"Heel!" Ian commanded again. "Hush!"

"My lord!" she cried, clutching at his saddle. "My lord, you must help us!"

"Us?" he asked.

"My father!" she said. "We were on our way home when bandits took us! You must help us!"

"Are you from the farm?" Ian asked.

"Yes! Oh, please! Please help us!"

"My lady, I am no match for a den of bandits," he said. "Do you have a lord near here?"

"There is no time!"

"My lady!" Ian admonished. "Calm yourself!"

"My father needs you! Please, my lord!"

"I will take you to your lord," Ian began.

"No!" she wailed. "There is no time!" Without warning, she turned and fled into the forest.

"My lady!" he shouted, but she was already gone. Ian

cursed and jumped down from the saddle. He quickly tied Brazen's reins around a tree limb.

"Hunter, guard!" he commanded before he took off after her. The tangled underbrush grabbed at him as he ran through it. He caught a glimpse of the woman ahead.

"My lady!" he called. He had to catch her before she made it back to the bandit camp. In all probability, her father was already dead. A pretty girl they would keep alive. Her aging father? Not likely.

Ian chased her through the forest. How could she run so fast through the tangled brush?

He burst into a clearing and froze. Several rotting bodies hung from a large oak in the center of the clearing. There, naked, hung the body of the woman he had just chased here. Her throat was ripped out and her right leg was stripped of meat to the bone. It was obvious that the body had been here for more than one day.

Ian's sword flew from its scabbard as he wheeled to look behind him. This was not the work of bandits! A stinking mass of arms and legs leaped at him from behind.

Ian screamed and threw his shield up barely in time to block the jaws of the hobgoblin. Its fetid claws scrabbled at his armor as Ian hurled the monster away from him.

Grotesquely human, the hobgoblin's body was barely half his in size, but its arms and legs were easily as long as Ian's. Matted black hair hung in greasy strings from its head, and oversized eyes bulged from a face with no true nose. The remains of the woman's dress still hung about its scrawny body.

"You stinking piece of filth!" Ian screamed.

The filthy creature shrieked and leaped at him with a speed that startled Ian. Its almost human mouth was apparently double-hinged and opened far wider than a man's to reveal horrifying fangs.

The thing landed on him, wrapping long fingers around his sword arm. Its long toes wrapped around Ian's ankles as the impact knocked him to the ground. Ian shoved his shield into the thing's face in a desperate attempt to keep its gaping jaws away from his throat.

The hobgoblin was insanely strong. Even through his heavy leather gauntlets, the thing was squeezing the life from his sword hand. Ian felt the hilt slip from his fingers as he struggled beneath the monster's weight. The creature's foul stench filled his nostrils.

Oh, gods! Ian thought. *I'm going to die!*

The hobgoblin grabbed the edge of the shield to pull it away. It shrieked in pain as the dragon scales sliced into its fingers.

Ian slammed the shield upward into its face. The thing fell back, and Ian rolled away and up to his knees. He reached for his sword, but the fingers of his right hand would not close on it.

The monster screamed in rage and leaped at him again. Ian swung the shield flat, with all his might. The dragon scales bit into the creature's belly. Foul-smelling blood and other, less pure liquids sprayed over him.

The thing fell away, shrieking. Ian was finally able to pick up his sword. The hobgoblin thrashed about, screaming, on the ground.

"Filth!" Ian shouted, raising the sword over his head.

"You killed her!" His sword bit into the monster's arm. It shrieked and tried to scrabble away from him.

"You *ate* her!" he screamed, again striking at the monster. "Damn you!"

"Damn you, damn you, *damn you*!" he shouted, punctuating each curse with blows from his sword. Tears ran down his face as he cut the monster into pieces. Blood and gore stained both the ground and himself as his sword struck again and again.

"Damn you!" he shouted. The hobgoblin no longer moved.

"Damn you," he said, dropping his sword. He turned back to the tree.

Ian pulled the dagger from his belt and sawed at the vines that were tied under the girl's arms. He caught her as she fell and gently lowered her to the ground. She smelled of rotting meat.

His stomach finally betrayed him. Ian was able to stagger to the edge of the small clearing before vomiting. He knelt by the brush for several moments while his stomach wrung out its contents.

Shakily, he returned to the grisly work of retrieving the bodies. He would have to go back for the mule to carry them out of here. He looked back at the dismembered corpse of the hobgoblin.

"Damn you to hell," he said.

It took Ian the rest of the morning to gather up the bodies and carry them back to the farm. He could think of no other place to bury them, and the girl, at least, had probably come from here.

He got a shovel from the shed. He would bury them in the fields he had tended. It was the least he could do.

He was four feet into the first grave when he heard the horses. Ian scrambled out of the grave as five armored men rode up. Their armor was not uniform, but they all carried the same blazon on their shields: a wyvern with a spear clutched in its talons.

"Who are you?" the lead rider asked. "What are you doing here?"

"Is this your farm?" Ian asked.

"I am Chief Erik its lord!" the man replied. "Answer me, boy!"

"I rescued these bodies from a hobgoblin's larder," Ian explained, gesturing toward the blanketed forms. "I have reason to believe that one of them is from this farm. I was just trying to give them a decent burial."

The self-proclaimed lord dismounted, and his men followed suit. He was a large man with coarse black hair and beard and piercing brown eyes.

"Step aside, boy!" he said. Ian did so. The lord knelt down and ripped open the first bundle. It was the woman. Erik ripped the blankets Ian had wrapped her in all the way

down to the eaten leg. He covered the woman back up and
turned back to Ian.

"*You* killed the hobgoblin?" he asked.

"Yes," Ian replied.

"I don't believe you," he said.

"You can go see for yourself, if you like," Ian said.
"Go down the road about an hour and then off to the left.
You should be able to find my trail pretty easily. I had to
cut away the underbrush to get them out."

The lord nodded to his men. Two of them mounted up
and rode off.

"You had best not be lying to me, boy," Erik warned.

"I am Ian Urqhart," Ian replied, "heir to the clan of the
Fire Sword. I am not in the habit of lying. Now, may I
finish digging her grave?"

"You may," Erik said. "But if you are lying to me,
'twill not be *her* grave. 'Twill be yours."

It was several hours later by the time Erik's men returned.
As Ian had worked, Erik's attitude had softened and he and
the other men had joined Ian's labors. They were laying
the last body to rest when the riders returned.

"Well?" Erik asked.

" 'Tis as he said, m'lord," one of the riders replied.
"We found the hobgoblin cut to pieces. A foul creature,
that one."

" 'Twould seem that I owe you a debt, young warrior,"
Chief Erik told him. "I have lost several men to that
beast."

"My father almost lost one as well," Ian replied. "I was
only defending myself, lord."

"Did you not tell me that you attempted to rescue
Lydia?" Erik asked. "Or what you *thought* was Lydia?"

"Yes, lord."

"She was one of mine," Erik said. "And you risked
your life for her. You are always welcome in my hall, Sir
Ian."

"Thank you, my lord."

"You must stay with us tonight," Erik added. "It is too late for you to travel on. My hall is only a few hours north of here."

"I would be honored," Ian said.

Especially if I can have a bath, Ian thought. He was anxious to scrub away the smell of death.

CHAPTER

------- Nine ------------

BATHED AND IN clean clothes, Ian watched as the jugglers finished their act and retreated from the room under a hail of vegetables. One thing could be said about these lesser clans. They were certainly . . . boisterous.

"Hold!" Erik shouted. "Hold!"

The din in the hall slowly quieted. Erik stood and lifted his cup to the hall.

"I would raise a goblet," Erik said, "to our honored guest. Ian Urqhart of Reykvid who, in single combat, did slay the hobgoblin that has plagued our lands this entire past winter."

"To Sir Ian!" the hall echoed.

"Sir Ian, if you are an example of the quality of warrior that your father trains," Erik added, "I think I speak for my entire clan when I say, 'tis a good thing you don't border us!" The rest of the hall burst into laughter.

"Your grace is too kind," Ian replied, smiling. "It was only by good fortune that I defeated the monster."

"I have found that, in battle, good fortune only comes to those who seize it," Erik said. "Still, no one can deny that you have done us a great service. Ask anything of me within my power, and it shall be yours."

"Your grace, the hospitality you have shown me is all I could ask," Ian said.

"So, where are you bound, lad?" Erik asked, taking his seat.

"Nowhere in particular," Ian lied. "My father once went wyvern hunting near Nalur's Ridge; I had thoughts of visiting there."

"You could have taken ship from Star Lake," Erik noted. " 'Twould have been far easier than riding overland."

"I am serving my time of errantry," Ian explained. "I don't think I should spend it comfortably aboard ship."

"Well said, lad!" Erik replied. "Your father has raised you well."

"Thank you, your grace."

"Do you know the route to Nalur's Ridge?" Erik asked.

"Uh," Ian replied, "I fear I do not."

" 'Tis a good thing you happened across us, then," Erik noted. "We can provide you with directions when you depart."

"Thank you, your grace."

"Pah! 'Tis nothing!" Erik said. "Steward! More wine!"

The steward came over and refilled their glasses. Fortunately, Ian's was still almost full. He had been carefully nursing his drink—Ian doubted that he had drank more than two goblets thus far.

"Where are those blasted jugglers?" Erik shouted.

As in all of the other towns Arik had visited, the Circle in Ravenhall was not easy to find. Even here, beyond Gavin's influence, the panic was spreading.

He had passed the Sign to everyone in the inn without recognition. Tomorrow, he would try the marketplace. Even if the Sign were not returned, perhaps it would lead the Circle to him, as it had in Star Hall.

Arik finished the last of his ale and rose to go to his room. He tossed a crown on the table, generous payment indeed, and left.

Arik turned his key in the lock and opened the door. Inside the room, laying in front of the door, was a note. Without pause, Arik entered the room and closed the door behind him, throwing the bolt as he did so. He scooped up the note and walked over to the bed to turn up the lamp.

The note said little.
Follow the Call tonight.

The Call led him into an unsavory part of town. Fortunately, at this hour, the streets were deserted of even the ruffians that must live in this area. Arik would not want to call attention to himself by getting involved in a brawl.

He followed the Call to a crumbling stone building. This was risky, calling the Circle inside the city. Still, it would have been even more dangerous to try to pass the gate at this hour. Especially in these times.

Arik circled the building, looking for a way in. Apparently he was going to have to enter through the open doorway in the front of the building.

Arik mounted the crumbling steps to the doorway. What he had taken for shadow was actually a black cloth draped across the doorway. As he brushed it aside and stepped across the sill, a shadowy figure stepped forward and placed the point of a sword against his chest. The Guardian.

"Who seeks to enter Circle?" the Guardian asked. He was cloaked so that Arik could not see his features. Even his hands were gloved.

"A friend from afar," Arik replied. Arik lowered his barriers, allowing the Guardian's probe to enter his mind.

"To what purpose?" the Guardian asked.

"To discuss a matter of grave urgency," Arik replied.

"Are you armed?"

"I am."

"Will you surrender your arms?"

"I will," Arik replied.

"Do so," the Guardian commanded. Arik unbuckled his sword belt and set it aside carefully. As he did, he felt the pressure of the Guardian's sword against his chest increase.

"Are you armed?" the Guardian asked again.

"I am not," Arik replied. He could feel the mind of the Guardian touching his own. Apparently the Guardian was satisfied.

"Enter in peace," the Guardian said, removing his sword from Arik's chest and stepping aside.

A single lamp, with the wick lowered so that it barely glowed, was the only illumination in the room. Arik stood for a moment, allowing his eyes to adjust, before he moved to the center of the room where a cloaked and hooded man sat, waiting for him.

Other shadows moved around the room, and Arik could feel their presence in the Circle. The Guardians of the Four Points had also been summoned for this meeting. Arik sat in front of the central figure.

"Why have you sought us out?" the High Magus asked.

"These are troubled times, Magus," Arik replied. "My lord seeks your aid in saving as many of the Circle as can be saved in these days."

"What does he ask?"

"I do not know," Arik replied. "I have a sealed letter to deliver to you, and I am to await a response."

"Give me this letter."

"Yes, Magus," Arik replied. He reached into his cloak and pulled out the letter. A gloved hand took it from him.

"Return to your inn," the Magus told him. "You will have our response in the morning."

"Thank you, Magus," Arik said, rising.

"So we part," the cloaked figure said.

"Until we meet again," Arik replied. He turned and walked back out into the night. With any luck, he could be back in Smithton within a sevennight. It had been a long mission.

Of course, he thought, *it could be worse.* After all, he could be on the quest that Ivanel had given to Ian.

Ian laid his saddlebags across Brazen's rump and wrapped Loudmouth's lead around the hitch on the back of the saddle. His night in Erikshall had been a pleasant one. Good food and drink and a relatively bug free bed.

"That will take you to the main road," Erik explained, pointing to the path that led northwest from the hall. "From there, just follow the road north and east to Nalur's Ridge. Take care, 'tis not much of a road in places. Never make the mistake of thinking you are safe.''

"I shan't," Ian replied. "The hobgoblin taught me that lesson well. Thank you, Chief Erik. Both for your hospitality and for the provisions."

"Safe journey, lad," Erik said.

"Thank you, your grace," Ian replied. He turned and rode away from the squalid little keep. Hunter bounded along beside him. After riding down the road a ways, Ian turned and looked back.

The keep was little more than a squat tower surrounded by an outer wall less than twenty feet high and no more than four or five thick. Still, it had afforded him secure shelter for the night, and he now had friends there.

Someone waved to him. From this distance Ian could not tell if it was a warrior or a serf. Ian waved back and then turned and rode away.

Nalur's Ridge sprawled across both sides of the river. The core of the town sat beside the ridge that gave it its name. Atop the ridge were the crumbling remains of an old keep. Ian's father had once told him that the farmers used the keep for grain storage.

Most of the land within the walls was nothing but empty fields. In fact, *all* of the land between the inner wall and the outer wall was unoccupied. And there was apparently no true keep. Just the town walls.

"Are there any inns in town?" Ian asked the guard at the gate as he approached.

"There are several in town, m'lord," the guard replied. "Just ask around."

"Thank you," Ian replied.

"Yes, m'lord."

Contrary to Ian's expectations, Nalur's Ridge was not a busy town. In fact, the town itself was smaller than Star Lake. Much smaller. Apparently most of the people of Nalur's Ridge lived out on the farms. Finding the Circle here was not going to be an easy thing.

Finding an inn was not difficult, however. Ian had barely ridden a block past the gate when four presented themselves on the corners of an intersection. He started to dismount at the first one on the right, and then an odd thought struck him.

That would be the one that almost everyone stopped at first. He guided Brazen across the street to the inn on the far left corner. This one would likely receive less traffic than the other three. If there was one thing that was true of the Circle, they liked to avoid crowds.

Ian dismounted. The inn was a clean stone building, like all of the buildings he had seen thus far. He walked in through the open front door.

A large, noisy crowd filled the common room. So much for less traffic. All conversation stopped, and every eye turned to Ian.

"Innkeeper!" Ian called, trying to ignore the attention.

"Yes, m'lord!" replied a portly man, hurrying in from a back room. He looked startled when he first saw Ian, but it passed quickly.

"How may I help ye, m'lord?" he asked.

"Do you have a stable?"

"Yes, m'lord!" The patrons began to return to their original conversations.

"I shall need to stable my horse and mule for a few days," Ian said. "And I need a room."

"Aye, m'lord," the man replied. "One horse, one mule and one room."

"That's correct."

" 'Twill be a measure of silver per night, m'lord," the innkeeper replied.

Ian fished a crown out of his pouch and handed it to the innkeeper. He passed the Sign along with the coin. The innkeeper took the crown and examined it, apparently without noticing the surreptitious gesture.

"I presume that includes grooming the horse," Ian began.

"Aye, m'lord," the innkeeper said.

". . . *and* the mule," Ian finished.

"Aye, m'lord," the innkeeper agreed. "I'll get yer key."

"I also have a dog," Ian added. "Where will he stay?"

"In your room, m'lord," the innkeeper said. "I'll not have my stablehands bitten. See that he stays off the bed."

"He knows better than that," Ian replied.

"A copper measure will get ye a meal and another will get ye an ale, m'lord," the innkeeper added. "Ye must be tired from the road."

"That sounds good," Ian agreed. "Get me my key and I'll put my dog away."

"Aye, m'lord."

A few moments later Ian was sitting in front of a hot bowl of stew and a mug of ale.

"Is there a market in town?" Ian asked one of the other patrons of the inn sitting near him—a blond-haired man with green eyes. Ian laid his hand on the table in the Sign.

"Aye," the man replied, taking no apparent notice of the Sign. "North of the center of town. Ye can't miss it."

"Thanks," Ian said.

"Lookin' fer anything specific?" the man asked.

"Just supplies," Ian replied.

"Ye'd be better off goin' to one of the farms," the man told him.

"I'll keep that in mind," Ian said. No doubt, if he were actually looking for supplies, that would be good advice. He would probably have better luck finding someone from the Circle in the marketplace, though. More people in less ground.

"In fact," the man added, "Wilhelm always comes out of the winter overstocked. I'd pay him a visit. Ye'll get a good price from him."

"Thank you," Ian began. Then he noticed that the man was passing him the Sign.

"Where is Wilhelm's farm?" Ian asked.

"'Tis not far," the man assured him. "I can take ye there myself a bit later. I'll be driving right past it."

"Thank you," Ian said. "You've been very helpful."

CHAPTER
------- TEN ------------

WILHELM OWNED A moderately large farm almost an hour's
ride from the town. He seemed to raise a little bit of everything. They had passed fields planted with corn and wheat.
Ian estimated about ten acres of each. The crops were just
about knee-high this early in the season.

Of course, there were other fields of potatoes, turnips and
onions. Those seemed to be the main staple crops of this
region. In Nalur's Ridge, however, corn seemed just as
popular, and hay even more so. Past the farmhouse, Ian
could see acres upon acres devoted to hay. Winter food for
the hungry herds.

Wilhelm's herd was kept further back, according to
Owyn, the man Ian had met at the inn. Wilhelm boasted
two hundred head of cattle—one of the larger herds in the
area.

Nearer the farmhouse, Wilhelm apparently also raised
pigs and chickens. A good score of swine wallowed about
in a pen, and chickens seemed to be everywhere. Next to
the house, roughly an acre was devoted to a vegetable
patch. Cabbages, beans and tomatoes dominated the garden.

The house itself was enormous, for a farmhouse. Ian estimated that it must be at least a ten-room house. More
surprising was the fact that the house was fashioned of
stone. Apparently, being a farmer in Nalur's Ridge was a
profitable enterprise. Two large stone barns sat behind the
house. Behind them sat another building that was reminis-
cent of a barracks.

"Wilhelm does all right for himself," Ian said over the
clatter of Owyn's wagon as he rode alongside.

"Aye," Owyn agreed. "He's one of our wealthiest citizens. Has a seat on the council, as well."

Owyn pulled his wagon in front of the farmhouse. Ian followed and dismounted.

"Just tie your horse to that fencepost," Owyn told him.

"Owyn Liefson!" a woman's voice exclaimed. Ian looked toward the farmhouse. A woman had opened the front door. She was beautiful, in a mature way. Her red hair was just beginning to frost with silver, and her form was still pleasing. Her aura was crisp and powerful.

"Good afternoon, Lady Olga," Owyn replied. "Is yer husband about? I've brought a traveller who is looking to buy provisions."

"So I see," Lady Olga replied.

"Ian Urqhart, my lady," Ian said.

"Come in, gentlemen," Olga said. "I shall tell my husband we have guests." Ian threw his saddlebags over his shoulder and followed Lady Olga and Owyn inside.

The interior of the house was just as grandiose as the exterior. Ian would have thought he was in the hall of a minor lord rather than a farmhouse. Expensive-looking rugs covered the floor, and ornate tapestries adorned the walls.

Lady Olga led them to a drawing room. Ian blinked in surprise at the bookshelves that lined one of the walls.

"Wait here," she instructed them. "I shall fetch my husband."

"Thank you, my lady," Ian replied. Owyn collapsed into one of the leather-covered chairs. Ian remained standing. His armor would not be gentle to the upholstery.

"I told you he was wealthy," Owyn said.

"Indeed," Ian replied. "I never would have . . ."

He was interrupted by the opening door. A man of middle age, presumably Wilhelm, entered the room. His graying hair still held traces of the blond it had once been, and his eyes were a piercing blue. He had the large build of someone who had worked hard all his life. His aura was even stronger than his wife's.

"You're lucky you didn't come a few minutes later," he

said, in a deep, strong voice. "I was about to inspect the herds. Owyn, I've a cow with calf I'd like you to take a look at later."

"Aye," Owyn replied.

"You must be the young lord I was told of," Wilhelm said, turning to Ian.

"Ian Urqhart, my lord," Ian replied. Wilhelm proffered his hand and Ian clasped it firmly.

"None of that," Wilhelm said. "There's no blue blood in my veins. Wilhelm will do."

"I've heard that, in the Wastes, 'tis not a man's parents that determine his nobility," Ian said, "but his character." Wilhelm smiled.

"A polite lad," Wilhelm said approvingly. "Olga tells me you need provisions for travel, but I suspect that's not all you're here for."

Ian glanced over to Owyn.

"Aye," Owyn replied, nodding. "He's Circle."

"I have a letter for the High Magus from my father," Ian said, searching through his saddlebags. He pulled out the sealed letter and handed it to Wilhelm.

"I'll need a response before I leave town," Ian said. "Can you see that this is delivered to the High Magus?"

Wilhelm took the letter and examined the seal.

"It already has been, lad," Wilhelm said, breaking the seal. "Have a seat."

"Uh," Ian replied. "Sir, my armor . . ."

"Hm? Oh!" Wilhelm replied. "Quite right—*don't* sit down!" He walked over and opened the door to the drawing room.

"Hans!" he shouted. Soon a young man roughly Ian's age came to the door.

"Yes, father?" he said.

"Fetch us a stool," he said. "Our guest needs a seat."

"Yes, father," the boy replied. He returned shortly with a stool.

"Take the men out to inspect the herd," Wilhelm told him. "Owyn and I will be along later."

"Yes, father."

Wilhelm closed the door and handed the stool to Ian.

"Thank you, sir," Ian said, but Wilhelm was already absorbed in the letter from Ian's father. He sat behind his desk and read all three sheets of it several times.

"Do you know what's in this?" Wilhelm finally asked.

"No, sir," Ian replied. "Only that I am to take your response to Hunter's Glen along with another letter from my father."

"This is . . . an ambitious undertaking," Wilhelm said. "Your father is a man of vision."

"Yes, sir. He is," Ian agreed.

"Would you excuse us for a moment?" Wilhelm asked, rising from his seat.

"Of course, sir," Ian said, also rising.

"No," Wilhelm said. "Make yourself comfortable. Pour yourself a goblet of wine. Owyn?"

The two of them left the room. Ian walked over to the wine cabinet and filled one of the crystal goblets with wine. Wilhelm lived well for a farmer.

Soon the door opened again and Wilhelm and Owyn came back in.

"By your father's instructions, I am to send a letter with you to your next stop," Wilhelm said, taking his seat behind the desk. He took some parchment from a drawer along with a bottle of ink.

"As I write," Wilhelm continued, "Owyn is going to ask you the news of the road. If anyone asks why you were here so long, that is what we spoke of. Do you understand?"

"Yes, sir," Ian replied.

As Wilhelm wrote, Ian related his journey to Owyn. He left nothing out, including his pursuit by Mathen and his battle with the First Knight. Wilhelm stopped writing during that portion of the tale.

"You killed the First Knight of the Hunt in single combat?" Wilhelm asked.

"Yes, sir," Ian replied.

"Well done, lad!" he said. "Although it disturbs me that they knew of you. Has anyone else followed you?"

"No, I kept watch behind me with the Art," Ian replied. "Mathen alone knew. He could not confide in anyone else because of my station. His only evidence against me was his ability to see my aura."

"One of our own," Owyn said, shaking his head.

"No," Wilhelm said. "One of the lost ones."

The Magus returned to his letter as Owyn continued to question Ian about his journey. Wilhelm stopped writing again when Ian got to the portion of his tale when he had encountered the hobgoblin.

"You defeated it?" Wilhelm asked. "Alone?"

"Yes, sir," Ian replied. "Although 'twas a near thing."

"On that recommendation alone, I could get you an officer's commission in the Guard if you've a mind to return," Wilhelm said.

"Thank you, sir," Ian replied. "But I've a hall to return to. I am my father's only heir."

"Hm," Wilhelm said, returning to his letter.

The rest of Ian's journey had been uneventful after leaving Erikshall. That part of the tale went quickly, but Owyn had some specific questions to ask about the road nearer to Nalur's Ridge.

"Do you know the way to Hunter's Glen?" Ian asked Jason.

"No," Owyn replied. "I've never heard of it before. Do ye have any idea where it might be?"

"Only that it is roughly a fortnight north of here," Ian said. "And that there is a small village by the name of Pine Grove on the way."

"Pine Grove I have heard of," Owyn said. His tone sounded ominous. "The road there is plagued with bandits, and the town, if you could call it that, is not much better. If you want my advice, do not stop in Pine Grove. Travel on."

"I've a better idea," Wilhelm said. The Magus had finished his letter and was sealing it with wax from a candle.

"What is that?" Ian asked.

"I know of a small band of merchants travelling north," Wilhelm said. "They'll be leaving in a few days. I am certain they could use another sword arm to protect them as they travel. Especially if it comes at no cost."

"That would be safer," Owyn agreed. "Although slower."

"Not as slow as if he dies on the way," Wilhelm countered.

"My mission is vital," Ian said. " 'Tis better to arrive late than never."

"I shall give you a letter of recommendation for the master," Wilhelm said. " 'Twill ease your way." He began writing on another sheet of parchment to which he applied his seal at the bottom. He handed both letters to Ian. The letter of recommendation was unsealed.

"Thank you, sir," Ian said.

"Your provisions should be ready by now," Wilhelm added.

"How much do I owe you for them?"

"Nothing."

"Sir, I cannot . . . !"

"Yes, you can," Wilhelm insisted. "Safe journey to you, Ian Urqhart. So we part."

"Until we meet again," Ian replied. "Thank you, sir. I wonder if I could prevail on you for one more thing?"

"Ask it," Wilhelm replied.

"Would it be possible for you to arrange for a letter to be delivered to my father?" Ian asked.

"That would be possible, yes," Wilhelm replied. "Would you like to pen it now?"

"If you don't mind," Ian said.

"Please," Wilhelm said, rising from his seat behind the desk. Ian carried his stool behind the desk and sat down. Wilhelm joined Owyn in the sitting area. Ian penned the letter as quickly as possible, but a lot had happened since he left home.

Two pages later, he was finished. He blotted the ink,

folded the parchment into thirds and sealed it with wax from the candle. His ring, pressed into the wax, completed the seal.

"Thank you, sir," Ian said. "How much will it cost to send the letter?"

"Nothing," Wilhelm said. "I am already sending a letter to your father. The same messenger can carry both. So we part."

"Until we meet again," Ian replied.

Ian shook Wilhelm's hand and left the room. Wilhelm walked back behind the desk and sat in his chair. He began writing another letter once Ian had left the room.

"I notice you did not tell Ian that caravan master Geoff is of the Circle," Owyn said.

"No," Wilhelm said. "He does not need to know that. When we are done here, you should get word to Geoff that he is not to let Ian know of his affiliation with us."

"I understand," Owyn agreed.

"When can you leave for Smithton?" Wilhelm asked.

"Tonight," Owyn replied.

Wilhelm simply nodded and continued writing.

The guard opened the inner door to the chamber and admitted Arik. Ivanel smiled at him. His chief scout looked road-weary.

"How was your journey?" Ivanel asked.

"Tiring," Arik replied. "Here are the letters of response."

"Do you know what they say?" Ivanel asked, taking them from him. He broke the seal on the letter from Star Lake.

"No, my lord," Arik replied. "I *do* know that they seemed to receive your letters well."

"Good," Ivanel said. "Have some wine while I read these."

"Thank you, my lord," Arik said. He poured himself a glass of wine as Ivanel read.

"Do you know this Johann of Star Lake?" Ivanel asked.

"Yes, my lord," Arik replied.

"Good."

The letter from Star Hall was similar. They would transport any refugees that arrived in Star Hall to Star Lake. Ivanel set that letter aside and broke open the letter from Ravenhall.

These people were more cautious. Their letter contained no names. Instead there were only instructions to deliver a letter containing the name of the contact in Star Hall to the same location, whatever that meant.

"Tell me about Ravenhall," Ivanel said.

"Very cautious," Arik replied. "I never saw a face, nor was I told a name."

"They have told us to deliver another letter to 'the same location,' " Ivanel said. "Do you know what that means?"

"Yes, my lord," Arik replied.

"Good," Ivanel said. "Arik, 'tis time you knew my plans, now that they have come this far."

"Yes, my lord?"

"We are setting up secret lines of transport to the Wastes for any mages who fall under the suspicion of the Hunt," Ivanel told him. "Ian is setting up those portions of the chain to the north."

"Where will they go, my lord?" Arik asked.

"That is up to Bjorn Rolfson," Ivanel said. "If anyone can help us, he can. We have begun the web. From here it will spread throughout the clans as each Circle contacts those adjacent to it."

"Are all the refugees to pass through Star Lake?" Arik asked.

"Yes," Ivanel said. "That should not cause too much trouble. A lot of traffic passes through Star Lake, and there are not that many of the magi."

"I see," Arik said. " 'Tis certainly a bold plan."

"Hopefully 'tis bold enough to succeed," Ivanel added.

"Hopefully," Arik agreed. "May I retire now, my lord? It has been a long journey."

"There is one more thing," Ivanel said. "Three families

of the magi have fled Reykvid. They are hidden at Hein-rich's old farm. Hervis is watching them. As soon as we hear from Nalur's Ridge, you are to take them to Star Lake.''

"When will that be?''

"With luck, we'll hear from them in a sevennight or so,'' Ivanel replied. "I want you to go out to the farm tomorrow and meet them. Then I have a letter for you to take to Foxmire.''

"That will be difficult,'' Arik noted. The border between Reykvid's lands and the Fox clan had been heavily pa-trolled ever since last year's war.

"I am confident you can do it,'' Ivanel replied.

"Thank you, my lord,'' Arik replied.

"Get some rest,'' Ivanel told him. "Tomorrow will be a busy day.''

Hervis came out to meet Arik as he approached the farm. In the last ten days, the young lesser Guardian had actually managed to get the farm into reasonable shape. Of course, he had yet to plant a crop.

"Greetings, Arik,'' he said.

"Hervis,'' Arik replied. "I have come to see the refu-gees.''

"They're in the barn,'' Hervis told him. "I'll take you.''

"Do not mention my name,'' Arik said.

"Of course, Guardian,'' Hervis replied.

One of the men was hauling a bucketload of earth from a pit in one of the stalls when they entered. Women were shoveling a pile of loose earth into sacks, apparently for removal later. Arik looked up to see where the rope was attached and saw a block and tackle hung from the rafters.

"You will remove *that* when you are finished with it for the day,'' Arik told the man who was working the rope.

"Y-yes, m'lord,'' the man said.

"This is Jarl Atkinson,'' Hervis said to Arik. He turned back to Jarl.

"This is our chief Guardian," Hervis explained. "He will be guiding you . . . from here."

"Are we leaving now?" Jarl asked.

"No," Arik replied. " 'Twill be at least another seven-night before we can leave. I have been away, arranging transportation and safe houses for you. We shall leave as soon as we receive word."

"Thank you," Jarl said. "We would all be dead now were it not for your help."

" 'Tis our duty," Arik said. "Nothing less. I wish to see the cellar."

"This way," Jarl replied. Arik followed him to the shaft in the stall. The sides were lined with wood. There were no gaps in the wall of the shaft, and the rungs set into the side of the wall did not so much as creak when Arik put his weight onto them.

Two other men worked below, expanding the cellar. It was almost finished. Wooden walls lined the cellar, as tightly fitted as the walls of the shaft had been.

"You've done well," Arik said.

"My brother and I were carpenters," Jarl informed him. "This is my brother Berek and my sister's husband, Arvis."

Arik nodded to them.

"This is the Guardian," Jarl explained to his relatives. "He says we'll be leaving in a sevennight."

"No," Arik corrected, "I said not *before* a sevennight. I've seen enough. Show me the door you have built for this cellar, Jarl."

"Yes, Guardian," Jarl replied. Arik followed the carpenter back up the ladder. The wooden trap door was sunk about six inches into the earthen floor of the barn. In an emergency, Jarl explained, it could be covered with earth and no one would be able to tell it existed.

"Very good," Arik said. "I will see you again when we are ready to depart. So we part."

"Until we meet again," Jarl replied.

"We are fortunate that they were carpenters," Hervis said once they had left the barn.

"Very," Arik agreed. He mounted and rode away from the farm. Ivanel would be pleased with his report on the progress here.

And then it was off to the Fox clan. Arik sighed.

CHAPTER

------- ELEVEN -----------

IT HAD TAKEN the wagons all morning to get ready for the trip to Pine Grove. Four wagons full of potatoes and vegetables, a fifth loaded with hay and another of woodcutting supplies—saws, axes and such. Four massive horses drew each wagon.

In addition, they were taking a dozen cows—two tethered to the back of each wagon. The caravan would be coming back loaded with the first batch of milled lumber this season. Ian hoped it didn't take them this long to get ready every morning, or it would take them all season just to get to Pine Grove.

Despite the delay, Ian was pleased. He had already completed the first third of his mission. With the caravan and its score of armed men as an escort, he had a good chance of completing the second third. His father would be pleased.

The only part of his journey that lay in doubt was the last portion. His father did not know exactly where to find Bjorn. Only that he lived in a lodge somewhere far to the north of Hunter's Glen.

Ian's only hope was that someone in Hunter's Glen would know how to find Bjorn.

Ian rode at the head of the caravan. In three days they had barely covered the distance that Ian could in one day of hard riding. They had just passed the last outlying farm of Nalur's Ridge yesterday.

Now they were beyond the area of relative safety that the garrisons at Nalur's Ridge patrolled. The surrounding forest had seemed to become darker—more ominous. Ian was uncertain whether or not that was simply his imagination.

"We shall make camp here!" the master announced. He was a heavy man, only some of which was fat. Ian had no doubt that the man could use the short sword he wore on his hip.

" 'Tis still daylight," Ian observed. As the only member of the caravan guard with a horse, he usually rode alongside the master.

"It won't be by the time we make camp," Master Geoff replied. "I don't want to be fumbling about in the dark. Our camp must be up by sunset."

"Bandits?" Ian asked.

"Aye, and worse," Geoff replied. Ian nodded. He had run into worse, already, on the way to Nalur's Ridge. He still shuddered at the memory of the hobgoblin's grisly lair.

"Form the wagons!" Master Geoff ordered.

Ian watched as the drovers arranged the wagons. They had not done this on the nights before. Two wagons were moved to flank each side of the road. One of the remaining two was placed at each end with a gap of about one wagon's length as a gate. The resulting enclosure was a square about thirty feet on a side.

The cattle were driven into the enclosure, and the horses were tethered to the outside of the wagons. The cattle were left free inside the makeshift corral.

Two of the drovers closed the pen with rope gates. Ian noticed that one of the cows was still outside the makeshift pen.

"They missed one," Ian said to the master.

"No, that's for our safety," Master Geoff replied.

"What do you mean?"

"Bandits are like wolves, lad," he explained. "They'll attack you if they're hungry, unless there's easier prey. Two of the guards will take that cow down the road a little ways and tether her to a tree. I doubt she will be there in the morning."

"But, that's . . . I mean . . . we've got over a score of guards!" Ian stammered. "You don't have to let them cow you like that!"

"Boy," the master replied sternly, " 'tis not my job to make the forest safe. I am only interested in getting safely to Pine Grove with my cargo intact. If it costs me half a dozen cows to do that, I'll pay the toll."

"I . . . see," Ian said.

"You think me a coward," Geoff said.

"No!" Ian replied. "No, not at all. 'Tis just . . . a different way of thinking. I am not used to it."

"Life is different in the Wastes," Master Geoff agreed.

"That it is," Ian said.

"Get your tent pitched next to mine," the master told him. "You have command of the first watch."

"Yes, sir," Ian said.

Foxmire was bustling with activity. Arik moved unnoticed among the busy throngs. So far he had learned that three events of great importance were about to occur here, which was the reason for the festival atmosphere.

Valther's cousin Locke was about to be named chieftain of the Fox clan. Valther had stepped down from that position.

What was interesting, was why. After Locke was named chieftain, he, Urall and Skald were all going to swear allegiance to Valther as king. This would put Valther in rule over three united clans on Reykvid's very border!

After Valther's coronation, he was scheduled to wed Urall's youngest sister, Freya. This would help to cement the new kingdom. Valther's heir would have blood ties to two of the three clans. Rumor had it that Valther's heir would eventually be wed to one of Skald's yet-to-be-born daughters to further strengthen the alliance.

On the morrow, the new royal couple would begin their journey to the new palace still under construction at Burton. From what Arik had heard, that palace was enough to rival the palace of Reykvid, with three concentric walls and enough barracks to house over two thousand troops.

This information alone was worth the effort of crossing the border from the Sword clan. Now, however, he had to find someone of the Circle in this madhouse.

Arik had already passed the Sign to over a score of likely prospects with no response. In one sense, the crowd helped to cover his actions. In another, he had to be more careful lest he alert the Hunt.

"Pardon me," someone said at one of the merchant's stalls next to him. "What think you of this blade?"

"I beg your pardon?" Arik said as he turned toward the man.

The man's aura was clearly visible, and his fingers were crossed in the Sign as he handed the blade to Arik, hilt first. His eyes were dark brown, as were his hair and beard. He was a few inches taller than Arik and more slender.

"You seem to be a man who is familiar with blades," the man replied. "I merely wanted your opinion on this one before I purchase it."

Arik took the dagger and examined it. It was unexceptional.

"I would not," Arik said. "The steel is not high quality. See the graininess in the metal? The blade will likely shatter if met with any force."

"I see. Thank you."

Arik handed the blade back, returning the Sign as he did so.

"My lord," the merchant said to his supposed customer, "my blades are the finest quality!"

"I don't think so," the man replied. "Good day."

The merchant fixed Arik with an angry glare. Arik merely smiled back and turned away.

"Are you in town for the coronation?" Arik's contact asked.

"Yes," Arik replied. "All three of them."

The other laughed.

"A new chief, king and queen," the other said. "Truly an auspicious occasion."

"They say trouble comes in threes," Arik replied. "Best to get them all out of the way at once."

The other laughed again.

"I had not thought of it that way," he said. "I am called Mavik."

"Sven," Arik said, extending his hand. Mavik took it firmly.

"If you have not secured lodging, I know of an inn nearby that still has some rooms available," Mavik said.

"And no doubt, you know the proprietor," Arik said, smiling. Mavik shrugged.

"You know blades," he said. "I know inns. This is a good one. You could do far worse."

"I meant no insult," Arik said. "Please, show me."

"Follow me," Mavik said.

Their destination truly was an inn. The sign over the street depicted a rabbit hiding under a bush while a fox sniffed the ground nearby. Mavik led him inside to a small table in the back corner. He motioned to the innkeeper as they entered, holding up two fingers. Their ale almost beat them to the table.

"Why are you here, Sven?" Mavik asked quietly once the barmaid had left.

"I have a letter for your High Magus from my lord," Arik told him.

"Do you know what it concerns?"

"Vaguely," Arik said. "My lord is arranging passage to the north for all those who flee the Hunt. It is an offer to help any of yours who need to . . . relocate."

"That is generous of him," Mavik said.

"It comes at a price," Arik added.

"And that is?"

"To take in other victims from elsewhere and pass them to us as well," Arik replied. "It would require you to expose someone as a contact for these other Circles."

"We give the name of this contact to you?" Mavik asked.

"No," Arik replied. "It is up to you to contact the other Circles. We do not want to know."

"That is wise," Mavik agreed. "Are you staying somewhere already?"

"The Sleeping Fox," Arik said. "Room twelve."

"May I have this letter?"

"Yes," Arik said. He took the letter from the inside pocket of his cloak and handed it to Mavik.

"I will contact you later tonight," Mavik told him. "After the ceremonies are over."

"I will be waiting," Arik said.

"So we part," Mavik said. "Finish your ale."

"Until we meet again," Arik replied. Mavik rose and left the inn.

That was almost too easy, Arik thought. That made him worry.

A knock sounded at the door to Arik's room. He got up from the chair and walked over.

"Who is there?" he asked.

"Mavik," came the reply. Arik drew his dagger and moved his weapon hand to where it would not be visible from the doorway. With his left hand he turned the bolt and opened the door.

Mavik was alone. Arik stepped away from the door, sheathing his knife.

"Come in," he said.

"You are cautious," Mavik noted. "That is good."

"No, that is necessary," Arik replied.

"I am to travel back to Smithton with you," Mavik told him. "Can you leave tonight?"

"Tonight?" Arik asked.

"Yes," Mavik said. "We have a family that must be smuggled out of the city. Since I am to return with you anyway, it seems like a good opportunity."

"Had I known, I would have rested before your arrival," Arik said.

"We need only travel an hour or so from the city," Mavik said. "Then we can make camp. Meet me outside of the south gate in one hour."

"Very well," Arik agreed.

"So we part," Mavik said.

"Until we meet again," Arik replied.

Arik waited impatiently out of sight of the south gate. Mavik was late. Could this possibly be a trap? Was the Hunt about to descend on him?

Not likely, he decided. If Mavik were with the Hunt, they would simply have taken him. They had no need to arrange such an elaborate trap.

On the other hand, it was possible that the Hunt had seized Mavik himself. If that were so, it was possible that they could learn that Arik was waiting here for him.

They would not learn that very quickly, though. Arik glanced toward the sky. A crescent moon was just climbing above the horizon. If Mavik had not arrived by the time it cleared the tallest tree, Arik would leave without him.

The clatter of a wagon interrupted his musing. Arik peered through the darkness. Soon the dark silhouette of a wagon became visible. It was too dark for Arik to see who drove the wagon.

He could see the aura, however. It was Mavik. Arik rode out onto the road.

"Sven?" Mavik called, pulling the wagon to a halt.

"Aye," Arik replied. Closer now, he could see that Mavik was alone in the wagon.

"Couldn't get them out?" he asked.

"They're in the back," Mavik said. "Give me a hand, will you?"

Arik dismounted and followed Mavik to the back of the wagon. Two large crates sat in the back of the wagon along with several smaller crates. Mavik rapped lightly on one of the crates thrice. He paused and then knocked twice before opening the crate.

Arik helped him remove the lid, not doubting that that coded knock would be changed long before he ever returned to Foxmire. A man sat up in the crate.

"Brin," Mavik said, "this is Sven. He'll be leading us to a safe place in Smithton."

"So we meet," Brin said.

"So we meet," Arik replied.

"Let's get Alysse and the baby," Mavik said. Again he knocked on the crate before lifting the lid. She handed the infant to her husband, and then Arik and Mavik helped her from the crate.

"Thank the gods he stayed asleep," Mavik whispered.

"The gods and a little catnip tea," Alysse replied.

"Brin," Mavik said, "you'll have to drive the wagon from here on out. My horse is a little further down the road."

"No problem," Brin replied. He and Mavik took the front seat while Alysse settled into the back, cradling her sleeping son.

"Are there any abandoned barns or such near here for us to camp overnight in?" Arik asked.

"None that I know of," Mavik said.

"Then we will travel through the night," Arik said. "And tomorrow as well. I don't like the idea of camping this close to the Hunt."

"Are you able?" Mavik asked.

"I am," Arik replied.

CHAPTER
------- TWELVE ------------

THE REPORTS WERE depressing. Three people had been indicted by the Hunt in outlying villages around Smithton during the last sevennight. From the reports, Ivanel concluded that at least two of them were innocent of the charges.

The third may or may not have been a mage. Once Arik returned from the Fox clan, Ivanel would send him to investigate. If there were any other magi still in that village, it would probably be best to relocate them.

However, Arik was a full day overdue and Ivanel was concerned. Had something gone wrong in the Fox clan? If so, had it been the Fox clan's border guards or the Hunt?

Ivanel had no illusions about that risk. If captured by the Hunt, Arik would make every effort to end his life before they could learn anything from him. If he failed to do so, however, no man could long withstand the persuasion of the Hunt. Ivanel, and the entire rescue operation, could be placed at risk.

Ivanel looked up as one of the guards knocked on his inner chamber door before opening it.

"My lord, the scout has returned," the guard said. Ivanel silently sighed in relief.

"Excellent," he said. "Show him in."

Arik walked into Ivanel's chambers, and the guard closed the door behind him.

"I expected your return yesterday," Ivanel said.

"I had to escort a family to the farm from Foxmire," Arik explained.

"Already?"

"Yes," Arik said. "They had run out of places to hide them in Foxmire. The Guardian of Foxmire took advantage of his trip here to bring them with him."

"Then we have saved another family," Ivanel said. "That is good."

"Have you heard from Nalur's Ridge yet?" Arik asked.

"No," Ivanel said. "I was also hoping to have heard from them yesterday as well."

"I'm certain that Ian is well," Arik said. "He's a good lad."

"Yes, I'm sure you're right," Ivanel agreed.

"Another four days shall see us in Pine Grove," Master Geoff said.

"I shall certainly be glad to see it," Ian replied. As they had travelled northward the forest had become more and more dense and overgrown.

"Aye," Geoff agreed. "However, it is always the trip back that is the most dangerous."

"Back?" Ian asked.

"Aye," Geoff said. "We will not have cattle to appease the bandits. However, they have also learned that we carry nothing of value to them on our return. Only milled lumber. We take no payment in coin."

"But your cargo is more valuable than lumber," Ian said. "Six wagons of lumber will not pay for all of this."

"No," Geoff agreed. "But twelve shall."

"Twelve?"

"Aye, why do you think my wagons run a team of four such powerful horses and carry two drovers?" Geoff explained. "The spare wheels we carry are not for repairs. We shall build six new wagons at Pine Grove. Then a team of two horses shall haul each wagon back. At Nalur's Ridge I shall sell the lumber and the six old wagons."

"You do this every trip?" Ian asked.

"Every trip," Geoff said.

" 'Tis a wonder that Nalur's Ridge is not crawling with wagons," Ian said.

"There are a lot of farmers in Nalur's Ridge," Geoff added. "They use many . . ."

He stopped talking when they reached the location where last night's cow had been left. He raised his hand, and the caravan slowly came to a halt behind him. He motioned for Ian to ride ahead with him.

On the previous nights, the cow had been taken. Not last night. Black crows covered the animal's corpse. Ian felt the gorge rise in his throat as they rode up on the site.

The cow had been torn apart where she stood. Blood and entrails covered the road. Bones dripped red as the crows fled their arrival. Most of the meat was gone. The angry buzzing of flies was everywhere.

"This is not the work of bandits," Ian said.

"Nor wolves," Geoff agreed. "Ready your bow."

Ian drew and loaded his crossbow as the caravan master dismounted. Master Geoff was right to be cautious. Wolves would not scatter their prey so. They would simply kill it and devour it in place. This was the work of something more vicious.

The caravan master returned to his horse and mounted quickly.

"Hobgoblins," he said. "At least three." Ian felt his blood chill. He still had occasional nightmares about the one he had faced.

"Three?" he said. "I thought hobgoblins were solitary creatures."

"Normally, they are," Geoff agreed. "This must be a mated pair rearing their young. One of the tracks was very small. Warn the others. *Nobody* wanders from camp tonight."

"Yes, sir," Ian said. They hurried to join the others. Even a *pack* of hobgoblins would not attack a large camp. However, a solitary straggler could easily be lured away from the main group, as Ian had learned.

The caravan travelled the rest of the day in almost complete silence. Every eye constantly scanned the forest around them.

However, the day, and the following night, passed without incident. On the morrow, everyone seemed to be in better spirits, although Ian noticed that they still travelled very closely together.

Owyn Liefson waited in the hall outside the lord's chambers. Lord Ivanel's castle was the most lavish building he had ever seen. Great stone halls, brass chandeliers, glass windows in some places. It was staggering. Even the council hall in Nalur's Ridge was not so ornate.

The door opened, and one of the guards stepped out into the hall.

"His grace will see you," the guard said, holding the door.

"Thank you," Owyn said, stepping through the door. He was inside a small foyer.

"Leave your weapons here," the guard told him. Owyn obediently removed his sword belt and hung it over a hook on the wall. Once he had done so, the guard opened the inner door for him.

"Owyn Liefson of Nalur's Ridge, your grace," the guard announced. A man with graying red hair and beard and no aura to speak of sat in a plush chair by a large fireplace. He rose to his feet as Owyn entered the room.

Owyn's heart climbed into his throat. He knew this man! He had come to Nalur's Ridge two years ago with a southern prince to hunt wyvern. While there, they had attempted to locate one of the magi. At that time, this man had given no evidence that he was of the Circle. Owyn had just walked into a trap!

"I am Ivanel," the man said, extending his hand, "chief of this hall. Enter and be welcome."

"I . . . I am Owyn Liefson of Nalur's Ridge, your grace," Owyn replied, using the title he had heard his escort use. He took the offered hand. Owyn was beginning to calm somewhat. If this *were* a trap, they would have sprung it already. Besides, Ian *had* been of the Circle.

"You may leave us," Ivanel told the guard.

"As you wish, your grace," the guard replied hesitantly. He looked suspiciously at Owyn before turning to leave.

"Please, sit," Ivanel invited, motioning to a chair across from the one he himself took. "How was my son when last you saw him?"

"In good health, your grace," Owyn said, taking his seat. "He was preparing to travel to Pine Grove when I left."

"A more lawless place there never was," Ivanel grumbled.

"Indeed," Owyn agreed. "However, he was travelling in the company of a large merchant caravan. He should have a safe journey. In fact, he should nearly be to Pine Grove by now."

"Excellent," Ivanel said. "I am pleased to hear he is well."

"Your grace?" Owyn asked hesitantly.

"Yes?"

"If I may ask," he said, "I remember *your* visit to Nalur's Ridge. Why did you not reveal yourself to us then?"

"That would not have been prudent," Ivanel replied. "You will recall that my prince was searching for a mage. I was not about to reveal to him the means of doing so. Or that I was of the Circle myself."

"I see," Owyn said. A knock sounded at the door, interrupting their conversation. The door opened and another man stepped in, unescorted.

His aura was as visible as the sword that hung at his side. His hair and beard were dark brown, and his brown eyes held the look of one who had killed before and expected to have to do so again someday. Guardian. Owyn returned his gaze evenly and nodded to him.

"Ah, Arik," Ivanel said. "This is Owyn Liefson of Nalur's Ridge. He brings us word of young Ian."

"So we meet," Arik said, extending his hand.

"So we meet," Owyn replied, rising to take the man's hand.

"See that he is given quarters for the night," Ivanel said.

"And a meal and a hot bath. Once he is settled, return here."

"Yes, my lord," Arik said.

"Owyn, would you join me at the high table for dinner?" Ivanel asked.

"I would be honored, your grace," Owyn replied.

"Good," Ivanel said. "Do you have a letter for me?"

Owyn removed two sealed letters from his saddlebags and handed them to Ivanel. Ivanel rose to take them.

"Arik will show you to your quarters," Ivanel said. "You must be tired from your long journey."

"*That* I am," Owyn agreed. "Thank you, your grace."

"This way," Arik said, opening the door into the foyer. Owyn left Lord Ivanel's chambers quickly. He was looking forward to that bath.

After Arik had left with the messenger, Ivanel sat in his favorite chair pondering the two messages. One bore an unfamiliar seal. The other was imprinted with Ian's signet. He should probably read the response from the Circle in Nalur's Ridge first . . .

To hell with it, he thought. He was more anxious to read Ian's letter. He had until dinner to read the other.

He broke the wax seal carrying Ian's signet. The letter definitely appeared to be in Ian's hand. Ivanel began to read.

> *Greetings, father,* the letter began. *I have arrived safely in Nalur's Ridge and have successfully contacted a local Circle.*
>
> *I almost did not make it here. The First Knight of the Hunt followed me all the way into the Boar clan from Reykvid.*

Ivanel almost rose from his chair at that.

Mathen! he thought. What business did the First Knight have following his son? He read on.

*Father, Mathen was one of us, although he did not
know it,* Ian's letter explained. *He was able to see my
aura and so realized that I was Circle. That knowledge has died with him, however. I confronted him
on the trail and was victorious. I do not believe that
he told anyone else of this.*

That was probably true. If the Hunt had indicted Ian,
Ivanel would surely have heard of it by now. Ian had *killed*
Mathen? That had been no mean feat! The First Knight had
been much more experienced in battle than Ivanel's son.

It will be good not to have to worry about that *man
again!* Ivanel thought. He read on.

Since then my trip has been relatively uneventful, Ian
continued. *Save for one encounter with a hobgoblin,
which I killed. This has earned me the friendship of
a lesser chieftain by the name of Erik, who will provide me with safe haven on my return trip.*

Ivanel smiled, sadly. Ian would not be returning from the
Wastes. However, the boy had no way of knowing that
Ivanel's letter to Bjorn included instructions for Ian to re-
main there until this madness had passed.

Ivanel wished he *would* see his son again so that he could
tell Ian how proud he was. To have slain first Mathen and
then a hobgoblin in single combat were two acts of con-
siderable valor. Even Ivanel had not realized that his son
had become such a formidable warrior.

How quickly they become men, he thought. He read further.

I am now preparing to depart for `Hunter's Glen,
Ian's letter said. *With the help of the Circle here, I
have secured passage with a merchant caravan for
the dangerous trip to Pine Grove. I will probably not*

be able to send a letter from there, but I will attempt to do so.

I miss you all, Ian concluded. *Give Eva my love and tell her I am safe. Your son. Ian.*

Ian's signet, pressed in ink, finished the two-page letter. Ivanel took a swallow of wine to soften the lump in his throat.

Some time, when he had not noticed, his son had become a man.

Ivanel sealed the first letter with a drop of wax that he deliberately left blank. He drew another sheet of parchment from his desk.

A knock sounded at the door, and Arik entered.

"Is our messenger settled in?" Ivanel asked.

"Yes," Arik replied. Ivanel handed him the letter from Ian. Arik took it and sat in one of the reading chairs.

Ivanel glanced at Arik from time to time as he penned the next letter. The Guardian showed almost no reaction as he read Ian's letter, although twice Ivanel noticed that Arik's eyebrows lifted almost imperceptibly.

Finally Arik set the letter aside and looked askance at Ivanel.

"Yes?" Ivanel asked, looking up from his letter.

"The First Knight?" Arik asked. "*And* a hobgoblin?"

"Indeed," Ivanel replied.

"The hobgoblin is itself surprising," Arik said. "But to defeat the First Knight of the Hunt! I fear that my money would have been on Mathen in that encounter. His experience in battle was much greater than Ian's."

"Arik, when did he grow up?" Ivanel asked.

"He hasn't yet," Arik replied. "Although he is much closer than I would have thought."

"Exactly."

"I'm certain that it happened here and there," Arik said. "In between things. Hopefully, he is correct and the whole of the Hunt is not onto him."

"I think not," Ivanel said. "Mathen would have had no support from Gavin with nothing but a 'feeling' about Ian. Not against one of the royal line. That is why he did not attack until *after* Ian had left Gavin's lands."

"True," Arik said. "Good. What of Nalur's Ridge?"

"They have given me a contact point for the refugees," Ivanel replied. "We have done it, my friend."

"Not until Ian finds Bjorn and gets his agreement as well," Arik said.

"We shall never know that," Ivanel replied. "All we know is that the refugees will find new homes in the Wastes. If Ian fails at this point, they will go *somewhere*. The Circle in Nalur's Ridge will see to that."

"I suppose that is also true," Arik agreed. "When do we lead the refugees to Star Lake?"

"Tomorrow," Ivanel said. "Before dawn. Take the two wagons with you to the farm and slip the refugees out before sunrise."

"Excellent," Arik said. "Hervis is about to go mad keeping them from throttling one another. That cellar is close quarters for that many."

" 'Tis the best we can do," Ivanel said. "Do you know where Colton lies?"

"I do," Arik replied.

"Travel through Colton on your way to Star Lake," Ivanel instructed. "The Hunt may have discovered the magi there. There may be more of our people in need of our help waiting for you there. Be cautious."

"Yes, my lord," Arik said.

"From Star Lake you will travel to Star Hall and Ravenhall. I shall have letters for you to take with you. After this trip, you will be able to stay home for a time."

"Until the next batch of refugees arrives," Arik noted.

"Exactly," Ivanel replied.

Chapter
------- Thirteen ------------

Arik watched as the refugees prepared to bed down in the wagons. Bairn knew they were empty enough. None of those fleeing the Hunt had many belongings left to them. Fortunately the weather was clear, although a simple tent covering would make the wagons comfortable even if the weather turned bad.

They had made good time today. They had ridden from before dawn until almost midnight. At first dawn, they would break camp and continue on.

"I had no idea there would be so many," Owyn said, interrupting his thoughts.

"What do you mean?" Arik asked.

"I imagined that people would trickle through," Owyn replied. "A family here and there. Maybe half a dozen at a time at the most."

"They will probably arrive that way at Star Lake," Arik said. "However, with only one ship to carry them to you, you'll no doubt see groups like this all the time. Is this a problem?"

"Yes, but we'll manage," Owyn replied. "We'll be buying a lot of wagons, though. And horses, for that matter."

"I'm sure you'll work something out," Arik said. "Now let's get some sleep. We've a long way to go yet."

Ian literally breathed a sigh of relief when the wagons pulled into the small village of Pine Grove—even though it quickly became obvious that Pine Grove was a village in name only.

The entire town consisted of four inns, a general store

and a blacksmith's shop. At the end of the only street that ran through the town sat a large sawmill. Except for the mill, each of these establishments boasted a large stable. In the case of the smithy, the stable was just a continuation of the smithy. The stables of the other establishments were separate buildings.

There had to be enough stable space for at least twice as many people as actually lived here. Ian wondered why that was.

"We'll make camp by the mill," Master Geoff told him. "I'd like you to stay through the auction, Ian. Sometimes that can get ugly. It'll be a lot less likely with you there."

"Auction?" Ian asked.

"Yes, the cattle will be sold at auction to the innkeepers," Geoff replied. "In that fancy armor of yours, you'll help keep the tempers down."

"When will that be?" Ian asked.

"Tomorrow morning," Geoff said. "Think you can bear to camp with us another night, lad?"

"I think I could bear that sooner than a night in one of these inns," Ian replied. Master Geoff laughed as they rode through the town.

"That is one reason that I prefer to make my own camp while I am here," Geoff agreed. "Not to mention, it keeps my property from walking off. I keep my watches just as tight in Pine Grove as I do on the trail. The only sword that will come to your defense in *this* town is your own."

"May I inquire directions to Hunter's Glen while you set up camp?" Ian asked.

"You may," Geoff said. "Just watch yourself, and leave your horse and your dog at camp."

"Yes, sir," Ian said.

Ian walked to the inn closest to the mill. There were only a few patrons in the common room. The inn smelled of stale smoke, alcohol and grease. There were a couple of other pungent aromas that Ian could not identify.

"G'day, m'lord!" the innkeeper said. "Will ye be needin' a room?"

"No," Ian said. "I was wondering if you knew the way to Hunter's Glen?"

"Can't say as I do, m'lord," the innkeeper replied. Ian turned toward the other patrons in the common room.

"Does anyone know the road to Hunter's Glen?" he asked. Most of the patrons ignored him.

" 'Tis somewhere north o' 'ere," one man said. " 'S all I know."

Ian felt a hand land on his shoulder. He turned and looked straight into a hairy chest covered by an open tunic. He glanced up to the red-bearded face of the man standing over him.

"If ye're not buyin', don't bother the customers," he said. "Now git!"

Before Ian could reply, he found himself propelled through the door of the inn by a single shove from the man's meaty hand. He landed in the dirt of the road in a jangle of armor and weapons.

Laughter followed him out of the inn. Ian scrambled to his feet.

How dare *he!* Ian thought, as his hand flew to the hilt of his sword. His face burned, and Ian felt his lips pull back from his teeth. He took a step forward and then stopped himself.

Ian took a deep breath and released his grip on the hilt of his sword, clenching and unclenching his fists. He closed his eyes for a moment.

Calm down, he thought. The only thing that had been injured was his pride. If he went back in there, Ian was certain that would change. No doubt, better fighters than he had challenged that brute.

He opened his eyes to see the bouncer watching him from the door to the inn. Ian made a rude gesture not at all befitting a young lord in the man's direction and turned away.

He crossed the street and walked into the next inn.

"Got tossed out on yer ear, eh, m'lord?" the innkeeper said when Ian walked in.

"Something like that," Ian replied curtly. "I'll have an ale."

"Smart thing walkin' away from *that* fight," the innkeeper said as he drew a mug of ale and set in on the bar in front of Ian.

"That'll be a silver half, m'lord," he said.

"A half-measure!" Ian objected.

"Aye," the innkeeper said. "Things are hard to ship inta Pine Grove. Ye should know that. Didn't ye just come in wi' the merchant?"

"I did," Ian confirmed, laying a Reykvid crown on the table. The innkeeper picked the coin up and examined it closely.

"Never seen one o' these before," he said.

" 'Tis from far south," Ian explained. "A full measure of silver." The innkeeper rang the coin against the tankard.

"A'right," he said. "I'll take yer southern money since ye're wi' Geoff." The coin disappeared, and the innkeeper laid a smaller but surprisingly well-crafted silver coin on the counter. Ian picked it up for a closer look.

The coin was from Nalur's Ridge. Apparently the farming town minted its own coin as well. He dropped it into his pouch.

"Do you know the way to Hunter's Glen?" Ian asked.

"Roughly," the innkeeper replied. " 'Tis a few days north o' here. A little to the west, I think."

"Does anyone know *exactly* how to get there?"

"Ye can ask," the innkeeper said, gesturing toward the other patrons.

"Am I going to get thrown out in the street?" Ian asked. He glanced over to a table where three people who looked an awful lot like the bouncer across the street sat without drinking.

"I'm not goin' ta toss out a payin' customer, lad," the innkeeper replied. "Even Jolaff wouldn'a do that."

Ian turned to the patrons. Like at the other inn, the few that were here looked to be lumberers. That explained the inns and the stables. Ian doubted that many of these people actually *lived* here.

"Does anyone here know the way to Hunter's Glen?" he asked. One man looked up from his stew.

"Aye," he said. "I live there." He spooned another bite of the stew into his mouth.

"Would you mind giving me directions?" Ian asked. The man shook his head and beckoned Ian over to his table. Ian walked over and sat down. The man was huge, at least as large as the bouncer who had thrown him out of Jolaff's inn. His blue eyes sparkled beneath a wild shock of blond hair. His beard was neatly trimmed, and he looked like he bathed more often than many in this town.

"Ian Urqhart," Ian said, extending his hand. The man sat up and back, studying him. After a moment he took Ian's hand.

"Urqhart?" he asked. "Any relation to Gavin?"

"You *know* Gavin Urqhart?" Ian asked.

"Know *of* him," the man grumbled. Apparently he did not have a very high opinion of Reykvid's king. "Hear he killed his father and then used someone who was once a friend of mine as the patsy fer it. My name's Lief, by the way."

"That's not quite true," Ian said. "I'm his cousin. Who was this friend?"

"Bjorn Rolfson," Lief said, dropping his voice to a whisper. "The stories from the south accused him of practicing. He was no more a mage than I am!"

Is that so? Ian thought. He surreptitiously passed Lief the Sign. The other took no notice of it.

"No, that lie was spread by Valerian," Ian whispered back in reply. "*He* was a mage. Gavin was in his power—he had no choice. Bjorn was exonerated. In fact, I'm trying to find him—to pay my respects. I'm serving my time of errantry."

"Well, ye're too late, lad," Lief told him.

"What do you mean?"

"He and his father were burned out of Hunter's Glen by

bandits,'' Lief explained. ''They were ne'er found. They're probably dead.'' Lief made the sign of the Hammer when he said this in respect for the dead.

''When did this happen?'' Ian asked.

''Nigh on two years ago, now,'' Lief said.

Ian furrowed his brow. That couldn't be right. It had been just a little over a year ago when Bjorn had brought Arcalion to Reykvid. He and his father had probably fled, arranging for a convenient ''bandit'' attack to cover their flight.

''Can you tell me how to get there anyway?'' Ian asked.

''Aye,'' Lief said. '' 'Tis not hard to find. You just head due north until you come to a road running northwest. Follow that, and it will lead ye into Hunter's Glen.'' Then Lief dropped his voice to a whisper again.

''Bjorn may have been cleared in Reykvid,'' Lief said. ''But he hasn't been here. I wouldn't spread it about that ye're lookin' for him.''

''Thanks,'' Ian replied. ''I appreciate it.'' The lumberer just nodded, returning his attention to his stew. Ian stopped at the bar, placing the Nalurian half-crown on the counter.

''Send that man another ale, please,'' Ian told the innkeeper.

''Right, m'lord,'' the innkeeper said, turning to draw another mug from the keg. Ian stepped out into the street.

Bjorn was probably still alive. The time that the lumberer had given for his death was *before* he had saved Reykvid from Valerian. The bandit attack and the lack of bodies sounded like a typical ruse.

Ian turned down the street toward the mill. Now that he had the information he needed, he didn't want to spend any more time in the town itself. At least Geoff's men were civilized.

Ian woke at dawn. Around him the camp was already busy.

''Awake?'' Master Geoff asked.

''I'll let you know,'' Ian replied, sitting up.

"Come get some breakfast," Geoff said. "It'll get you going."

"Thanks." Ian rose from his bedroll and stumbled over to the cookfire. The drover who doubled as the camp cook handed him a plate. Ian blinked in surprise. There were eggs on the plate.

"Where . . . ?" he began.

"They have a few chickens here in Pine Grove," Geoff explained. "I bought up the whole batch this morning. Thought it would do the men some good to have a real breakfast."

"You are an easy master to work for, Master Geoff," Ian said. The merchant smiled.

"Well, if you're ready to quit this errantry business, I could sure use a fine guardsman such as yourself," Geoff offered.

"Thank you, sir," Ian said. "But . . ."

"I know," Geoff interrupted. "You have a clan to rule someday. We'll have the auction first off. Then you can collect your pay and be on your way."

"Pay?" Ian asked.

"You didn't know you were getting paid?" Geoff asked.

"No," Ian said. "I thought I was giving my service in exchange for being allowed to travel with you."

"Gods," Geoff said, looking heavenward. "He works this hard when he thinks 'tis for naught! One measure of gold for half the trip."

"Two measures for the entire trip?" Ian asked. "How can you afford to pay your men that much?"

"Not my men," Geoff explained. "They get a single measure. Their captain is paid three. You, as my sergeant, are being paid two, halved for half the trip."

"I cannot accept," Ian said.

"You damned sure *can*," Geoff said. "Gods, listen to me! I'm arguing a man *up* in pay! You'll take your pay. I'll not have people speaking ill of me."

"I would not . . ." Ian began.

"Not you, lad," Geoff interrupted. "The other men.

Take the measure. The grief 'twill save me is worth it.''

"If . . . you insist," Ian conceded.

"I do. Come to the stand when you're finished eating."

"Yes, sir," Ian replied. In all honesty, the measure of gold would be helpful. Still, he did not feel quite right taking it.

Ian was happy to finally ride away from Pine Grove. He turned back in time to watch the last of the wagons disappear back into the forest behind him on their way back to Nalur's Ridge. Ian smiled—Geoff was a good trade master.

The forest was a lot thinner this far north. From what Ian had learned, the bandits began to thin out northward as well. There simply wasn't enough up here for them to raid.

That didn't mean the forest was safe, though. Ian still remembered the cow that had been torn apart by the hobgoblins. He would be well advised to take caution. His father and a lot of other people were counting on him to make it to Hunter's Glen alive.

"*Eighteen* people!" Johann exclaimed.

"Quietly!" Arik whispered. They were speaking in one of the upstairs rooms, so there was little chance of being overheard. Even so, it was best to be cautious.

"Where am I supposed to put that many people?" Johann said, more quietly. It was a valid concern. Arik had left Smithton with thirteen and had added another five at Colton. Snatching them from the teeth of the Hunt had been a near thing.

"You have not been preparing a place?" he asked.

"Not for that many!" Johann said.

"Normally they will come in smaller groups," Arik said. "These have been . . . accumulating."

"I suppose you're right," Johann said.

"Even so, you will accumulate them here, Johann," Arik said.

"How so?"

"How many ships are you using?"

"I . . . can't say," Johann replied.

"Fair enough," Arik said. "Assuming you are using one, Nalur's Ridge is a fortnight away, if I recall correctly."

"A little over that, usually," Johann confirmed.

"And about half that back, with the current," Arik added.

"Aye," Johann agreed.

"That means for three sevennights, people will accumulate here from all over the clans," Arik concluded.

"Gods above," Johann whispered.

"You will have to prepare some sort of holding facility," Arik said. "You will possibly have groups twice this size awaiting ship."

"Or larger," Johann agreed.

"What shall we do with these, now?" Arik asked.

"We only have to keep them a day," Johann said. "They will ship out on the morrow. I can keep them here for that short a time. Then we will start building a shelter."

"We used the refugees themselves to build ours," Arik told him. "They have plenty of time on their hands, and it takes little skill to use a shovel."

"We'll remember that," Johann agreed.

"Shall we bring them in the back?" Owyn asked.

"No, bring them in the front," Johann replied. "A few at a time. 'Twill arouse less suspicion that way."

"Agreed," Arik said. "I shall go fetch the first family."

Owyn watched as the refugees climbed aboard the longship. The town of Star Lake had not yet begun to stir from its slumber. In a little over a fortnight he would learn what measures Wilhelm had arranged to transport these people to Hunter's Glen.

Captain Oslaf was of the Circle, as was his entire crew. He was not a large man, but one would underestimate him at their peril if the cords of muscle on his broad neck were any indication. Not only their captain, he was their High Magus as well.

"That's the last of them," Arik said.

"That's enough," Oslaf replied. "I don't get paid for a cargo of refugees. If the groups stay this large, other arrangements will have to be made."

"I'm sure the Circle can arrange something," Arik replied. "Now that we have a place to send them."

"We're working on it," Johann assured the captain.

"We'll be pushing off at dawn," Oslaf said, turning to Owyn. "You had best be aboard by then."

"I shall come aboard now," Owyn replied. He turned back to Arik.

"Thank you again for your help," Arik said to him.

"We must work together in these perilous times," Owyn replied.

"I must depart as well," Arik said to Johann. "I have other bridges to build in this underground roadway of ours. Expect more arrivals soon."

"We will be prepared," Johann assured him.

"So we part," Owyn said.

"Until we meet again," Arik replied.

With that, Owyn turned and walked up the gangplank to join the refugees.

CHAPTER

------- FOURTEEN ------------

HUNTER'S GLEN WAS a much nicer sight than Pine Grove had been. As far as Ian had been able to tell, though, there was no actual town. A few farms nestled among the low, rolling hills had been cleared from the surrounding scrub forest.

After asking at a few farmhouses, Ian had found a farmer who kept a couple of small rooms off his barn for travellers. A silver measure a night for a room barely large enough to lie down in was a bit extreme, but Ian had little choice.

The price did include meals, however, and farmer Jonas's wife was an excellent cook, if breakfast had been any indication. Hopefully, he would leave Hunter's Glen before he spent too much of his pay from the caravan.

To that end, he had gotten directions to what probably passed for the heart of Hunter's Glen. A smithy and a provisions store. Jonas's boys had tried to follow Ian into town, but Jonas had reminded them of their chores and set them to work, leaving Ian free to try to locate the Circle.

He found the smithy easily enough, as Jonas had promised. He rode in front of the shop and dismounted. Sven, the smith, was a huge man. His face was clean-shaven for working with the fire, and his blond hair was cropped short for the same reason.

The smith was stripped to the waist, working with a piece of iron. Ian could not tell what it was going to be yet. He waited patiently until the smith set the bar aside.

"Can I help ye?" the man asked, looking up from his work. Ian smiled. He was in luck—Sven had a clearly visible aura.

"I am Ian Urqhart," Ian said. The man blinked in surprise, but quickly covered it.

"My horse needs to have her hooves trimmed and reshod," he continued. Ian patted her flank, resting his hand on her rump in the Sign. Sven gave no notice.

"I'll take care of her, m'lord," he said. "She should be ready by midday."

"How much?"

"A measure," he said. Ian presumed he meant silver. He reached into his purse and handed the coin to the smith, again passing him the Sign. Again, Sven took no apparent notice of it.

"Thank you, m'lord" was all he said as he took the piece of iron that he had been working and put it back into the forge. It was clearly a dismissal.

Ian wandered out of the shop, more than a little confused. The man had definitely had an aura. A powerful one at that.

Still, not everyone who had the Gift was Circle. Also, Sven might be an outcast—barred from the Circle. If that was so, he would not acknowledge Ian's Sign.

As Jonas had said, the provisions store was right next to Sven's shop. In this case, "right next to" meant that it was the next building, not that it was close. Hunter's Glen seemed to be very spread out.

Ian walked down the street and in through the front door of the shop. He walked up and set his hands on the counter, passing the Sign with his right.

"Can I help ye, m'lord?" the shopkeeper asked. The man was also blond-haired, but his was longer than Sven's, and he also wore a closely trimmed beard. He seemed to take no notice of the Sign, either, although he also had a visible aura. It was much weaker than Sven's had been.

"Yes," Ian said. "I need some supplies. Some salt, a flintstone, and a coil of rope. Do you have polishing oil and saddle soap?"

"Wouldn't be much of a store without the soap," the merchant said. "And the farmers here use the oil on their tools."

He showed Ian where to find what he was looking for, and soon they had accumulated a sizeable pile of merchandise on the counter. Ian bought a couple of sacks to put it in.

"That comes to three silver measures, m'lord," the merchant said.

Ian laid three Reykvid crowns on the counter and rested his hand palm down on the countertop, again passing the Sign. Again, there was no response.

A few moments later, Ian was carrying the sacks back toward Jonas's farm. Midday was still a long way off. He could make it there, share the noon meal and return to pick up Brazen.

For whatever reason, the Circle in Hunter's Glen was being coy. Perhaps they would be a little more open when he came back.

Ian woke abruptly. A hand over his mouth and nose stifled his instinctive cry of surprise. Someone held his shoulders and arms. Ian was actually grateful for this. If he had sat up, he would have driven in the dagger point that was at his throat.

Gods above! he thought.

"If you cry out," a voice whispered hoarsely, "or speak above a whisper, you will die. Do you understand?" Ian tried to mumble assent through the hand that cut off his air. He must have succeeded, for the hand was removed.

"W-what do you want?" he whispered, ashamed of the fear that he knew was in his voice. Thank the gods his father could not see him now! He would disown him as a coward.

"No," the unseen voice replied. "What do *you* want, Urqhart? Why have you come here seeking the Circle?"

"I carry an important letter for the High Magus," Ian said. "The lives of many of our people depend on me to deliver it."

"Who are *our* people, Urqhart?"

"Those of the Circle," Ian replied. "Those from all over the clans who flee the Hunt."

"What does this letter say?"

"I . . . don't know," Ian replied. "My father charged me to deliver three letters. One to the Circle in Nalur's Ridge, one here and one to Bjorn Rolfson."

"Bjorn Rolfson is dead," the voice whispered. "He and his father were burned out by bandits two years ago."

"I know better than that," Ian objected, a touch of anger replacing the fear in his voice.

"Bjorn returned with Arcalion to save us from Valerian a year ago," he added. "If anyone 'burned him out,' it was you to cover his tracks. My father claims that he now lives in a lodge far north of here."

"Is that so?" the voice said. The dagger pressed a little harder against his throat.

"Please, read the letter," Ian said, the fear returning to his voice. "Please—many lives depend on it." Ian waited for a response. After a time the voice spoke again.

"Very well, Urqhart," the man said. "We will read your letter. If you leave Hunter's Glen before we respond, we will kill you. Do you understand?"

"I do," Ian said.

"Leave the letter by the well out front in one hour," the voice told him. "If you attempt to wait and see who comes to collect it, you will be killed."

"I understand," Ian whispered.

"If you attempt to leave this room before the hour is up, you will be killed."

"How am I going to know?" Ian objected. "I have no glass."

"We will be reasonable," the voice said. "Do not attempt to follow us."

"I won't," Ian replied. The door opened, and Ian caught a glimpse of a cloaked figure slipping out into the moonlight. In the sudden light Ian could see that it was not a dagger at his throat but a sword. The door closed again. The hands holding his shoulders released him, and a huge figure slipped out the door. Sven, no doubt. Finally, the sword point left his throat and the last man slipped out into the night.

Well, he thought, still trembling. *I got in contact with the Circle, at least.*

Ian had no idea how long it had been. He just hoped that something close enough to an hour had passed. He cautiously opened the shutter over his window and peered out at the moonlit night.

The moon had just passed full four nights ago and still shed quite a bit of light. Ian saw nothing outside.

He pulled his saddlebags from under the cot and pulled the letters out. He carried them over to the window and read the names on them by the light of the moon.

He took the letter to Bjorn and placed it back in the saddlebags before replacing them under the cot.

Here's hoping, he thought. He opened the door to his room and stepped outside. Nothing happened.

Ian breathed a sigh of relief and crossed around to the front of the barn. No one attacked him—no arrow found his flesh.

So far, so good, he thought. He walked over to the stone well and laid the letter on its lip, placing a stone on top of it to keep it from blowing away or falling in. Then he turned and quickly headed back to his room.

Bairn, let them be reasonable, he thought.

Ian woke the next morning, surprised that he had managed to fall asleep after last night's visit. Someone was pounding on his door.

"Ian!" a young man's voice called. It was Karl, Jonas's youngest son.

"What?" Ian asked, still groggy with sleep.

"Mama says come to breakfast," he shouted.

"On my way," Ian replied, swinging his feet onto the floor. Outside he could hear the scamper of excited feet.

A slip of parchment by the door caught his eye. Someone

had slipped it under the door during the night.

Ian picked it up and opened it. The message inside was very short.

Follow the Call, it said. *Tonight.*

Well, they were going to let him see their gathering site. Either they had decided to trust him, or to kill him. Ian would find out which tonight.

Ian sat on the edge of his cot, fighting sleep. He was tired from helping Jonas around the farm all day, but it had saved him his crown for the day's let on the room. Now he waited for the Call.

And waited. The sun had set long ago, and the waning moon was climbing high into the night sky before it came.

He felt it, like an urge, compelling him to follow. Ian rose from the cot and stepped outside, a small bundle of black cloth in his arms.

Hunter's Glen was asleep. Ian followed the Call as it led him down the deserted road. Inside a few homes he could see lamplight flickering through the shutters closed tightly against the night and its denizens.

A few dogs barked at his passing, but Ian reached out and touched their minds, calming them as he passed.

Friend, he thought. *Sleep.*

His trip through the town was uneventful. Most people were sound asleep at this hour. Those few who were not sat safe inside their houses with no desire to venture out into the darkness.

Outside town Ian checked to make certain he had not been followed. No one was in sight. At the forest's edge, he unfolded his black cloak and draped it over him, hanging the hood low over his face.

He continued on—deeper into the forest. The Call led him like a beacon. He followed.

He knew the moment he passed the barrier of the lesser Guardians. At this point, the Circle had been notified of his arrival. Ian slowed his pace, still following the silent Call.

They were gathered in a small clearing, cloaked and

hooded. There were seven in all. The High Magus and the Guardian in the center, the other five surrounding them. The four lesser Guardians out in the forest would bring the Circle to a total of eleven souls. Not bad for a small town like Hunter's Glen. The Call ceased—he had arrived.

Ian approached slowly. He stopped just outside the wall of Power that was the Circle. The Guardian stepped forward and placed the point of his sword against Ian's throat.

"Who seeks to enter Circle?" the Guardian asked. Ian was certain he had felt this sword before.

"A supplicant," Ian replied. He released all of his guards and felt the mind of the Guardian touch his own.

"Are you armed?"

"I am not," Ian replied. He wasn't *that* stupid! There was a short pause as the Guardian weighed Ian's reply.

"Do you swear to preserve the sanctity of our Circle with your life?" the Guardian asked.

"I do," Ian replied.

"Enter in peace," the High Magus said. The Guardian stepped aside to allow him to pass. Ian added his own Power to the Circle and stepped across. He walked forward and knelt before the High Magus.

"Show yourself," the Magus commanded. Ian reached up and pulled his hood back, revealing his face, and his identity, to all of those within the Circle. If he betrayed them, they would all now know whom to kill.

"We have discussed your father's proposal," the Magus said. "Do you know of it?"

"No," Ian replied. "I was charged only to deliver the letters."

"Then 'tis time you knew," the Magus said. "He has requested that we send you to Bjorn with the one who will lead those who come to us fleeing the Hunt to safety. Here is our letter to Bjorn."

Ian reached up and took the sealed parchment from the Magus.

"Fjalin, our Guardian, shall ride with you," the Magus told him. "According to your father's letter, the first of those who flee the Hunt are probably already on their way.''

"Does Fjalin know the way to the lodge where Bjorn lives?'' Ian asked.

"No,'' the Magus replied. "None of us do. You shall have to find it as best you can. May Bairn guide you in your travels. You will meet the Guardian north of town after dawn. Guardian, show yourself.''

Fjalin removed his hood for a moment. Bright blue eyes beneath blond hair met Ian's gaze for a moment. Then the hood was drawn back up.

"So we part,'' the Magus said.

"Until we meet again,'' Ian replied. He put his hood back in place and rose to leave the Circle. He tried hard not to tremble as he walked away.

I did *it!* he thought. Now that he knew his father's plan, he was especially proud. Those fleeing the Hunt now had a place to go.

Ian met Fjalin north of town after dawn. He had said his farewells to Jonas's family, giving each of the three children a Reykvid penny to remember him by. Even gruff old Jonas himself had told him that Ian would always be welcome to let his barn.

Brazen had benefited from two nights of rest in a dry barn. She practically danced underneath him as Ian rode out of town. Hunter bounded along beside him, still treating this as just a grand outing, which, to him, was all that it was. Loudmouth was as recalcitrant as ever.

Before Ian had travelled a quarter mile into the forest, Fjalin stepped out from behind a tree. Hunter immediately barked and charged.

"Hunter!'' Ian called, halting the dog in mid-charge.

"Attend!'' he commanded. Ian dismounted as Hunter returned to his side.

"Good morrow, Lord Ian,'' Fjalin said.

"Good morrow,'' Ian replied. "Don't you have a horse?''

"There are no horses in Hunter's Glen," Fjalin replied. "Save for Lief the lumberer's team."

"Well, we can at least load your pack onto Loudmouth," Ian suggested.

"Loudmouth?"

"My mule," Ian replied. Fjalin smiled.

"An apt name," he said. "Very well." Fjalin shrugged out of his pack and handed it to Ian, who tied it onto the mule's back.

"EEEYAWW!" Loudmouth objected.

"A *very* apt name," Fjalin amended.

"Hush, Loudmouth," Ian said. "You had two days' rest in Jonas's barn."

"You really don't know where to find Bjorn?" Ian asked.

"I fear not," Fjalin replied.

"Then how are we going to find him?"

"We know they went north," Fjalin said. "And I also know that, at the time they left, they could not have travelled more than a moon before settling in for the winter. And they were heavily burdened with supplies."

"On foot?" Ian asked. Fjalin only nodded.

"And I know that they are living in a lodge," Ian added. "That's not much to go on."

"It will have to do," Fjalin replied.

"Well, we'll never find them just sitting here," Ian noted. "Are you ready?"

"I was the one who was waiting," Fjalin pointed out, smiling.

Chapter

------- Fifteen ------------

Brianna Klauswyf wandered through the marketplace. It was a beautiful spring day, and she had picked up most of tonight's dinner. On several occasions, Klaus had offered to hire a cook to save her this chore.

Their new wealth wasn't going to rob her of the pleasure of cooking for her family, however. She had allowed him to hire the maid, but shopping and cooking were two chores she reserved for herself.

Ever since the war against Reykvid, they had done well. The previous year they had harvested an unusually good crop. When the war had begun, Brianna had been afraid they would lose everything. That had not been the case.

Instead, Klaus had been able to buy the mill next to their land from the widow of the miller. The poor man had died during the war defending the city wall alongside Brianna's husband. Klaus had been wounded in that battle, but had recovered.

The extra money from the mill had enabled Klaus to hire workers to help him with the extra land he had bought after the war. The next year's crop had been even better than the last. With so many farms burned out and unplanted, their harvest had sold for top measure.

This winter, Klaus had bought yet more land around their farm and had hired extra hands to plant it. They would not get as high a price for their crop as they had gotten last year, but that was actually a good thing. The land was healing from the war, and so more farmers had crops to bring to market.

Klaus had helped with that by hiring workers to help

133

their neighbors plant and rebuild. He was a good man and a good father to their children.

"Can we go *home* yet?" Jason asked. Brianna smiled. He was ten summers old and short on patience.

"Soon, love," she said. "I just need a few more things for dinner." She smiled down at her son, who was dutifully holding his baby sister Hilda's hand. Her daughter of seven summers smiled up at her. Little Oslaf was asleep in his carriage.

". . . they caught another one!" Brianna overheard an old woman saying at the merchant's stall next to her.

"No!" another woman said. "Another mage?"

"Aye," the old woman replied. "A wealthy man, I 'ear. Owns a big farm south of town."

Brianna glanced over at that. Their farm was south of town. Which of their neighbors had the Hunt flushed out?

"They say," the old woman continued, "that 'e and 'is wife enchanted the old miller's widow so that she would sell the mill to them instead o' to 'er own blood."

"No!" Brianna said. She and Klaus owned the only mill south of Foxmire. These women were talking about them! They were not mages!

"'Tis true!" the old woman insisted. "The 'unt took the 'usband this very morning. They found a chest in the barn wi' a black 'en's leg and black robes and masks, they did. I even 'ear they found a 'uman skin in it."

This couldn't be happening! How could such a thing be happening?

"They 'aven't found 'is wife yet, though," the old woman continued. "I 'ear they'll be burnin' the 'usband on the morrow."

Brianna's vision dimmed and her stomach seemed to fall out from inside her. She felt a hand steady her by the arm.

"Are ye all right, dear?" the old woman asked.

"Oh! Y-yes, I'm fine," she lied. "That's terrible!"

"Aye," the old woman agreed. "But the 'unt sniffed 'em out. They always do. Everything will be all right, dear."

The Hunt was searching for her—*her*! They were going to burn her husband! Klaus, who had shared his good fortune with all of his neighbors. It wasn't right!

She fought to stop the tears that were trying to fall. She couldn't let these people see how upset she was. The Hunt would find her and her babies! Oh, Hrothgar, how could this happen to *them*?

It had to be Wiglaf, the old widow's nephew. He had wanted to buy the mill, but Klaus had offered Gretchen more money and had promised to allow her to continue to live in the millhouse and to support her. Wiglaf would not have been so generous. What would happen to Gretchen now?

She turned back to the stall to finish her business. If she bolted, who would notice? Was she being watched even now?

"Sad business, that," the merchant said.

"Y-yes," Brianna agreed. "That poor widow."

I'm the widow now, she thought. Tomorrow they would burn Klaus and she could do nothing to stop it. She had to save her babies.

The crowd at the east gate bumped and jostled its way out of the city. Brianna had bought a cheap shawl to help hide her identity. To avoid the appearance of wealth, she carried her baby, having discarded the carriage in a convenient alley. Thank Hrothgar that she always did the shopping in her old clothes.

The guards at the gate chatted among themselves, ignoring the throng that flowed out past them. There did not seem to be any special watch out. Perhaps they would be able to slip out of the city unnoticed.

And then what? What was she going to do once she made it out of Foxmire? Where could she go? Their friends would have nothing to do with them, if the old woman was right. Where could she go?

She could hide the children in one of the burned-out farms a little southeast of town. Then she could go home and see for herself if what they said was true.

Oh, Hrothgar, let them be wrong! she thought. *Let me go home and find Klaus worried sick about where we've been.*

Somehow, she didn't think that was going to be the case.

"Why are we here?" Jason asked. Brianna had found an unused barn that was almost intact. She and the children sat in the loft while she waited for the sun to set. Little Hilda and the baby slept on a pile of moldering hay.

"It's about what those old hags were talking about, isn't it?" he added.

"Jason Klausson, watch your tongue!" Brianna scolded. She had no idea he'd heard them. Thank Hrothgar he had kept his tongue until now!

"Papa . . . Papa's dead, isn't he?" Jason asked.

"No, honey," Brianna said, taking him into her arms. "He's not dead. We don't even know if this is all true. When the sun goes down, I'm going to go home . . ."

"No, Mama!" Jason shouted.

"Hush!" Brianna hissed. "Do you want the whole world to know we're in here?"

"Mama, you can't go back there," Jason whispered. "They'll catch you!"

"I'll be careful, honey," she said. "Your mama knows that farm better than they do. But you've got to promise me that no matter what happens, you won't say anything about this to Hilda."

"I'm not stupid, Mama," Jason said.

"I know you're not, love," she said. "I know."

The farm looked deserted. There were no lights in the windows. Brianna approached carefully, crawling through the hay fields toward the back of the house.

There should be a light on somewhere. If Klaus were home, every window would have a light in it and he would be up worrying about her and the children. Even disregarding the stories of the old women, something was not right here.

Before she reached the house, she heard voices speaking quietly. She couldn't quite make them out, though. She crawled closer.

". . . think she'll show?" one voice said.

"No," another replied. "Once these mages know they're found, they slip through cracks even a rat couldn't fit through."

Oh, gods, it was true! Brianna laid her face down in the dirt of the hay fields. Poor Klaus. What were they doing to him?

"Think she'll get away?" the first voice asked.

"Maybe. Locke's got half the guard out searching the abandoned farms, though. She'll not have an easy time of it."

The farms? Oh, gods! Her babies! Heedless of sound, Brianna rose to her feet and ran back through the hayfields. She had to get to the barn before they found her babies.

East of the city were the bogs that gave Foxmire its name. If there was any place nearby where they would be safe from the Hunt, it was here.

Brianna carried the sleeping Hilda, and Jason followed her carrying Oslaf. Their feet sank into the soft earth beneath them, and the smell of decaying vegetation was strong.

"I don't like this place," Jason said.

"Let's hope the chieftain's guards don't like it either," Brianna said. "It's not so bad in the day. I used to get in trouble for playing here when I was a little girl."

"Really?" Jason asked.

"Truly," his mother corrected. "Now be quiet. There are people trying to find us."

They were deep into the bog by the time Brianna found what she was looking for. An old willow, far older than Brianna, sat on a small hillock. She led Jason beneath its draping branches.

The hole was no longer there. Over the years, earth had washed into the hollow, filling her childhood hiding place. But the earth was soft and came away easily in her fingers just as it had so many years ago.

Soon there was a hollow beneath the willow's roots large enough for all four of them to squeeze into. Her new shawl, caked with mud, would hide the entrance from prying eyes.

Little had she known, as a little girl playing in the marsh, that her favorite hiding place would one day save her life.

Strange, how life turns on us, she thought.

Jason crawled into the hollow and Brianna handed Hilda, and then Oslaf, in to him. Then she crawled backward into the muddy pit and stretched her muddy shawl across the entrance.

Once the sound of Jason's breathing told her he was asleep, she finally wept—quietly.

"This is hopeless," Ian said after their first day of travel. "They could be anywhere. Just draw a half-circle north of Hunter's Glen for a moon's travel and they could be anywhere within it!"

They had passed absolutely no sign of human habitation. When he had left Hunter's Glen Bjorn had had over a moon to flee before winter set in. Ian would never find him! He would fail in the quest with which his father had entrusted him when it mattered the most.

"I would say a quarter-circle," Fjalin replied. "Pointing north for three sevennights travel and cut off the first sevennight from Hunter's Glen. They would not stop so close."

"That's still a *lot* of ground to cover," Ian objected, afraid to let his hopes rise.

"True," Fjalin said. "But I knew Bjorn. My guess is that he would have travelled due north for the first few days."

"That could narrow it a little," Ian granted.

"So," Fjalin said, drawing with his finger in the dirt. "If this is Hunter's Glen, we go due north for three days."

Ian watched as Fjalin drew a small circle and then a straight line up from it about a hand in length.

"Then we draw our quarter-circle outward," he said, drawing two lines up and to the right and left of the first, connecting them at the top with an arc.

"We scratch out the first sevennight of travel and that leaves us this," he said. Ian looked down at the section of the circle that was left. It resembled a slice of pie that someone had eaten the end from.

"A fortnight's travel due north puts us in the center of this area," Fjalin pointed out, drawing a dot in the center of the pie section. "We start searching from there." Fjalin drew lines out from the center in the direction of the four cardinal points and the four points between.

"The animals will tell us where there are people," Fjalin concluded.

"So, after the first sevennight we start asking the animals," Ian observed excitedly. Where there were people, there would be Bjorn. They *could* do it!

"Exactly," Fjalin said.

Mavik slipped into the Hidden Hare. Arvad was serving his midday patrons. Mavik caught the eye of the innkeeper and wandered to the table in the far back corner. Soon Arvad came back to his table carrying a tankard of ale.

"Something is amiss?" Arvad asked quietly.

"I need to speak with you," Mavik replied.

"Finish your ale and meet me at the cellar door," Arvad said.

"That'll be a copper measure, m'lord," he said more normally.

"Robbery as usual, Arvad," Mavik replied conversationally, tossing him a coin.

"Aye, but you rogues won't let me charge more," Arvad quipped back, before turning to attend to his other customers.

Mavik finished his ale and walked back out into the street. He turned down the alley as if taking a shortcut. He glanced behind him before stopping at the rear door. It wouldn't do to have someone notice his departure and stealthy return to the inn, after all.

He knocked thrice on the door, paused and knocked once more. Arvad opened the door and stood aside as Mavik quickly slipped in. Together they descended the steps to the cellar.

"Have you gone mad?" Arvad asked.

"My apologies, Magus," Mavik said. "This matter could not wait for long."

"What has happened?"

"The Hunt has taken a victim," Mavik replied.

"Gods," Arvad groaned. "Who is it?"

"Klaus Hanson," Mavik said.

"Who?"

"He is not one of us, Magus," Mavik explained.

"What is the evidence against him?" Arvad asked.

"False, of course," Mavik replied. "Accusations from a prominent merchant and the contents of a poorly hidden chest. The Hunt found black cloaks and a black silk bag with the feet of a black cock and a black hare within."

Arvad snorted derisively. The cloaks were used by the magi, but the bag and its contents were nothing more than superstitious trappings. If a person were found with such things it should be taken as proof that he was *not* a mage.

"I suspect that owning something this merchant desires is Klaus's true crime," Mavik said.

"There is nothing we can do for him," Arvad said.

"It is not Klaus that I am concerned with," Mavik said, "although I grieve for him."

"Then who?"

"He has a wife and three children," Mavik replied. "They have not been seen since he was taken. It is becoming apparent that they have fled. Magus, may I extend the protection of the Circle to these people?"

"Do you know where she is?" Arvad asked.

"No, but I can almost certainly find her before the Hunt does."

"Children . . ." Arvad mused. It was bad enough to falsely execute an innocent man. To indict his children as well for nothing more than greed was an abomination.

"Magus?"

"Yes," Arvad said. "If she will swear and if she passes our tests, you may extend our protection to her."

"Thank you, Magus," Mavik said.

"Now go," Arvad told him. "You must find her before the Hunt does."

"Yes, Magus," Mavik said. He hurried up the stairs and back out into the alley.

Fjalin taught him how to read the animals. You didn't so much single out a specific animal as you listened to the patterns their thoughts made. For instance, one did not single out a lone hawk, but all of the birds within one's Power.

It was possible to focus on a single creature. Some of the most adept could even see through the eyes of a creature in such a way.

But for what Ian and Fjalin were trying to do, the broader picture was best. So, on their sixth day of travel, Ian began trying to sense the patterns of the wildlife around them.

He learned from the hares where the foxes and wolves lived, and from the hawks which fields bred the most mice. He learned where the lynx hunted that the hares and the foxes both tried to avoid.

The grouse and pheasants also told him where the lynx and the hawks hunted. Even the little mice told him where to find tasty berries and roots. But none of the animals thought of Man.

"Not many people up here, are there?" Ian said, opening his eyes.

"No," Fjalin agreed. "We travel into the lands where the sun is gone for most of the winter. Few people live this far north."

"Apparently, there are about to be more," Ian said.

"The magi have fled to such places before," Fjalin said.

''When the ungifted have hunted us in the past. It is usually temporary. They will forget us again.''

But what about when one of our own hunts us? Ian thought, remembering Mathen. But he was dead, thank Bairn.

Chapter

------- Sixteen ------------

"Mommy, I'm *HUNGRY*," little Hilda cried.

"I know, precious," Brianna said, hugging her daughter. "After dark, I will go and gather some food for us."

"When can we go home?" Hilda asked. Brianna choked back a sob. By this time Klaus had been burned by the Sacred Hunt and that dog Wiglaf would have seized their property. Damn him to *Hell*! Right now, Brianna wished that she *was* a magess. She would rot Wiglaf's flesh from his bones while he lived if she could.

"We *can't* go home!" Jason shouted.

"Shut up!" Brianna hissed. "Do you want to bring the Hunt down on us, too?"

"No," Jason muttered. He was not yet a man, but was beginning to feel like one. Oh, how she wished he could have the chance to become one! He had his father's dark eyes and her golden locks. He would have made a handsome man in his prime.

"We'll be all right," Brianna assured them, although she didn't believe it herself. It was only a matter of time before the hunters found them. Who would help an accused magess?

No one, she thought. *No one at all.*

Mavik watched the dead willow. It was nearly sundown. That was no way for someone to have to live. Especially children. The first rainstorm would wash them right out of that hole.

Still, the woman had proven resourceful. She had successfully hidden her family from the Hunt for three days in that little hollow. If Mavik had not been able to ask the bullfrogs and the herons where she was, he himself probably would not have found her.

The sun slowly sank below the horizon. The shadows lengthened and then finally disappeared in the twilight. Mavik saw movement at the willow.

The woman, Brianna, crawled out from under the tree. Mavik almost had to stifle a laugh. With her clothes, hair and face mud-plastered from the marsh she almost looked the superstitious picture the common folk held of the magi.

Still, it was no laughing matter. Brianna made her way through the marsh, just as she had last night. She planned to go to some nearby farm and steal dinner for her children. Tonight, though, those plans could not be allowed to continue.

The Hunt had realized that the thief who had been raiding the farms in this area for food was probably Brianna Klauswyf. They would be waiting for her.

Silent as a ghost, Mavik followed her through the marsh. He needed to wait until she was far enough away that her children would not hear them before he approached her. The night darkened quickly, giving him the cover he needed. Only the barest sliver of the waning moon hung in the sky.

As soon as they were far enough away from the willow, Mavik broke into a silent jog and quickly crossed the distance between them.

Brianna's scream never passed her lips. Strong arms seized her from behind, pinning her arms to her sides, and a leather-gloved hand clapped over her mouth.

Hrothgar, save me! she thought instinctively. But he would not—his priests had already burned her husband. She began to weep. She would be left dead in this accursed swamp and her children would starve, or drown in the marsh.

'Tis not fair! she wailed silently.

"Brianna Klauswyf," a man's voice whispered behind

her. "If you cry out, I will have to kill you. Do you understand?"

Her breath, and her tears, stopped. He knew who she was! But . . . he was not of the temple?

"Do you understand?" he asked again. She nodded. As his hand left her mouth, she took in a deep breath and then felt the cold steel edge of a knife against her throat.

"Please, m'lord," she said in a trembling voice. "I won't resist, if 'tis my body you want . . ."

"Perhaps another time," the man replied, with a touch of amusement in his voice. "If you've a mind to. I have brought food for you and your children."

Brianna's mind spun. Food? She began to turn. His arms tightened about her, and the knife pressed against her throat.

"Do not move!" he ordered in a harsh whisper. She froze in his arms.

"The Hunt has realized that you've been robbing the local farms," he said. "This area is no longer safe for you."

Brianna laughed bitterly. *Safe?* What place was safe for her?

"Brianna," the man whispered. "Do you want to live?"

"Who are you?" she asked. There was a pause.

"I cannot answer that yet," the man replied. "Let us say that, if the Hunt took me for the fire, they would not be taking an innocent man."

"What . . . ?" Brianna said, momentarily confused before the realization hit her.

"Oh, gods," she sobbed. She had been found by the dark ones themselves. She had wished to be a magess earlier. Had they heard her? Or were they here to exact their own vengeance?

"Oh, gods," she said again. "Please don't hurt my babies. We've never hurt you."

"Brianna," the man whispered. "I have brought you food. I have come to offer you our protection."

The protection of the dark ones? At what cost? Her body? Her soul? Her children?

"W-why?" she asked.

"We are not what you think we are," the man said. "Even though you are not one of us, we can not stand by and watch three children be put to the fire. Not if we can stop it. But we will not help you if you do not want us to. You may have the food. But if you wish, I will depart here now and never return."

"W-what is . . . the cost?"

"A fair question," the dark one replied. Somehow he did not seem as . . . evil as she would have expected. But then, it was said that evil always came in a pleasant guise. However, Wiglaf had not come in a such a guise, and there was no denying the evil of his greedy soul.

"If you accept our help," the man told her, "you can never live among the common people again. You will have to swear never to betray us. And if you break that oath . . . you will die. Once you come to us, you can never leave alive. Do you understand that?"

"Yes," she said. If she were to leave, she could betray them. That she understood. However, he still had not answered her question.

"But . . . what must I *do*?"

"You must ask for our help," the dark one said. "You must submit to the Rite of Acceptance. You will be questioned in the Circle. If you give your oath falsely, you will be killed and your children will be raised as our own. We can tell if you lie, Brianna."

"I . . . believe you," she said. She had no doubt that they could read her very soul. "But . . . what do you *want* of me?"

"Only your oath," the man replied. "We want nothing more than your loyalty to that."

Oh, gods, could it be *true*? Or was this some trick of the dark ones to steal her children from her? It was an easy decision. If the Hunt found her, then her children would be burned alive.

"It seems I have little to lose," she said.

"And everything to gain," the man agreed. "Will you accept our help?"

"Gods forgive me, yes," she sobbed.

"Saving your life, and your children's lives, is something you need not beg the gods' forgiveness for, Brianna," the dark one whispered. "You will see. We are not the monsters we are painted to be."

"It seems I shall find that out," she breathed.

"Yes," the dark one agreed. "I shall return tomorrow night. Meet me here, south of the willow you have made your home. If you are not here, I will know that you have decided to refuse our aid and shall depart without malice. Do you understand?"

Brianna nodded. They were giving her every opportunity to refuse their help. Of course, once she accepted it, the decision was unchangeable.

"I am going to release you now," he said. "Do not turn around until you hear me leave. Do you understand?"

"I do," she said. The knife left her throat, and his arms released her. She felt a hand on her shoulder.

"Here," the dark one said, handing her a package from behind her. "You will find enough food for a sevennight in here. Longer if you're careful. If you decide to reject our assistance, at least you will have food for a time."

"Thank you," Brianna said, taking the pack.

"Until we meet again, Brianna," the dark one said. Then she felt his presence move from behind her. She turned around in time to catch a glimpse of a black-cloaked figure vanishing into the swamp.

"Gods forgive me," she whispered to herself.

Brianna crawled out from their shelter beneath the willow just before sunset.

What am I doing? she wondered. Here she was, about to deliver herself, and her children, willingly into the hands of the dark ones.

Still, the food had been good. Last night, she had eaten

some and then waited for what seemed like forever before she returned to her children. She had suffered no ill effects and, for the first time in four days, her children were not hungry. She had even made enough milk for her youngest.

I am doing what I have to, she told herself. The temple had given her no choice. *They* had driven her to accept the help of these . . . people.

She walked south, to the place where he had . . . approached her before. She waited. The shadows disappeared in the deepening twilight, and she still waited.

What if he does not come? she thought. To her surprise, she found that the thought frightened her. It was the first time she had felt anything resembling hope. To have it torn from her now would be more than she could bear.

She gasped in a mixture of surprise and relief when strong arms seized her from behind. His hand over her mouth muffled her initial cry of surprise.

" 'Tis I, Brianna," he said. "Do not fear." She relaxed in his arms, and he removed his hand from her mouth. Tonight, he did not hold a blade to her throat.

"Fear is all I know now," she said. She was surprised at how close to tears she felt.

"I know," he said softly. The sympathy in his voice *sounded* genuine. "We can change that. Will you let us help you?"

"Yes," Brianna whispered, surprised at how easily that answer came tonight. "I accept your help, willingly."

"Good," he said. "Do not turn around."

He released her. Then he reached around her to hand her three bundles of cloth.

"When I leave, return to your tree," he said. "Bring your children out and place the hoods over your two oldest. Then place the third over your own head. When you have done this, I will return. Oh, and don't forget the food. No sense letting it waste."

Brianna could not help but laugh at such a commonplace concern. For some reason, it seemed so ludicrous, so out of place.

"I'm sorry," she said when the short fit had passed. But there was no answer. She turned to find that the dark one had already left her.

Feeling more than a little foolish, she returned to the tree. It took a few moments, but she managed to bring the children out into the warm night air.

"Mommy, I'm scared," little Hilda said.

So am I, Brianna thought.

" 'Tis all right, Hilda," Brianna said. "We're going to go somewhere."

"Home?" Hilda asked.

"No," Brianna said. "We're going . . . to a friend's home. Where it will be warm and dry and safe."

"Where?" Jason asked. Brianna turned and frowned at him. Jason hushed.

"But first, we have to put this on," Brianna continued, holding out the hood. "Because our friends don't want anyone bad to see us. All right?"

Hilda just nodded, and Brianna pulled the hood over her head. There was a drawstring at the bottom. Brianna tied it loosely. Then she turned to Jason.

"You're not gonna put that over my head!" Jason objected.

"Jason Klausson," Brianna said. "Would you rather spend the rest of your life living in a muddy hole? You do as I say."

"Who are these friends?"

Brianna grabbed her son by the arm and pulled him out of Hilda's hearing.

"They don't want us to be able to identify them to the Hunt!" Brianna whispered sharply. "They're going to help us, but not if it gets them burned at the stake! Now you do as I say!"

"Yes, mama," Jason grumbled. Brianna pulled the hood down over his head and pulled the drawstring snugly around his neck.

"It's too tight!" he complained. She checked. She was able to slip her finger under the edge easily.

"Hush!" she whispered. Then she tied the string into a double-square knot. She wasn't going to have him untying it and getting himself killed. She had no illusions that their benefactors would hesitate to do so.

Finally, she slipped the hood over her own head and pulled the drawstring taught, tying the knot in the same double-square around her own throat. Then she waited.

She did not wait long. Soon she felt a hand on her shoulder that quickly moved to inspect her hood. Her heart leaped at the sudden sound of her baby crying.

"Shhh-sh-sh," she heard someone hush softly, and then a light humming. Brianna smiled beneath the hood. It was a tune she herself had hummed to the baby on occasion. The crying quieted.

"We will have to carry you, Brianna," the dark one whispered to her. "The swamp is no place to walk blindly."

"I understand," she said. His hand took her by the arm.

"Lay back," he said. His hand guided her as she lay down on the ground. Suddenly, something beneath her lifted. It was soft, like cloth. To her hands it felt like canvas. There was a hard post under the cloth on either side of her. They were carrying her on a cot of some type.

"Let's get out of here quickly," the dark one said, presumably to others he was with. "The Hunt is right behind us."

They carried her for a long time. She wasn't certain, but she thought that the people carrying her traded with others at least twice. She no longer heard her children.

She also had not heard the sound of footsteps in water for some time. Instead, judging from the jarring of their steps, the ground felt firm beneath them. Occasionally she could hear the sound of twigs and leaves underfoot.

It was obvious that they had left the swamp and gone into a nearby forest. She turned her head, listening to the night sounds. A hand touched her shoulder.

"Not long now," the dark one assured her. So—he was

still with her. Somehow, she found that comforting.

True to his word, they soon stopped, and her bearers set her down gently on the ground.

"Come," he said. "Take my hand."

She reached up and felt his hand take hers to help her to her feet. He gently turned her to face a certain direction.

"Come with me," he said. "Careful." She followed his lead, stepping carefully. They stopped.

"Who comes?" an unfamiliar voice asked. Brianna started in surprise. The speaker had made no attempt to soften his voice. Apparently, they felt secure here.

"One not of us who seeks our protection," her guide answered. "For herself and her children."

"Let her approach," the voice said.

"Take four steps," the dark one whispered in her ear. "Then kneel."

Brianna nodded and he released her. She carefully took the four steps and then knelt.

"Who are you?" the voice asked.

"I am Brianna Klauswyf," she said.

"Do you seek our protection?" the voice asked.

"Yes," she said. "If not for me, please for my babies." There was silence for a time.

"Do you not wish our protection for yourself as well?" the voice finally asked.

"If you will give it," Brianna said.

"Will you submit to the Rite of Acceptance?"

"I will," Brianna said.

"Do you know the consequences if you fail?"

"I will die," Brianna replied. "Will my children still be safe?" There was another pause.

"We will care for them as our own," the voice assured her. "Now bow forward and expose your neck to the Sword of Judgement."

Brianna bowed forward. Soon she felt the cold steel edge of a blade against the back of her neck. She shuddered at the touch. She knew that its bearer would strike her head from her shoulders if he felt it necessary. Then she felt something strange—almost as if there were something, some*one* sharing her mind.

"Do you feel the touch of the Guardian?" the voice asked.

"I . . . think so," she said.

"Are you ready, Guardian?" the voice asked.

"I am," the dark one replied. It was he who held the blade. The one she did not know began to question her.

"Brianna, do you accept our protection willingly in full knowledge of who we are?"

"I do," Brianna said. The sword did not waver.

"Do you swear to protect with your life any of our secrets you may learn?"

"I do." Still the sword held steady.

"Do you swear to protect with your life the identities of any members of the Circle?"

"I do." There was a pause. Brianna trembled, but the sword did not move.

"So be it," the voice said. "We accept you into our fold. Be it known that if you betray any part of this oath, your life will be forfeited to us."

She remained silent.

"Guardian, we commend our new sister to you," the voice said.

"I accept the charge," the dark one replied.

"Then we shall take our leave," the voice said. "Brianna, so we meet and so we part, until we meet again. May Bairn watch over you on your journey to your new home."

Who is Bairn? Brianna wondered. She heard the sound of people walking, and then nothing. Finally the sword left the back of her neck.

"You may stand," her benefactor told her. He helped her to her feet and, for a moment, fumbled with the knot at her throat.

"Gods, woman!" he said. "I am going to have to cut this."

"All right," she said. She felt the blade of a dagger slide

under the hood and cut the cord. Then he removed her hood.

She looked around. She was in an old, run-down shack. From the heavy dust which now bore their tracks, she could tell that this place was not used often. A single lantern lit the room.

She turned to the dark one to find that he had removed his own hood. For the first time she looked upon him. His dark eyes gazed kindly at her from beneath equally dark hair. Panic suddenly gripped her.

"Where are my children?" she cried.

"Safe," he said. "About now, they should be bundled up in their blankets, fast asleep. I will take you to them."

She exhaled—a sigh of relief. Then an odd thought struck her. She looked back up into the man's face.

"Am . . . I a magess now?" she asked.

The man threw back his head and laughed.

CHAPTER

------- SEVENTEEN ------------

TRUE TO THEIR word, Brianna's children had been safe and asleep when she had been brought here last night.

She did not know where "here" was, however. She had been placed in a crate and loaded onto a wagon. When she had been released from the crate, they had once again hoodwinked her. She had been able to tell by sounds and smells that they were back in the city.

They had descended a flight of steps and now appeared to be in a cellar of some sort, and, from the noises overhead, Brianna was almost certain it was attached to an inn somewhere.

Wherever they were, it was obvious that this room had been used for this purpose before. Straw mats on the floor served as beds for her and the children. A table, low enough for people sitting on the floor to use, served for the few meals they had eaten here. A lamp on that table was the room's only illumination.

In another room, with only a curtain for a door, a large wooden tub had given them all the first bath they had enjoyed in many days. It was a welcome change from the swamp.

The room's only door opened without warning. Little Hilda ran to Brianna's arms for protection while Jason walked over to the door.

"Hello, Jason," the Guardian's familiar voice said. He was cloaked and hooded again, as he had been ever since that one time last night when he had allowed Brianna to see his face. Another person followed him in. Brianna thought she recognized the form of the plump woman who had been tending to them all day. She was also cloaked and hooded.

"Hello," Jason said. "Why do you dress like that?"

"Because I'm so ugly," the Guardian replied. "Good evening, Brianna."

"Is it evening?" she asked, smiling at his teasing of Jason. It was obvious that her son did not believe his answer.

"Just barely," he said. "We will be leaving soon."

"Where are we going?" Jason asked.

"Smithton," the Guardian replied. "To another safe house. I will travel with you."

"Here's another draught for the baby, dear," the woman said, her voice proving her gender. She handed Brianna a small bottle.

"Thank you," Brianna replied. Little Oslaf had picked up a wheeze during their stay in the swamp. The magess had brought down teas and poultices for the baby all day. He was already starting to sound a little better.

That wasn't magic, though. Brianna had tested the tea herself before giving it to her child. It had been nothing more exotic than a weak tea of echinacea and comfrey mixed with honey to sweeten it. Exactly what the family's apothecary might have given her.

"And I've made some more for tomorrow," she said, setting a larger bottle on the table. "The tea won't keep longer than that, but you should be able to get more in Smithton if he hasn't gotten better by then. Just shake the bottle and warm it a bit before you give him any."

"Thank you very much," Brianna said again. The woman nodded and turned to leave the room.

"We've loaded some things for you in the wagon," the Guardian said. " 'Tis not much. Some old clothes and a few other little things. We did come up with this, though."

From somewhere beneath his cloak he produced a child's doll. The body was just stuffed linen, but the head was painted wood with flaxen hair. When he tried to hand it to Hilda, she just edged further around Brianna, away from him. Hilda's gaze was firmly bound to the doll, however, except for furtive little glances toward the Guardian.

Brianna reached out and took it from him.

"Thank you," she said, handing the doll to her daughter. Hilda took it, glaring mistrustfully at the hooded man who had given it to her.

"We've got to go," the Guardian told Brianna. "Night will have settled in fully by now. Come with me."

"Jason, come along," Brianna said. She carried little Oslaf, and Hilda clung tightly to her skirts, as if afraid her mother might disappear if she let go.

The Guardian led her out into the main part of the cellar. For some reason, he hadn't hooded them, and Brianna saw that this side of the door was a wine rack.

"Jason, Hilda," the Guardian said, "you have to stay completely quiet from here on. Do you understand?"

Jason nodded in reply. Hilda gave no response, just stared at him mutely.

"Just like that," he said. "Come on."

He led them up a flight of stairs and out into an alley. They moved away from the street, further back into the shadows, and stopped before a seemingly blank section of wall. He peered through a knothole for a moment and then, to Brianna's surprise, opened the section of wall inward like a door.

"Wow!" Jason said. The Guardian whirled and clapped his hand over Jason's mouth before the boy, or Brianna, could even flinch.

"Shhh!" he hissed angrily. Jason nodded, obviously frightened, and the Guardian removed his hand from Jason's mouth.

"Hurry in," he whispered to them. He followed, closing the door behind them.

"Up in the wagon," he said, not in a whisper but still in a soft voice. He lingered at the hidden door, presumably locking it somehow.

Two large, coffin-sized crates sat open in the wagon, along with a few assorted trunks and other boxes. One of these crates had been Brianna's transport last night.

"Jason, you and your sister get in one of those together," the dark one told them. "Brianna, you and the baby can ride in the other. I'll let you out when we're outside of town."

"Mommeee . . . !" Hilda began to wail when Jason tried to separate them. Again, the Guardian clapped his hand over her mouth with the swiftness of a striking snake.

"Calm her down," he ordered Brianna, "or she will get us all killed."

"Mommy will be right here, honey," she whispered. The Guardian removed his hand from the little girl's mouth.

"I want to stay with you," Hilda whispered.

"There's not enough room, honey," Brianna told her daughter.

"See these air holes?" the Guardian said. Hilda nodded.

"I can put the boxes next to each other and you can reach your fingers through to your mommy," he said. "And Jason will be with you. Will that be all right?"

Hilda thought for a while and finally nodded.

"Good," the Guardian said. "But no talking. Understand?"

Again Hilda nodded.

"Jason, I'm counting on you to keep both of you quiet," the dark one told her son. "Can you do that for me?"

"Aye," Jason said.

The Guardian moved the empty crates together so that the tiny air holes matched. He helped Jason and Hilda into one and then held little Oslaf while Brianna climbed into the other.

As he was sealing the lid on the children's box, Hilda's tiny fingers wiggled through the air holes. Brianna reached up and stroked them.

"Mommy's here," she whispered. "Stay quiet." Then the lid was placed over her own box, and she could no longer see. She continued to stroke her daughter's fingers as the wagon began to clatter away.

• • •

Arik sat up from his meal. Someone had just touched his mind. He opened himself and let the touch penetrate further.

It was Hervis. Arik relaxed. There was no sense of urgency—just a gentle summons. Good, he could finish his meal.

Soon, he thought back. The contact faded. Arik took his time with the last few bites of roast and boiled potatoes he had been eating. Eva had not lost her touch in the castle kitchens. It was too bad that Ivanel could not wed her without causing a scandal. After all, a baron of the Realm could not wed a lowly kitchen maid.

Still, it was no secret how the two felt about each other. And the woman had practically been Ian's mother since his own had died in childbirth.

Oh well. 'Twas none of his business, anyway. Arik swallowed the last bite of potato and washed it down with his last swallow of ale.

It was only a few hours to dusk. He would have to hurry out to the farm if he wanted to be back by sundown. Dark clouds to the north threatened rain. Perhaps by sometime tomorrow.

Arik hoped it wasn't more refugees. He would hate to have to lead them out in the rain.

It was nearing sunset when Arik arrived at the farm. The first crop of corn was beginning to poke out of the uneven rows of the fields. Hervis might make a farmer, yet. The lesser Guardian had come out to meet him in response to the silent greeting that Arik had sent ahead of him.

"More refugees?" Arik asked.

"Aye," Hervis said. His tone was grave. "A woman and three children."

"What is amiss?" Arik asked.

"They are not Circle," Hervis replied.

"Who brought them?"

"Mavik of Foxmire," Hervis said. "He brought them in hooded. Except for the infant, of course."

"Does he vouch for them?" Arik asked.

"He claims the woman has been through the Rite of Acceptance," Hervis replied.

"In that case," Arik said, dismounting, "she should not mind facing it again."

The children were asleep when Brianna heard the door open above. Two men climbed down the ladder into the small underground room. They were not hooded.

One was fair of hair and face. Blue eyes frowned out at her from beneath his blond hair as if she were an inconvenience. She undoubtedly was.

The other, dark of hair, frightened her. There seemed to be no emotion at all in his cold, dark eyes.

"You are Brianna Klauswyf?" this one said, quietly.

"I am," she replied.

"Come with us," he said.

"But, my children . . ." she objected.

"Come with us," he repeated.

She bowed her head and climbed up the ladder. They followed behind her. She crawled out onto the floor of the barn and got to her feet. They emerged behind her, and the dark-haired one sat a heavy bale of hay on top of the trap door after he closed it.

What was going to happen? Were these men going to kill her and keep her children?

"What are you doing?" she asked.

"You must face the Rite of Acceptance," the dark one replied.

"But I have already done that!" she cried.

"Not with us," he pointed out. Brianna felt tears gather in her eyes. Was she to be tested at every stop? What if one of these men decided she could not be trusted? What would happen to her children then?

"If . . . if you kill me, will you care for my children?" she asked. The dark one looked back at her with the first hint that Brianna had seen in his face of something that might be called tenderness.

"I swear it," he said. "Now kneel."

Brianna knelt before the fair-haired one, who had taken a seat on the barn floor while she had talked with the Guardian.

She bowed her head forward and closed her eyes. She felt the sword rest across the back of her neck.

"Who are you?" the fair-haired one asked as she felt the mind of the man wielding the sword touch her own.

"I am Brianna Klauswyf," she said.

They asked her the same questions that had been asked of her in the shed outside Foxmire. Issued the same threats should she betray them. Finally, it was over.

"Guardian, we commend our new sister to you," the fair-haired one said. His tone sounded relieved.

"I accept the charge," the darker one replied, his flat voice betraying no emotion.

"Then we shall take our leave," the first one said as he rose to leave the barn.

"So we part," he said just before leaving.

"Until we meet again," Brianna replied, surprising him a little. He smiled and left the barn.

"Did Mavik teach you the Sign?" the dark-haired man asked.

"No," Brianna replied. He nodded approvingly at her response.

"You have now been tested by two Guardians of separate Circles," he said. "We will have time on the trail to teach you that and a few other things. My name is Arik, and I will be guiding you to Star Lake in the morning. Return to your children and get some rest. You will be woken early."

"Yes, Guardian," she replied.

As he had promised, the Guardian had woken her early, before dawn. Brianna helped him to load the wagon. It was apparent that he had been up even earlier, lashing a tent over the crude frame set up over the wagon.

On the roof overhead, Brianna could hear why. Heavy

rain pounded on the roof of the barn as if nature itself intended to wash away her refuge.

"We are going to travel in this?" she asked.

"It should let up some before long," Arik replied. "For now, it will provide us good cover under which to depart."

That was true. No one would be out in this weather if they could avoid it.

"I fear that Hervis's corn crop is ruined, though," he added with a wry smile.

"Why is that funny?" Brianna asked. "I would think you would be concerned for your friend's loss."

"Hervis is no farmer," Arik replied. "Before now he has lived as a hired sword for travelling merchants. He was tasked by the Circle to guard this safe house and now has to *learn* how to be a farmer. This is going to infuriate him."

"This farm is *not* his livelihood," the Guardian assured her. " 'Tis his disguise. One he is not fond of, in fact. The other farmers got their corn in early enough to survive the storms. Hervis is going to have to work twice as hard to get another crop laid in now."

"Oh," Brianna said, also smiling.

"Get the children," he said. "We're ready."

"Yes, Guardian," she said.

"Stop calling me that," Arik said. "Until we get to Star Lake, I am your husband."

"Yes, m'lord," she said, smiling mischievously.

"Now what do *you* think is funny?" he asked.

"You are my third husband within a sevennight," she said. "If this gets out, my reputation shall be tarnished."

Arik simply looked astonished for a moment. Then he smiled and began to laugh. Brianna laughed with him.

"I fear . . .'tis a bit late . . . for that," Arik said between bouts of laughter. "The Hunt has tarnished that far worse than I could."

At the mention of the Hunt, Brianna's laughter ceased. Her head bowed—but it had felt good to laugh again for a moment.

"My apologies," Arik said. She felt his arm reach across

her shoulders. "I understand. We have all lost friends and loved ones to . . . these people."

"Mavik was right," she said.

"How so?"

"You are not what I have been taught," she replied.

"No," Arik agreed. "Get your children. We have to go."

They ate their meal in the tent atop the wagon. Even though the rain had let up two days ago, it was much easier just to leave the tent up on the wagon than it was to make camp every night.

"So, the MageLords went to war among themselves," Arik was saying as Jason listened intently. "And our people, the common mages, led as many people as they could to safety in the caves that Bairn had ordered they prepare."

"How did Bairn know the war was coming?" Jason asked.

Brianna cleared away the empty plates, pretending not to listen to Arik's story. She had given Arik permission to tell her son this as much for her own benefit as anything else. She was learning a great deal about the magi. More than the temple would want her to know, she was certain.

"No one knows," Arik said. "Bairn seemed to know much about what was to come. He taught us better how to hide from the MageLords and from other men as well. He taught us that in the times to come after the passing of the MageLords, men would fear us in their place and that we must be prepared to hide from them as well. He warned us of the Hunt before it ever was."

"I bet Bairn was a MageLord!" Jason said excitedly.

"No!" Arik replied vehemently, startling Jason—and Brianna.

"No," he said more softly, reaching out and patting Jason's shoulder to reassure him.

"Bairn was not a MageLord," Arik continued. "No MageLord ever cared for his people. The MageLords cared only for their Power. Bairn taught us that Power was only a prize if it made the lives of those around you better. He taught us that with Power came the responsibility to use it well—to never use it for ill. He may have been powerful, but his beliefs, if nothing else, separated him from the MageLords.''

''What happened then?'' Jason asked.

''The war of the MageLords almost destroyed the world,'' Arik said. ''Then, at the height of the war, their Power died.''

''Why?''

''No one knows,'' Arik said, ''but Bairn had foretold this as well. Once their Power died, the MageLords passed on, leaving the world at peace.''

''But the Mother was sorely injured. For a generation, there was no sun in the sky. Only black clouds hiding the sky. And then the rains began and fell for another generation.''

''After the rains came the Time of Winter,'' Arik continued. ''For over a hundred years, the world slept under a blanket of snow and ice.''

''What did the people eat?'' Jason asked.

''They lived on the supplies that the magi had stored in the caves,'' Arik said. ''And what they could hunt. No one grew crops or planted fields. Men forgot how to do such things.''

''Even the mages?''

''No,'' Arik said. ''The magi were driven from the caves during the Time of Night, before the rains.''

''Why?''

''Because the people became afraid of us,'' Arik said. ''They told tales of the MageLords and began to look on us as them. We were forced to flee into the darkness and survive as best we could. But Bairn appeared to the magi and led them to places that had been prepared for them as well.''

''We preserved our knowledge,'' Arik added. ''Taught our children to read and made books of all the things we knew. How to plow a field and plant a crop. How to smelt metal and mine the ores from which they came. We made ourselves the keepers of man's knowledge.

"When the snows finally melted and people began to come out of the caves, we were waiting. The few of us who had survived taught them how to plant crops and everything else we had preserved. We showed them how to build houses and tools until they drove us out again."

"Again? But why?"

"People forget," Arik replied. "Especially when they fear something."

"That's stupid," Jason said.

"No, that's human," Arik said.

"So is sleep," Brianna interrupted. "And 'tis time for you to be in bed."

"But, mama . . ." Jason began.

"Don't argue," Arik said. "Your mother is right. We must start early in the morning."

"All right," Jason said. He lay down, and Brianna covered him with a blanket before kissing him on the cheek.

"Goodnight," she told him.

"Goodnight," Jason said. He yawned mightily.

"Goodnight, Arik," he added.

"Goodnight, Jason," Arik said. "Sleep well."

Brianna left the wagon to bank down the cookfire and Arik followed her out to let Jason fall asleep.

"You are a good storyteller," she told him.

"It is an important skill for us," Arik replied. "These stories are written down and passed on to all of our children. It is how we preserve our history."

"Is it true, then?" she asked. Arik shrugged.

"We believe it is," he replied. "But, after so many centuries, how can we be sure? There is at least some truth in it."

"So it is the truth you live by," she observed.

"That it most certainly is," Arik agreed.

"How sad," she said. "If more people knew . . ."

"We would not be hunted," Arik completed. "But there are always those who fear what they do not understand. There always will be. The Hunt would begin again, eventually."

CHAPTER

------- EiGHTEEN ------------

IAN AND FJALIN stopped when the sun was at its highest point in the sky. They dismounted and tied the horses to a nearby pine.

"Just like we practiced in camp last night," Fjalin told him.

"Right," Ian said, facing south and taking a seat on the ground. He closed his eyes and bowed his head, taking a deep breath. As he breathed in, he drew on the Power, raising all of it that he could.

Fjalin crossed the barrier, adding his own Power to it and blending his consciousness with Ian's through the Circle. Fjalin took up the traditional position of Guardian, behind Ian to the left.

Together, they spread their consciousness out into the surrounding web of Life, sending out a single question. *Man?*

The circle of their query expanded outward. They touched the minds of badgers and mice, hares and foxes. Upward, they touched the minds of sleeping snowy owls and robins, hawks and doves.

To the southeast, they touched the mind of a foraging brown bear. Ian made note of that—they would not want to travel too close to him tomorrow.

Finally, they reached the limits of their combined Power. Their search had covered an area a little less than a day's travel across. In that entire area they had found no recognition of man, save where they themselves had crossed.

Ian released the Circle and allowed the Power to drain from him before opening his eyes.

"Nothing," he said.

"'Tis what we expected," Fjalin reminded him.

"I know," Ian said. "But . . ."

"I understand," Fjalin said. "Still, this is faster than searching the entire area."

"What now?" Ian asked.

"Now we go back to camp," Fjalin replied. "And tomorrow we check northeast."

"We need to watch out for that bear," Ian remembered.

"I plan on it," Fjalin agreed.

Once again, they stopped when the sun was high above them. Ian hitched Brazen to a tree and sat on the ground, facing south. Ian framed the question in his mind.

Man?

Their consciousness expanded outward in a circle around them, sweeping over all the small minds in its path, asking that one question.

As yesterday, the only recognition they felt were from those animals they themselves had disturbed. Ian pushed the question out further, but there was still no response.

Suddenly, just as he was about to drop the Power, he felt it. A glimmer of recognition far to the east, on the very border of their circle. *Man.*

Ian almost lost his concentration, so great was his surprise.

Focus! he commanded himself. Or was it Fjalin who commanded him? It was hard to tell when one was in Circle. Ian focused his attention to the east, and the Circle shifted as well.

Man? he asked.

Man, came the reply. A single mind, small and keen. Ian focused on that mind and found himself gliding on the wind with the one he had touched.

Show me, he told the hawk. *Show me Man.*

The hawk's territory was large. Today he hunted far to the west of the nest where his mate waited with their young. But, far to the east and north of his nest, he had seen men.

Several men with many very large, dark animals too big for the hawk to eat. There had been no meat that day.

Thank you, Ian thought, but the concept was alien to the animal. The hawk merely returned to his own business. Ian let the Power fall away.

"Did you see?" Ian asked.

"I did," Fjalin replied. "Men."

"Men with cattle," Ian added. "We've found them!"

"No," Fjalin replied. "We have found men—probably a lodge. Probably *not* the lodge we are searching for." Ian sighed. Fjalin was probably right.

"Now what?" he said, a little less excited.

"We go back to camp," Fjalin said. "Tomorrow we will break camp and return here before heading east."

Bairn, let it be them! Ian thought as he mounted his horse and led the way back to camp.

The next day's travel took them to the edge of the hawk's territory. However, today the search gave them no new information. Ian could not even find the hawk that had first told them of the men.

"He's probably back at his nest," Fjalin said. "That would be further than we can reach."

"If that hawk had not been as far west as he had been yesterday . . ." Ian began.

"We would still be searching," Fjalin finished. "We might still be after this, if these people are not who we're looking for. However, they will probably know of other lodges in the area."

"Or it could be them," Ian said.

"It could be," Fjalin admitted grudgingly. "I, for one, am not going to hope too much for that, however. I don't think you should, either."

" 'Tis hard not to," Ian replied.

"In another five or six years," Fjalin said, "when you're my age, it won't be so hard."

There was a slight edge of bitterness to Fjalin's voice. Ian wondered what the Guardian meant, but he decided not to ask. Instead, he simply returned to his task of settling the animals in for the night.

Arik drove the wagon through the streets of Star Lake. Brianna sat beside him, playing the role of the dutiful wife, minding the children as he drove.

He was uneasy, more so than when he had made this trip before. Well, the Circle was going to have to accept this woman eventually. Tonight he would deliver her to Johann unhooded. She had passed the tests of two Guardians, after all.

That was all their law required before she be taught the Sign, their greetings, and their history. Once she knew those things, she was capable of finding Johann by herself, so it was not as if Arik were betraying the Circle in Star Hall.

He just hoped they saw it that way. He pulled the wagon to a stop outside of Johann's inn.

"Wait here," he told Brianna. "I'll be back quickly."

"Yes, husband," she said. Arik smiled at her as he climbed down from the wagon. She was learning quickly, as were her children. Soon, she would have the skills to drop out of sight as quickly as any who had been raised in the Circle.

The boy might even have a touch of the Gift. It was difficult to tell at his age. In another two years, though, it would be time to begin his training, if his mother allowed it. If he *did* have the Gift, it would emerge then.

The inn was not overly crowded. Arik strode up to the counter and caught Johann's eye. The innkeeper finished his business with one of the customers and came over to him.

"Another batch?" he asked.

"Aye," Arik replied.

"You keep getting here just in time for the ship," Johann said. "They'll go out tonight."

"That's good," Arik said.

"Don't bring any more here after tonight," Johann said.

"We're preparing a place outside town for them. I'll show you after the ship leaves."

"Is it outside the gates?" Arik asked.

"Yes," Johann replied.

"That is better," Arik said.

"Yes, it is," Johann agreed. "How many this time?"

"Four," Arik replied. "A mother and three children."

"I can give you a room until the ship leaves," Johann said.

"They are not Circle," Arik added. Johann just looked at him for a moment.

"They have passed the Rite?" he asked.

"Twice," Arik confirmed.

"Then you've taught them the Sign and our history?" Johann asked.

"Some of it," Arik said.

"Then they *are* Circle now," Johann said. "I will be sure to pass that on to the captain, however. Bring them in."

By the end of their second day of travel, Ian and Fjalin had found more animals who knew of man. The hawk had returned to his nest for the night, and both he and his mate knew of the men who lived to the north and east.

Some of the deer further on also knew of the men who lived in the great stone house. Ian could barely contain his excitement.

"It *is* a lodge!" he said.

"Everyone lives in lodges up here," Fjalin said, unimpressed. "It does not mean that it is *his* lodge. Or that he still lives there, if it is the same one."

"Can you try to call for him?" Ian asked.

"Not tonight," Fjalin said. "We are still much too far. Tomorrow we shall travel east for another half day and then turn to the northeast. Tomorrow night, I will try to touch Bjorn."

"Great!"

"For now, let's just make camp," Fjalin said.

• • •

Again Arik watched as another batch of refugees took ship for Nalur's Ridge. This group was smaller, but was still over half the size of the last group he had sent off. Ten instead of eighteen.

"Goodbye, Brianna," Arik said. "So we part."

"Until we meet again," Brianna said. "Thank you for everything."

"Goodbye, Sven," young Jason said, hugging Arik around the waist, remembering to use the name Arik had told him to call him by in Star Lake.

"Goodbye, Jason," Arik said. "So we part."

"Until we meet again," Jason said. "But we won't, will we?"

"We will someday," Arik said. "We all meet again in one life or another."

"Come along, Jason," Brianna said. "We have to go."

Arik watched as they climbed up the gangplank. Brianna turned and waved to him at the top. He waved back, and then she turned and was gone.

"Thank Bairn for children, eh?" Captain Oslaf said. "They know not the hatred of their elders."

"Indeed," Arik agreed.

"The woman is not Circle?" Oslaf asked.

"As I have been reminded," Arik said, "she *is* Circle. She passed the Rite of Acceptance from two Guardians and has been taught the Sign and some of our history."

"True," Oslaf agreed. "But some of our passengers might not be comfortable with her presence. I shall keep a close watch over her."

"I would recommend that," Arik agreed.

The hold of the ship was cramped with people. Brianna sat against one wall of the hold, cradling little Oslaf in her arms. Hilda nestled tightly against her right side. Jason sat to her left with his left arm over the cloth bag that held what few possessions they had.

"Hello, dear," an old woman said to her. She came over

and sat near Hilda, who clung more tightly to her mother.

"Are all of these your children?" the old woman asked.

"Yes," Brianna replied cautiously. What did this woman want of her?

"I am Ingrid," the woman said. She looked back toward the old man with whom she had been sitting.

"Nolan is my husband," she added. "We are from Ravenhall."

"My name is Brianna," Brianna said. The woman seemed to just want to talk. She began to relax.

"Where was your Circle, dear?" Ingrid asked.

Brianna glanced around the hold of the ship. No one else was paying any attention to them.

"I was . . . not Circle," Brianna replied.

"Oh, I'm sorry," Ingrid said.

"If you're not Circle, then why are you here?" a young man demanded. Brianna looked across the hold to a young man with red hair.

"Hans!" an older, red-haired man said sternly. He resembled the younger man—apparently his father.

"Watch your manners!" the boy's father commanded. The young man fell silent but continued to glare at Brianna. She looked away nervously.

"My husband was falsely accused by a man who wanted our lands," Brianna explained, as much to the young man as to Ingrid. "They found a chest in one of our barns with . . . incriminating evidence within."

"As if *anyone* would leave such a thing lying about in a barn," Ingrid said. "How did you come to be here, Brianna?"

"The Circle in Foxmire found me before the Hunt did and offered me their protection," Brianna replied. "I accepted."

"Was your husband . . . lost?" Ingrid asked.

"Yes," Brianna whispered.

"We lost our daughter Gretchen in Ravenhall," Ingrid said. "She was . . . a little younger than you."

"I am so sorry," Brianna said, taking the old woman's hand. "Were there . . . any children?"

"No, thank Bairn," Ingrid said. "She had not yet wed, although our Guardian was courting her."

"You shouldn't be here!" the young man shouted, rising to his feet. Brianna cowered back, clutching Oslaf and Hilda to her. Jason jumped to his feet to stand between his mother and this sudden threat.

"Hans!" the red-haired man shouted.

"She could betray us all!" Hans said. "Besides, she is not one of us! The Circle in Foxmire should have let the Hunt have you."

"Hans!" the man whom Brianna assumed was his father shouted. "That is *enough*!"

"She's an outsider!" Hans said, turning just in time for his father's fist to strike him in the face.

"Jason!" Brianna whispered. "Sit down." She leaned forward and pulled him down by the hem of his tunic.

Hans looked up from the floor of the hold at his father. He held his bleeding mouth and looked up at his father in disbelief.

"If I ever," the boy's father said in a cold, low voice, "hear you speak of letting the Hunt have someone again, I will beat the life out of you myself."

"Who is speaking of turning someone over to the Hunt?" a harsh voice asked from above. The captain of the ship climbed down the ladder from above. This was going too far.

"He didn't mean it!" Brianna said. "He's just upset . . . about me."

"Is that true, boy?" Captain Oslaf asked.

"Y-yes," Hans stammered.

"That woman is every bit as much Circle as you are," he said. "She had to pass the Rite of Acceptance twice to be here and would have died if she had failed it. And *she's* not the one I hear talking about turning people over to the Hunt. If I ever hear that again, it will be *your* throat I slit before I dump you over the side! Is that clear, boy?"

"Yes, Magus," Hans said.

"Are you all right?" Oslaf said, turning to Brianna.

"Yes," Brianna replied. "Thank you."

Without responding, Captain Oslaf climbed up the ladder back to the deck. The hold door shut loudly.

"If we start hating people who are not 'one of us,' " the older man told his son, "we are no better than the Hunt. This woman and her children have lost just as much as we have. Now you shut your mouth and go to sleep, boy."

Brianna looked up to the man who turned to face her. Wild red hair and beard framed a pair of ice-blue eyes that looked down at her.

"I am sorry," he said. "My son is ... overcome with his own loss and can't see another's right now. Thank you for defending him to the Magus."

Brianna just nodded. They were all alike here. All of them, even she, had lost loved ones to the Scared Hunt. Although, now, she had a very hard time considering it sacred.

"Was it his mother?" she asked softly.

"Aye," he said. "And his younger sisters. We ... saw it happen."

"Oh," Brianna said. At least she had not *seen* Klaus burned. She didn't think she could have borne that.

The ship began to rock beneath them as the longship pulled away from the dock. Brianna nestled back and cuddled her children to her as she settled back to sleep.

Where will this journey end? she wondered, just before she fell asleep.

CHAPTER

------- Nineteen ------------

IAN AND FJALIN found the strange pond just after midday. It was almost perfectly round, with a small spit of land thrusting into it from the south. All around the small lake, the decaying remains of shattered trees lay. Their bases all pointed toward the pond.

"I know what this is!" Ian shouted excitedly.

"What?" Fjalin asked.

"This is where Valerian destroyed Bjorn's cottage!" Ian said. "My father was here when it happened. Valerian called down a star from heaven, and it blasted a huge hole in the ground and flattened the trees all around it."

"In Bairn's name!" Fjalin said. "One man did *this*?"

"For nothing but spite," Ian confirmed. "The cabin was empty."

"Gods above!"

"We must be close to the lodge!" Ian said. "Can you try to call for Bjorn?"

"I can try," Fjalin replied in a subdued voice, still staring at the small pond.

Fjalin took a seat on the grass surrounding the pond and closed his eyes. It had been a *long* time since he had touched Bjorn's mind. He took a deep breath, drawing as much of the Power into himself as he could. Then he reached out.

Bjorn? he thought, trying to picture his friend's once-familiar face in his mind.

Bjorn? He couldn't be certain, but he thought he felt something. It was weak.

Bjorn! he called silently. The touch grew stronger.

Fjalin? came the reply, so strongly that Fjalin could almost swear he had actually heard it.

"Fjalin?" Bjorn said. "What in Bairn's name are you doing *here*? And who is this with you?"

Fjalin's eyes snapped open. That had *not* been in his mind!

Bjorn stood before him. Fjalin glanced over to Ian, who stood open-mouthed, staring at Bjorn. Something was wrong, though. Fjalin could see no aura.

"Bjorn?" he said, climbing to his feet. "But . . . how?"

"A trick I've picked up," Bjorn explained, as if describing nothing more exciting than a new way of setting one of his traps. "I'm not really here. See? You can't touch me."

Bjorn held out his hand, and Fjalin gingerly reached out to touch it. Sure enough, his own hand passed through Bjorn's as if it were a ghost before him.

"You have no aura," Fjalin said.

"Truly?" Bjorn asked. "That is interesting. However, so is finding you on my doorstep. If you have gone to this much trouble to find me, it must be urgent."

"It is," Fjalin assured him. "Ian here is carrying some important letters for you."

Bjorn's shade turned to face Ian, who was still staring slack-jawed at Bjorn.

"Who are you?" Bjorn asked.

"I-Ian Urqhart," the boy replied. Bjorn visibly flinched at the name.

"My father is Ivanel," Ian added. "He sent me with extremely important letters to give to you."

"So," Bjorn said. His expression became dour. "It begins."

"You've . . . been expecting us?" Fjalin asked. Right now he would not be surprised by anything.

"I have been expecting *something*," Bjorn replied, sounding suddenly weary. "You seem to be it. Travel northeast from here. You can make the hall before dark, although 'twill still be late. I will send someone out to meet you.''

"Thank you," Fjalin began, but Bjorn's shade had vanished, as if it had never been. Fjalin looked over to Ian, who was looking back at him as if he'd just seen a ghost.

"I take it," Ian said, "that you didn't know he could do that, either."

They met the guide from Bjorn's lodge at the edge of a cleared field. To Ian's eye, the land looked like pasturage, but there were no cattle to be seen.

Probably in for the night, he thought. Even though the sun was still high in the sky, Ian knew that it would be near sunset back home. This strange land with its short nights was unsettling.

The man who met them was no less so. He was a veritable bear of a man. A blond bear, with blue eyes and a heavy beard and an aura that was at least twice as powerful as Ian's or Fjalin's.

"I am Herrold," the man told them. "Lord Bjorn sent me to fetch ye."

"Lord Bjorn?" Fjalin asked.

"Our chief died this past winter," Herrold explained. "Bjorn is now our chief. Come—we still have a long way to go."

Without another word, the man turned and strode away. Ian bent over toward Fjalin from the back of his horse.

"I've never *seen* an aura that strong," he whispered to Fjalin.

"Nor have I," Fjalin agreed.

"Hurry up or I'll leave ye here!" Herrold shouted back at them. Fjalin and Ian hastened to follow.

Herrold led them across field after field of pastureland. Each field was carved separately from the forest with a border of thick trees and brush around it. Judging from the size of the fields, Ian would guess that the lodge owned at least a hundred head of cattle.

They emerged from the last line of trees to see a large

stone lodge flanked to the north by four smaller lodges. Judging from the smell, the smaller buildings were barns. The lodge kept its cattle indoors. If the winters here were as bad as Fjalin had said, Ian could understand why.

As they approached the lodge, the doors opened and a few guards emerged. Ian swallowed. Herrold was apparently *not* the most powerful mage in this place. A couple of the guards were even stronger than he, judging by their radiant auras.

And then Bjorn stepped out to greet them.

Fjalin stopped in his tracks. Ian dropped Brazen's reins, and she stopped as well. Both men stared at Bjorn.

His aura surrounded him like a man standing before the sun. If it had been physically visible, it would have been blinding. Even the auras of the unbelievably powerful magi around him seemed washed out in comparison.

"Fjalin!" Bjorn said, walking up to them. "So we meet! It has been a long time."

"Your . . . aura," Fjalin said.

"I will explain later," Bjorn assured him. "For now, let us get you inside and get your animals tended to. We can better talk over a tankard of ale."

Bjorn turned toward Ian.

"Ian Urqhart," he said. "So we meet. How is your father?"

"H-he is well, my lord," Ian stammered.

"Dismount, lad," Bjorn said. "Let's get that horse tended to. How old are you, by the way?"

"Fifteen summers," Ian replied as he climbed down from his mount. Some of the guards led the horses away toward the barn.

"A bit young to be sent on such a perilous journey," Bjorn noted.

"I am serving my time of errantry," Ian explained. "This was my quest of manhood."

"I would say you've earned it," Bjorn replied. "Come. You've both travelled a long way. Let's get you inside and to bed. We can talk on the morrow once you've rested."

"Y-yes, my lord," Ian said.

"And don't call me that," Bjorn added. "With old friends, or their sons, I am still merely 'Bjorn.' "

Once the lodge had settled down for the night and the guests were in their beds, Bjorn broke the seal on the letter from Ivanel that Ian had given him. Inside was another sealed letter, addressed to Ian. That was curious. Bjorn set it aside.

Old friend, the letter began. *When we last parted outside Reykvid you said that I could call on you for help when the time came for our people to flee the clans. I fear that time has come.*

Bjorn nodded as he read. *This* was what he had been expecting.

The madness is spreading like fire, the letter added. *Mage and ungifted alike are being burned by the dozens in the Hunt. I have sent my son on this quest to establish a line of safe houses through the Wastes to you. If you are reading this, he has succeeded.*

That was impressive. According to Ivanel's letter, Ian had successfully established an underground highway all the way to Bjorn's lodge. Bjorn frowned. This would pose them no small problem.

Soon, Ivanel added, *you will see the first groups of those who flee the Hunt arrive at your location. In all likelihood, they are already on their way to you. I hate to burden you with this duty, but their lives are now in your hands. I know of no other who can aid them better than you.*

Bjorn wondered how many were on their way. Dozens? Scores? Hundreds? Certainly more than he could simply absorb into the lodge here. Even so, he could not simply turn them away. Bjorn read on.

Ian does not realize it, the letter said, *but in a way, you have already received your first refugee. I have enclosed another letter for Ian, instructing him to remain with you until such time as I send for him. I will not have this madness claim my only son. Please keep him safe for me.*

I would also ask, as my friend, that you conduct his Rite of Manhood. I think you will agree that this quest has aptly demonstrated his readiness.

The fate of our people now lies in your capable hands. May Bairn watch over you and guide you in the coming days.

Until we meet again. Ivanel.

Bjorn set the letter aside. So, Ian would be staying on as well. No doubt the boy would not be happy to learn this. Still, Bjorn had to figure out what to do with him.

Ian was no doubt an excellent warrior. If he had travelled alone through the Wastes to Hunter's Glen, he could be nothing less. But what other skills did he possess? To what task could Bjorn assign him? Bjorn had little use for someone who was trained only in combat and governing a clan.

Or do I? he thought. Bjorn smiled. This could solve *both* of his problems.

Ian waited impatiently. He had slept fitfully last night in a strange place with much on his mind. He was anxious to discuss his father's message with Bjorn and start on his way home. However, Bjorn had been in council with the clan elders all morning discussing, no doubt, the letter from Ian's father.

Ian looked around the lodge. All of the magi here were incredibly powerful. One old woman, named Freida, carried an aura almost as powerful as Bjorn's.

"Master Urqhart?" a voice said from behind him. Ian turned to see Herrold standing behind him.

"Yes?" Ian asked eagerly.

"Our chieftain would like you to join him in council," Herrold said.

"Finally!" Ian said. "I'll get Fjalin . . ."

"No," Herrold replied. "Just you for now. I will find Fjalin."

"Oh," Ian said. "Very well."

He left Herrold and walked to the back of the great hall, where the only permanently walled rooms in the lodge could be found. One set of these were the chieftain's rooms. A few others were for storage, and the smallest was the council chamber.

The guard opened the door for Ian as he approached. Ian walked into the chamber. Bjorn and four older men sat around a plain table. One of the men had a powerful aura that was as red as blood. It was not as powerful as Bjorn's or even Freida's, but it pulsed like a beating heart. Ian swallowed.

"Please," Bjorn told him, "sit down."

Ian took a seat at the end of the long table.

"H-have you read my father's letter?" Ian asked.

"Yes," Bjorn said. "We will discuss that in a moment. Honored sirs, will you excuse us? I will call for you in a moment."

The four elders nodded and rose from the table. They smiled sympathetically at Ian before they departed. Ian did not like the feel of this.

Once they had left, Bjorn rose from the table, a folded sheet of parchment in his hand. He walked over and handed it to Ian.

"In your father's letter to me," he began, "was enclosed another letter—for you."

"For me?" Ian asked. He glanced at the wax seal on the letter. It was his father's.

"Yes," Bjorn replied, returning to his own seat. "I thought you might like a little privacy in which to read it."

"Thank you," Ian said, breaking the seal on the letter and unfolding the parchment.

My dearest son, his father began. *If you are reading this, you have safely arrived at Bjorn's lodge. Words cannot convey how proud I am that you have completed this dangerous and difficult quest. Today you are a man.*

To that end, I have asked that Bjorn conduct your Rite of Manhood. I wish that I could be there to see your moment of glory.

But your quest will not be over after this, Ian read. *These are difficult times, my son. Madness sweeps across the land like a wildfire. Until it passes, I have asked that Bjorn make a place for you in his lodge. I am sure that he can use your help in dealing with those who follow you.*

Ian felt tears come to his eyes and a lump rise in his throat. He had been looking forward to beginning his journey home today or tomorrow. Now he knew that he wasn't going home.

I am so very proud of you, my son, his father said. *I wish you all my love. May Bairn watch over you and keep you until we meet again.*

Ian's hand shook as he laid the letter on the table. He swallowed, trying to break the lump that had formed in his throat.

"I . . . guess," he began, but his voice cracked. He stopped speaking and cleared his throat.

"Did you know . . ." he began again, but his voice broke against the words yet again. Ian felt a hand on his shoulder, and he looked up to see Bjorn standing next to him.

"I knew," Bjorn said. "I will leave you alone for a few minutes."

Bjorn left the room. The door closed behind him, and Ian was alone.

Then the tears came.

"How is he?" Theodr asked. His aura pulsed with the Power of the red cord he had taken two days ago. Once he achieved control of the yellow and violet, his aura would settle into the steady golden glow that Bjorn's and Frieda's had.

"As well as can be expected for a boy who has just learned he is not going home," Bjorn replied. "We will give him a few moments alone before I disturb him."

"Will you take the refugees?" Fjalin asked.

"We do not have room for them here," Bjorn replied. "Not for as many as will be coming. We will discuss that in council."

Fjalin did not ask any more questions. Bjorn's answer troubled him, though. If he would not accept those who fled the Hunt, what would be done with them? Hunter's Glen could not absorb them. The Bjorn he knew would never turn people away like this.

"Excuse me," Bjorn said after a moment. He walked to the door of the council room and knocked lightly before entering. He was inside for a few moments more before again opening the door.

"We can begin," he said.

Ian watched as the four elders returned to the council room with Fjalin. Fjalin sat down beside him, an expression of concern on his face.

Ian turned his attention back to Bjorn.

"Well," Bjorn began. "Your father's letter has presented us with a problem."

"What is that?" Ian asked.

"Look around you," Bjorn said. "You have seen our lodge. How many do you think we could take here without burden?"

Ian thought for a moment. There wasn't much free room left in the lodge.

"A score?" Ian said.

"Probably two," Bjorn said. "Certainly not the scores upon scores that will likely arrive."

"Can't you build another lodge?" Ian asked. Bjorn smiled.

"You are a sharp lad," Bjorn said. "But this land will not support a clan of that size. We can not extend our croplands and pastures beyond a quarter day out and still work the land."

Ian felt the beginnings of panic. If Bjorn turned the refugees away, what would become of them? There was nowhere else for them to go.

Don't panic, he thought. These people were willing to help. They just didn't know how. He had to think of something.

"What about outlying farms?" Ian asked. "You could build farms a half day out. The victims of the Hunt could work that land under your protection."

"But the winters here are very harsh," Bjorn pointed out. "Each farmhouse would almost have to be a lodge in itself to withstand the winter."

"You could build another lodge," Ian suggested. "The farmhouses could be built for the summer only, and the farmers could winter in the second lodge."

"That is not a bad idea," the man with the red aura said. He sounded mildly surprised. Ian felt the panic ebb somewhat. These people *would* be able to help them!

"Not a bad idea at all," Bjorn said with what almost sounded like pride in his voice. "Was I not right about him?"

"I think you were," Theodr agreed, still sounding surprised.

"We can use Ian's suggestion of summer farms to extend the capacity of the two lodges," Bjorn said. "Instead of doubling the number of people we can support, we could increase it fourfold."

"Or more," Theodr agreed.

"We shall have to discuss this more once Ian leaves," Bjorn said to the elders. "That could help to offset the cattle and seed we are going to lose."

The elders muttered and nodded in agreement. Ian did not hear what they said, though. Something Bjorn had said caught his attention.

"Leaving?" he asked. "But my father's letter said I was to remain here."

"True," Bjorn said. "But there is no room for your people here. I will have to make a place for you elsewhere."

"I . . . do not understand," Ian said.

"Even with your suggestion, we don't want the refugees to settle here," Bjorn explained. "Not if the Hunt might follow them. Therefore we *are* going to build another lodge. A sevennight from here."

"We will send people to help build it and to get the first crops laid in," Theodr added. "That will be their new home. They will be a new clan."

"Fortunately," Bjorn said, "we have someone to lead this clan. Someone who has been raised and trained to govern his father's clan. You."

"Me?" Ian shouted in surprise. "I can't lead a clan!"

"I disagree," Bjorn said. "You are no longer a boy. And you did solve a serious problem for *our* clan just now with your suggestion of summer farms. With no more than a moment's thought, I might point out. Your quest through the Wastes has proven you an able warrior. I think you will make a fine chieftain."

Ian sat back down in his chair. He hadn't even realized that he had risen from it. *Him?* A clan chieftain? In the Wastes?

"But I know nothing of life here," Ian said quietly.

"Theodr will go with you," Bjorn said. "He will be your senior advisor. Listen to him well. He *does* know life up here."

"When do I leave?" Ian asked. It seemed there were no more objections he could raise.

"On the morrow," Bjorn said. "We must get your crops planted quickly if you are to make it through the winter. Half the men of the lodge will travel with you."

"Very well," Ian agreed.

"Today," Bjorn said, smiling, "we will have your Rite of Manhood. The women are already preparing the feast. 'Twill be a grand night, Ian Urqhart. I hope you're up to it."

Ian hoped he was, too.

CHAPTER

------- TWENTY ------------

IAN STOOD NAKED while three old women drew bright blue patterns on his body. The woad was still warm from the brewing as they brushed it onto him.

Apparently here, in the far north, the Rite was a little more . . . barbaric. Ian would be released as soon as the women were done, with only a knife in his possession. He was to return with a slain buck. Bjorn had added that, in his case, time was short. He should try to be back by sunset.

Right, Ian thought. *Go kill a fully grown buck with nothing but a knife. And be sure to get back in time for supper.*

The women stepped back from him. Apparently they were finished. One of them pulled back the hide that covered the doorway and Ian stepped out into the hall, still naked.

Bjorn was waiting. He handed Ian his own knife. Ian had no doubt he looked quite the barbarian with a mask of blue woad drawn around his eyes and mouth and intricate patterns of blue laid down with the Power over his body.

"Return as soon as you have found and slain the buck," Bjorn told him. "Beware of wolves and bears. Bairn watch over you."

No kidding! Ian thought. He simply nodded to Bjorn. The guards opened the doors at the end of the lodge.

"Go," Bjorn commanded. Ian walked quickly from the lodge, trying to ignore some of the glances the women were giving him. No doubt the blue woad stood out brightly against the red flush he felt spreading over his body. There were a few quickly hushed giggles.

Ian broke into a measured, distance-eating run as soon

as he left the lodge. If he had to bring back a buck by sunset, walking was a luxury he did not have time for.

He stopped in the first stand of trees outside the lodge, looking for a stick or a branch he could use as a spear. He wasn't about to try killing a buck with just a knife. The deer's horns would give it the reach in *that* battle!

He finally selected a dead branch lying on the ground. It was still solid, apparently only having been dead long enough to season it—not long enough to rot.

He quickly stripped the remaining bark from it with the knife and began sharpening the end as he walked. As he worked and walked, Ian reached out with the Power.

The same method that he and Fjalin had used to find Bjorn could be used to find deer. Slowly he extended his consciousness while his hands worked with the wood.

It was more difficult to use his Art while working on another task, but Ian forced himself to concentrate. Slowly, the land yielded its secrets to him.

He found deer back at the lodge, but Ian suspected that it would not be smiled upon if he killed one of the lodge's tamed sled deer.

There! To the northwest, almost at the limit of his Power, was a herd. Gods! They were almost half a day away. Ian broke into a jog, still carving his spear.

Ian warily peered out from between the bushes. This was a surprisingly large herd. One buck and four does. The buck was *not* small. Of course—he would not be small with so many females to defend.

The wind carried his scent away from the herd. Ian hefted the smaller of the two spears he had made, gauging its weight and balance.

He stood from behind the bushes and hurled the small spear. It flew true, catching the animal just back from its left foreleg. The buck threw up his head from grazing and barked in pain as the does fled away from Ian.

Ian raised his heavier spear and stepped into the clearing as the buck turned to face him. Ian's spear fell from the animal's side. It had not penetrated as deeply as Ian had hoped it would.

I'm going to die, Ian thought. The deer lowered his rack and snorted. Ian dropped into a crouch just as the deer charged.

Ian leaped to the side and rolled away as the deer charged past. Unfortunately, the beast was agile and turned quickly to face him.

Ian stepped forward and thrust with the spear, grazing the animal alongside the neck. Blood sprayed out from the wound.

The deer dropped his head and charged again. Ian barely dodged the deadly antlers. The animal would die, eventually, but not before he tried to take Ian with him.

Crazed with pain, the animal thrashed his head around, raking the ground where Ian had lain just a moment ago. Ian scrambled away from the animal, and the deer reared to charge at him once more.

Ian spun and thrust his spear into the animal's chest, more in an attempt to keep him away than to kill him. The crazed deer forced his way up the shaft and Ian ran to the side, twisting the spear inside his chest.

The animal fell to his side, twitching. Ian released the spear and hurried back to where he had left his knife.

The buck was still bleating in pain when Ian returned. Ian grabbed the antlers, forcing the animal's head down, as he knelt and cut the deer's throat.

Soon, the deer's death throes stopped and the brown eye rolled up, revealing a crescent moon of white. The animal was dead. Ian glanced at the sky. The sun was halfway in its descent toward the horizon. Ian had, at most, a quarter day to carry a deer that weighed as much as he did half a day's travel back to the lodge.

"I guess it wouldn't be a trial if it were easy," he grumbled. He lifted the deer and hooked its hind legs into the branches of a nearby tree to let the blood drain out before he carried it back.

•   •   •

The sun had already set by the time Ian carried the animal back to the lodge. The clan waited by a large fire burning outside the lodge over which a spit waited for the animal he carried. Ian collapsed to his knees and dropped the deer from his shoulders. Bjorn was by him in a heartbeat.

"Are you injured?" he asked.

"No," Ian said. "Just damned tired. Although my back swears I've broken it."

"Ten points," Theodr announced from behind Bjorn.

"Ten?" Bjorn asked, turning away from Ian. Theodr indicated the points on the deer's rack, counting off ten.

Bjorn rose and turned to face the assembly.

"Ten points!" he announced. There was a collective gasp and then a loud cheer. It made Ian's head hurt.

"Get up, Ian," Bjorn said. "You're a man now. Face your peers."

Ian groaned and rose to his feet. Right now he just wanted a hot bath to ease his tired muscles. He wasn't even particularly hungry, although he had not eaten all day.

"Do you see those women waiting over there?" Bjorn asked. Ian looked over to where a small group of young women waited.

"Yes," he said.

"Pick one," Bjorn said.

"What for?" Ian asked.

"To bathe you and tend to that sore back you mentioned before the feast," Bjorn explained.

"Oh," Ian said. That sounded good. A hot bath and someone to rub his back and shoulders.

"And to spend the night with you," Bjorn added.

Ian looked back at Bjorn without speaking. Then he looked back to where the clan's young women waited. He swallowed nervously.

Couldn't I just go kill another buck? he wondered.

Ivanel sat in his drawing room chair with a warm glass of mulled wine. It was late, but he had been unable to sleep. His thoughts had kept him awake wondering about Ian. It had been over a moon since Ivanel had received word of his son's arrival in Nalur's Ridge.

During that moon, half a score of people had been indicted by the Hunt in the lands of his own clan alone. They had managed to save only one in three with their new chain of safe houses. But even that small number of escapes was beginning to raise questions. Ian had to succeed, or all of this was for naught.

If all had gone well, Ian had left Hunter's Glen and was now searching for the lodge where Ivanel had last known Bjorn to live. Even if Ian found him, Ivanel would never know if his son had arrived safely.

He took another sip of the wine. He should have sent someone with Ian to bring word back to him. Still, whom would he have sent? Not to mention that sending *anyone* with Ian during his time of errantry would have aroused suspicion.

"Greetings, old friend," someone said. Ivanel started, spilling his wine.

Bjorn stood in front of him. Ivanel set the goblet on the small table next to him and rose to his feet, wiping at his tunic with a kerchief.

"Bjorn?" he said. "How did you get in here?"

"I'm not truly here," Bjorn said. He held out his hand. Ivanel reached for it, and his hand passed through Bjorn's like smoke.

"Gods above!" Ivanel said.

"'Tis truly a simple rite," Bjorn assured him. "I thought you would like to know that your son, Ian, has arrived safely."

"H-how is he?" Bjorn might call it a simple rite, but Ivanel had *never* heard of anyone who had been able to do anything like this! Anyone save Valerian, that was.

"Well," Bjorn replied, smiling. "He passed his Rite resoundingly. Killed a ten-point buck by himself with a spear. Right now he's sleeping . . . with the rewards of his exploits."

Ivanel smiled in return, remembering his own Rite. Then the smile faded.

"Does he know?"

"Yes," Bjorn replied. "I gave him your letter this morning."

"How did he take it?"

"Well, I think," Bjorn said. "He wept for a time. It is a hard thing for a young man to accept. He will get over it."

Ivanel nodded.

"Is that all you came to tell me?" Ivanel asked.

"Not all," Bjorn said. "I want to ask you about this madness you spoke of in your letters. Tell me *exactly* what is happening."

"Do you mind if I sit?" Ivanel asked.

"Not at all," Bjorn said. His shade affected to take the seat across from Ivanel. Ivanel sat down, took a long drink from his wine and then took a deep breath before speaking.

"Things are not well with the clans, my friend," he began.

It was almost midday by the time they were ready to leave. Three wagons, drawn by oxen, had been loaded with tools and seed for Ian's new fields. Another cart was filled with hay for the oxen.

Yet a fifth cart was filled with food for the fifty men and ten women who were travelling with Ian. The women drove the carts. The men, with the exception of Ian and Theodr, would walk.

"Remember," Bjorn told him, "travel due west for at least seven days before you stop. We don't want you too close. Theodr will help you pick a site. Get your fields planted quickly. If need be, you can finish your lodge *after* the harvest. But you must have food."

"Yes," Ian agreed.

"Bairn ride with you," Bjorn said.

"Until we meet again," Ian replied. He turned to mount his horse as Bjorn walked away.

"My lord?" a woman's voice said to him. Ian turned, smiling at Raven. She had been named for the silky black hair that fell over her shoulders—a rare thing among Bjorn's people. That and her bright gold eyes made her seem more like the bird she was named for than a mere woman.

"Raven," he said. "I was wondering if you would come."

"I could not allow you to leave without saying goodbye," Raven replied, smiling. "Not after . . ."

"I shall miss you," Ian said, filling the uncomfortable pause.

"And I you," Raven agreed. "I have brought you this."

Ian reached out to take the scrap of cloth she offered him. It was white cotton backed with lace—intricately woven and delicate.

" 'Tis beautiful," Ian said. "What is it?"

"It would have been part of the hem of my wedding gown," Raven said. "I thought you should have it. Take it for luck on your journey."

"You . . . are to be wed?" Ian asked.

"I hope so," Raven said. "Someday."

She would likely not have to hope long. She was beautiful, and her beauty was rare. No doubt she had many suitors in the lodge.

"Thank you," Ian said. "I shall keep it always."

"Farewell, Ian," Raven said. She kissed him quickly on the cheek and then turned away and quickly walked back toward the lodge.

Ian swallowed around the lump that had formed in his throat. He turned and mounted his horse. As he turned back to survey the people under his command, he looked down at the fragile piece of cloth in his hand.

He wheeled the horse about and spurred her in the ribs. Raven heard the beating hooves and stopped, turning to look at him. He reined Brazen to a halt and dismounted.

"What is it?" Raven asked.

"You said this is from your wedding gown?" Ian asked.

"Yes."

"It must have taken you a long time to make this," he continued. "If I keep this, will it make your gown late?"

Raven laughed.

"Do not worry about that, Ian," she said. "I should have it finished by spring. Not that I have anyone yet to wear it for."

"Wear it for me," Ian said before he even realized what he was going to say.

"For you?" Raven said softly. His words had surprised her as much as him. Still, they had been true.

"Yes!" Ian said. "Raven, I love you. *I* want your hand."

"Herrold!" Raven said, turning toward the lodge.

"Aye?" Herrold asked, stepping from his post by the lodge door. He looked suspiciously at Ian. Ian swallowed. Had he just violated some custom?

"Would you find my father?" she asked. "Please?"

"Aye," Herrold said. His tone changed from guarded to puzzled. Raven turned back to Ian.

"You have to ask my father," she said. "Can you wait?"

"Until the stars burn out," Ian replied.

Raven's father was as black-haired as his daughter, but his eyes were a deep brown that revealed nothing of what the man behind them was thinking.

"What is it, daughter?" he asked once Herrold finally brought him out. Raven said nothing. She merely turned to Ian.

"I . . ." Ian began. His voice broke, and he had to stop to swallow.

"That is," he continued, "Sir, I wish to ask for your daughter's hand." He rushed the last words before he could lose the strength to speak them.

"No," Raven's father replied. Ian felt something inside him wither.

"Father?" Raven said quietly.

"Is this your wish as well?" he asked, turn.
daughter.

"It is," she replied. Ian began to hope again.

"No," he repeated, crushing that hope. "Not the n
ing after you've performed his Rite." He turned back
Ian.

"I've nothing against *you*, lad," he said. "If you still
want her hand come spring, and she still wishes you to have
it, I shall grant it to you, but not on the morning after your
Rite."

"I . . . understand," Ian said. Raven's father smiled.

"I doubt *that*," he said. "But you're willing to live with
it. That's a good sign. So we part, Ian."

"Until we meet again," Ian replied.

"Oh, thank you, papa!" Raven cried, throwing her arms
around her father's neck.

"Don't thank me yet," he said. "Say goodbye to the
young lord and then come inside. Your mother will want
to talk to you."

"Yes, father." She turned back to Ian as her father
walked into the lodge.

"You *will* come back in the spring?" she asked.

"I swear it," Ian replied.

Their first day, or rather half day, of travel passed une-
ventfully. Ian looked around as the men set up camp and
the women prepared the evening meal. Three large cook
fires dominated the center of the camp. The ten oxen grazed
in a makeshift corral bounded by the five wagons. Ian
smiled—he had learned that trick from Master Geoff.

A little of the fear at leading these people had passed.
They accepted him as their chief on this journey—that
helped.

Of course, the real test would come not on a good day,
but on a bad.

HELD THE children close as they slept. The hold ние longship stank with the smell of too many bodies in too little space for far too long. For five days, she and her children had shared this cramped little space with six others—mages all.

Brianna looked around at the people sleeping in the hold as the ship rocked in the river currents. They lay about in various groups like sacks of grain scattered in the ship's hold. These people certainly did not seem like the monsters the temple painted them to be. It was no way to have to travel.

Brianna smiled as she watched Nolan and Ingrid sleep. The old couple could almost have been her own parents. The way Ingrid doted over her and the children heightened that illusion.

She misses Gretchen so much, Brianna thought. Ingrid was taking advantage of Brianna's presence to ease the ache of that loss. But that was all right. If Brianna's presence could ease the old woman's suffering a little, so be it.

They had all lost so much. Fathers, mothers, husbands, wives, siblings—so very much. Poor Stefan had had to watch while they raped and burned his wife. Fortunately, Hans had been spared the sight of watching his mother tortured. Still, he had seen the temple cut the throats of his younger sisters.

And they call us monsters! she thought.

At least the mages didn't brutally murder children in front of their parents and siblings. Nor did they falsely ac-

cuse and kill entire families for their p
had tried to do to her and her children.

That thought brought a burning ache to her boso
had been such a good man. He had provided well for
and the children, both by hard work and by being a loving
husband and father. And *they* had taken him from her and
the children forever.

Silently, so as not to wake the children, Brianna wept.

They arrived in Nalur's Ridge ten days after the ship had
left Star Lake. Brianna took a deep breath of the warm night
air. The closeness of so many unwashed bodies in the hold
of the longship had long ago become overpowering. It was
good to smell clean air again.

Brianna hoped that their new hosts could offer them a
bath. A place to wash their clothes would be nice too. Like
herself, most had very little in the way of clothing, and the
clothes they did have smelled as bad as their wearers.

"Can I carry that for you?" someone asked her. Brianna
smiled up at Stefan's son, Hans.

"Yes, thank you," she said.

"I'm . . . sorry about that first night," Hans said quietly.

"I understand," Brianna said, reaching out and squeezing his arm gently. "Thank you."

"Everybody ashore," Captain Oslaf interrupted. "The
wagon's here."

Brianna followed Stefan and Hans off the boat. Nolan
and Ingrid followed her with Ingrid leading little Hilda by
the hand.

"Come along," a man said to her. He helped her and
her son Jason into the wagon. Ingrid handed Hilda up to
her before climbing into the wagon herself with the man's
help.

"Looks like we've room enough for everyone," he said.
"Good. Come along. Quietly, now."

Brianna settled into the wagon next to Nolan and Ingrid.
She smiled a tired smile across at Stefan and Hans. They

...med glad to be off

...sked, echoing all of their

...an replied. "With beds and a
...on't want to draw too much at-

...onto the driver's bench and soon they
we.......... down the empty streets of the town.
Brian........ with the baby on her lap as they rode
through ....

"Someplace safe" turned out to be another secret cellar
beneath still another barn. This one was different, though.

The large cellar was divided into smaller doorless rooms.
Each small room held two stacked beds—four beds in each
room. One could literally reach from one bed to the other.
Still, it was more privacy and comfort than the other safe
houses had offered.

Another room, with an actual door, housed a large
wooden tub with a wooden tap in the ceiling above it—
presumably leading to a cistern. Brianna breathed a sigh of
relief at the sight of it. They could wash themselves, and
then their clothing, in here.

"How long will we be here?" Stefan asked their guide.

"Less than a fortnight," their guide replied. "Then you
will travel north to Hunter's Glen."

"Is that where we'll be staying?" Brianna asked.

"No," the man said. "You will be travelling on from
there. I don't know where."

"Are you Guardian?" Brianna asked. The man did not
reply, simply turned to stare at her. Ingrid leaned over to
her.

" 'Tis not proper to ask that, child," she whispered.

"Oh!" Brianna said. "I'm sorry." She still had so much
to learn!

"You are not Circle," the man said.

"No," Brianna replied.

"Yes, she is," Stefan objected. "She has passed two

Rites of Acceptance. The Hunt took her husband. She's one of us now.'' The man nodded.

"You have my sympathy,'' he said. "I am glad that you and your children have found safety with us.'' He turned to address them all.

"You may expect daily visits,'' he said. "If there is anything you need, ask. Don't be shy. Goodnight, and welcome to Nalur's Ridge. So we part.''

"Until we meet again,'' everyone else replied. Their guide then turned and climbed back up the ladder to the surface.

"All right,'' Stefan said, once he had left, "who gets the tub first?'' Brianna laughed.

"Well, this is it,'' Ian said, looking around at the site they had selected the day before.

"Are you sure?'' Fjalin asked.

"It meets our needs,'' Ian replied. "We have a stream that can be dammed for a millpond to the east. The hilltop will make a nice site for the lodge once we clear all the trees from it.''

"We can put the barns north of the lodge,'' he added. "And the farmers tell me the land seems good. We don't have the time to go searching for something better.''

"Then I suppose I shall be leaving,'' Fjalin said.

"By the time you get back, I should have some of the land cleared and the first fields planted,'' Ian said. "With luck I'll even have the lodge and the barns started.''

"Good luck, Ian,'' Fjalin told him. "So we part.''

"Thank you for everything you've done, Fjalin,'' Ian said. "There will always be a place for you in my hall. Until we meet again.''

Ian watched as Fjalin walked away into the forest. When he could no longer see his friend, Ian turned and walked back to the camp.

"All right!'' he shouted. "Let's get to work! I want to start planting our first field within a sevennight!''

•   •   •

Ian rose with the dawn. Around him, the camp was beginning to stir. In three days they had stripped the small hilltop bare of trees. Today, the men would begin clearing what would soon become their first field of crops.

Pine logs, stripped of their branches and bark, were stacked across each other to dry and season. These would eventually become the roof of the lodge and the barns.

Nothing was wasted. The branches that were too small to use for lumber were being cooked down into pine tar by the women. The tar would be mixed with pine needles and clay to form the paste that would be used to fill between the logs of the roof. Then the remaining pine tar would be brushed over the logs themselves.

Small logs would either be cut into planks or into firewood for the winter. Excess pine needles, and there were a *lot* of those, were being saved as kindling and as eventual fuel for the pottery kilns.

Even the ashes were being saved, along with their own waste, to be plowed into the new fields. Stones gathered from clearing the ground were stacked in piles throughout the camp. These, and others gathered later, would become the walls of Ian's hall. *Nothing* was wasted.

Still, stones gathered from the fields would not be enough to build a hall. They needed to find another source of stone. Ian walked over to the tent Theodr shared with his wife Freida.

"Theodr?" Ian called from outside. The older man lifted the flap and stepped out into the cool morning air.

"Yes, lord?" Theodr said. Ian had stopped asking Theodr to quit calling him that. His new advisor had pointed out that it was important to build Ian's authority if he was to maintain order here.

"We need to find another source of stone," Ian said. "The stones from the fields are not going to be enough."

"No, they will not," Theodr agreed. "This area is not as rocky as the land around Bjornshall was."

"What should we do?" Ian asked. "I hate to send one

of our teams of oxen with a wagon to haul stone. We need them for clearing the fields.''

The men were able to cut down the trees faster than their five teams of oxen could pull out the stumps. Especially since the oxen were also being used to haul the logs. The oxen were their weak link in clearing the fields.

Ian wished that Bjorn had sent more with them. With the resources at their disposal, they could only clear a little over a quarter acre of land per day. At that rate it would be two moons before their first field was completely cleared.

"Let us wait and see how much stone the plowing turns up when we get to that point," Theodr suggested. "We may yet have the stone we need."

"Very well," Ian agreed. "But we have to get the first barn started in another moon, at the latest. We can wait another moon after that to start on the lodge, but no longer."

"I would rather not wait that long," Theodr said.

"Neither would I," Ian said. "But we must get our crops planted first."

"Aye," Theodr agreed.

"Is everyone ready here?" Master Geoff asked.

"Yes," Nolan replied. "We're ready whenever you are, Master Geoff."

"Good," Geoff said. "We'll be moving out soon. Remember your story?"

"Yes," Nolan said. "We were burned out of our farm by bandits. We're travelling to Hunter's Glen with our daughter and grandchildren to start over. We have family there."

Brianna smiled in the back of the wagon. Nolan and Ingrid had just become her "parents"—at least for this trip. Ingrid had actually seemed pleased at the role.

"Most of my men are not Circle," Geoff cautioned them. "Do not forget."

Brianna's smile faded. Could they successfully hide

openly among the ungifted like this? Or would this journey end in the fire?

"How . . . long will the trip take?" Brianna asked.

" 'Tis a dozen days to Pine Grove," Master Geoff replied. "Another six from there to Hunter's Glen. In good weather, that is."

Brianna felt her heart sink. Over half a moon. And even then, their journey would not be over. How far did they have to go to escape the Hunt? And in what kind of place would they finally come to rest?

The ground was cleared for the barn. Loudmouth had been pressed into service hauling stone from upstream. They could not load the wagon as heavily with the mule as they could have with oxen, but they needed the oxen to clear fields.

The smell of pine smoke mixed with the mouth-watering aroma of venison. Ian had begun sending out hunting parties two days ago. The deer meat would help extend their rations. That could become important when the refugees began to arrive.

Ian watched as the men dug the foundations for the barn. He had assigned twenty men to the construction of the barn. That left him thirty to continue clearing fields.

Oddly enough, this had not slowed down the rate at which they could clear the ground. Another quarter acre had been cleared again today. The limiting factor there was still the oxen.

Once the barn was finished, Ian would assign those same twenty men to start the lodge. By then, they should have almost ten acres under crop.

If all went well, by the time winter hit, they would have three times that under cultivation. A score and a half acres of farmland would not feed an entire lodge, however. Come spring, they would have to clear even more land—build more barns. There was still much to be done.

Even so, watching this place grow from the wilderness gave Ian a strange sense of pride. Soon the stone walls of the first barn would begin to rise where before had stood only forest. A place of safety for the magi.

It was a great work. Ian was finally beginning to feel like a chieftain.

"Who?" King Gavin asked, blinking against the light from the open door. In his windowless room, he had no idea of the hour, but it felt early.

"Temple Father Olaf and the First Knight of the Sacred Hunt, your majesty," the guard repeated. "They request an audience with you immediately. Forgive me, but they claim that it is *most* urgent."

"Tell them to wait in the garden," Gavin ordered. "I will send for them shortly."

"Yes, majesty," the guard said, bowing before leaving Gavin's presence.

Mathen? Gavin thought. It had been over three moons since the First Knight had inexplicably left Reykvid. And now, upon his return, he wanted to see Gavin on a matter of dire urgency?

Gavin called for his valet. Whatever was afoot, he wanted to find out quickly.

Gavin looked up as the door to the council chamber opened. A guard held the door as Father Olaf and First Knight Mathen entered the room.

Gavin rose from his chair as they advanced and bowed. They did not kneel, which befitted their station as priests.

"Greetings, Father Olaf," Gavin said. "And Sir Mathen. Please, be seated. It is good to see you back safely, Sir Mathen, although you left us at a most inopportune time."

"Father Olaf has explained that to me, majesty," Mathen replied. "I regret that it was necessary. However, I have uncovered something that threatens us all. Something which only you, the king of Reykvid, have the power to help us with."

"This sounds grave, indeed," Gavin said, retaking his seat on the throne. "What is it?"

''Majesty,'' Mathen replied, ''a MageLord walks the earth.''

Gavin felt the blood in his veins turn to ice. A Mage-Lord? Certainly not again! Gavin closed his eyes against the memories of the atrocities committed against him and by him under Valerian's control.

Did we not truly kill Valerian? he wondered. The mere thought was almost enough to unman him.

''What proof have you of this?'' Gavin finally said.

''No proof, majesty,'' Mathen said. ''Only what I have seen with my own eyes. If I may?''

''Proceed.''

''Majesty,'' Mathen began, ''much of what I am about to say may be difficult to believe, but I ask that you bear with me.''

''Go on.''

''Majesty, the mageborn bear a Mark, placed upon them by Hrothgar,'' Mathen said. ''Most cannot see this, but it surrounds them like a pale, glowing shadow. The reason that I have been made First Knight of the Hunt is that I can see this Mark upon them.''

Gods above! Gavin thought. *He's a mage himself! And he doesn't even know it!*

Long ago, Bjorn had told Gavin about the aura that surrounded the magi when they worked their craft. An aura that was visible only to the mageborn with their arcane senses. Mathen was one of the very mages he hunted with such fervor!

Gavin almost wanted to laugh, or perhaps weep, with the irony of it. He doubted the First Knight would find his revelation humorous, however.

''Father Olaf?'' Gavin asked, instead. ''Are you aware of this?''

''Yes, your majesty,'' Olaf replied. ''Mathen has always had an uncanny ability to ferret out the mages. He has also maintained the innocence of several who were wrongly accused. To my knowledge he has never been wrong.''

"Very well," Gavin said. "I will accept this as truth, then—for now."

"The strength of the Mark varies," Mathen explained. "The more powerful the mage, the stronger the Mark."

Gavin nodded. That also fit with what Bjorn had once told him.

"And the vermin can hide the Mark for a time," Mathen said. "Although it seems to be difficult for them to do it for very long."

"And this Mark is what has led you to believe that you have found a MageLord?" Gavin asked.

"Yes, majesty," Mathen replied. "If I may continue?"

"Please."

"When young Ian Urqhart was leaving, I saw the Mark rise about him as he rode away," Mathen said.

"What!" Gavin shouted, rising to his feet. "That is the very day you left as well, is it not?"

"Y-yes, majesty," Mathen said.

"Is Ian your so-called MageLord?" Gavin asked.

"No, majesty," Mathen replied. "His Mark was not unusually strong. In fact, I have seen the Mark much stronger on others."

"Have you killed Ian?" Gavin asked coldly.

"No, majesty!" Mathen replied. "I would never take action against one of the royal line. I only sought to follow him, to see if he could lead me to others of the mages."

Gavin sat back in his chair. Ian a mage? Then what of Ivanel?

"Does his father carry this Mark?" Gavin asked.

"No, majesty," Mathen said. "At least, not that I have ever seen. It may be that Ian's mother was a magess. Baron Ivanel may not even know."

Gavin nodded. That was possible. Still, there were Ivanel's strenuous objections to the Hunt. And it had been Ivanel who had convinced him to release Bjorn and banish him rather than keeping him imprisoned. Then there was the matter of the fleeing magi who had inexplicably slipped through Ivanel's grasp in Smithton. Gavin did not like the direction in which his thoughts led him.

"So, where did Ian lead you?" Gavin asked.

"Into the Wastes, majesty," Mathen told him. "He travelled far into the Wastes."

"Where?"

"I doubt that you would recognize the towns..." Mathen began.

"I know the Wastes well, priest!" Gavin snapped. "Where did Ian travel?"

"My apologies, majesty," Mathen replied. "He travelled to Nalur's Ridge. From there he hired on with a caravan bound for a small lumbering town called Pine Grove."

"Gods above," Gavin whispered. "And from there to Hunter's Glen?"

"That... is correct, majesty," Mathen said. Gavin's apparent guess had taken the priest off guard.

"Is that where you found this MageLord?" Gavin asked.

"No, majesty," Mathen said. "I followed Ian north from Hunter's Glen. He did meet with another mage in Hunter's Glen, however. A blond man, almost as young as himself."

That would not have been Bjorn. Bjorn would be in his early twenties by now.

"Go on," Gavin commanded.

"Ian travelled north for some time," Mathen said. "Then he, and his companion, began searching. I eventually followed them to a strange place that looked as if the forest had been swept away by a giant."

Gavin knew the place Mathen was talking about. He had been there when Valerian had destroyed Bjorn's cabin and the forest around it for hundreds of feet. Ian had gone searching for Bjorn!

"There I saw them conjure forth a man," Mathen said. "He was blond of hair and beard and about your majesty's height, I would say. He simply appeared before them. They spoke for a time and he disappeared."

"And that's when you saw the Mark?" Gavin asked.

They had conjured someone to them? Bjorn? Or someone worse?

"No, majesty," Mathen said. "I saw no Mark on him at that time. Ian and his companion travelled on, however. By the end of the day, they arrived at a stone hall. There were many people there—all with the Mark very strong upon them. Stronger than I had ever seen before. And then *he* came out of the lodge to meet them."

"Who is *he*?" Gavin asked.

"The man they had summoned earlier," Mathen replied. "Majesty, the Mark surrounded him as though he had called down the sun itself and wore it about him."

Gavin felt gooseflesh rise on his arms and the back of his neck. Those had almost been Bjorn's exact words when he had described the aura around Valerian. As if one were looking at the sun.

"I believe you, Mathen," Gavin said. "I also believe that Ian's father knows of this."

"He may be innocent, majesty," Mathen said. "I have never seen the Mark upon Ivanel."

"No," Gavin said. "He is not innocent. But I cannot explain how I know this." Only Gavin, Ivanel and Wilhelm had known of Bjorn's survival. If Ian were hunting Bjorn, Ivanel was the one who had sent him.

"Shall we take him, majesty?" Mathen asked.

"Absolutely not!" Gavin shouted. "You will never, *never* act against one of the royal line! Not unless the temple of Hrothgar feels it has the ability to stand against the armies of Reykvid!"

"No, majesty!" Father Olaf said. "We would never act against one of royal blood without your explicit command!"

"*I* shall deal with my uncle," Gavin said. "*And* my cousin. Who else has been told of this?"

"No one, majesty," Mathen said.

"Keep it that way," Gavin commanded. "Or else we risk warning our prey before the trap is sprung."

"Yes, majesty," Mathen replied. "I understand that all too well."

"We will discuss this more after I have tended to matters here at home," Gavin said. "We will likely have to take action against this . . . MageLord you have found."

"I agree," Mathen said. "Majesty, I am delighted that we are of one mind regarding this. I must confess that I had feared you would scoff at our warnings."

"I do not scoff at much where the magi are concerned," Gavin said, "and less where the MageLords are concerned. You may go. I will send word for you soon."

"Yes, majesty," Mathen said. "Thank you, majesty."

Gavin sat thinking, long after Olaf and Mathen had left. Bjorn! Bjorn, a MageLord.

But was it truly Bjorn? Or had a weakened and injured Valerian taken Bjorn's form to escape them? Had the man they killed in his place truly been Valerian—or Bjorn? Was Valerian even now gathering his power and his forces in the north, just waiting for the right time to strike?

In the end, it did not matter. Whether it was Bjorn or Valerian, if this person held the power that Mathen described, he had to be killed.

But first, Gavin had traitors to deal with at home.

"Guard!" Gavin called.

"Yes, majesty?" the guard replied, opening the door.

"Summon a messenger," Gavin commanded. "I am going to have a letter for him to deliver."

"Yes, majesty," the guard replied.

CHAPTER

------- TWENTY-TWO ------------

THE FOREST OUTSIDE Nalur's Ridge looked forbidding. Outside of the city's protection, the trees and brush looked as if they hadn't seen an axe in generations, if ever.

Master Geoff's habit of leaving a cow out for the bandits every second night did little to calm Brianna's nerves. So far, five nights into their journey, things had gone well.

Only another sevennight, Brianna told herself as she lay down between Hilda and the baby. In another sevennight, they would be out of the heaviest part of the forest and on their way to Hunter's Glen.

The name sounded pleasant. Supposedly it was a small farming village. Brianna could almost see the farms lying amid grassy, gently rolling hills just from the name alone.

As she was drifting off to sleep, beginning to dream of working a new farm with Klaus, a shout woke her. Brianna rose up to listen.

Another shout followed quickly. And then another. Soon it sounded as if the entire camp were shouting. Then she heard the ring of steel against bronze.

They were under attack! But Master Geoff had said that the bandits left them alone if he placated them.

"Nolan!" Brianna called, crawling to the back of the wagon where the old couple slept.

"Nolan!" she said, shaking the old man's shoulder. "Ingrid! Wake up!"

"Oh, dear!" Ingrid said, waking to the sound of the battle.

"Mommy!" Hilda cried. Brianna turned back to her children. Hilda looked past her and screamed.

Brianna looked back to see a hairy, unwashed face preceding its smelly owner into the back of the wagon. Ingrid screamed as Nolan swung a hammer at the man's face. The bandit fell away, only to be quickly replaced by another.

Brianna scrambled on all fours to her children. Jason was also picking up a makeshift club. Brianna started to forbid him, but checked herself. If the bandits had surrounded their wagon, they would all be fighting soon enough.

The cloth of the wagon ripped next to Brianna. She grabbed Hilda and Oslaf and dragged them to the other side of the wagon.

Jason swung the shovel he had found edge-on into the bandit's face. The man screamed and fell back from the wagon. The cloth behind her ripped, and Brianna started to drag her children away from the intruders when strong hands grabbed her arms.

She flung Hilda and Oslaf away from her as the men dragged her from the wagon. Once outside she could see that the bandits had indeed surrounded the wagons of the fleeing magi. Geoff's guards were fighting their way to them, but they were horribly outnumbered.

Brianna kicked the man in front of her in the groin. He collapsed to the ground as the man behind her got a better grip on her arms. The man holding her arms was strong, but Brianna was no weak rich woman. She and Klaus had started out poor, and she had spent many years working alongside him on the farm.

She threw her weight to the right, knocking her captor off balance. Then she pushed back, slamming him against the wagon. When he let go, she turned, balled up her fist and punched him with all her strength on the temple.

He toppled like a felled tree. Brianna began to climb back up on the wagon. What was happening to her babies?

Someone grabbed her by the hair and pulled her from the wagon. She screamed, more in surprise than fear, as she fell to the ground. The impact knocked the wind from her and someone grabbed her wrists, pinning her to the ground.

Another man landed on top of her. Brianna gagged at the sour smell of his unwashed flesh.

"Oh, aye!" he said. "I tol' ye they had women!"

The man grabbed the collar of her bodice and ripped the garment open, exposing her flesh. His filthy hands groped at her exposed flesh, making her want to vomit.

Fortunately, the man was so distracted by her womanhood that he had forgotten her legs. Brianna's knee rammed into his groin with all her strength. The man's eyes rolled up into his head, and he collapsed on top of her.

"Bitch!" the one holding her wrists shouted. Brianna rolled, allowing her arms to cross as the unconscious bandit rolled off her.

"Gimme a 'and, 'ere!" the bandit shouted.

Brianna pulled her knees up under her and threw her weight back, pulling the bandit toward her. His grip on one arm slipped, and Brianna ripped her hand from his grasp. She slashed her fingernails across his eyes, and the man flinched away.

Someone grabbed her free arm from behind. Again she found herself pinned to the ground.

"Mind 'er legs," the first bandit warned. "She's a feisty one."

A great shout of rage from behind them surprised the bandits. They released her and turned to face the red-haired and bearded giant that waded into them with a double-bitted woodsman's axe.

One swipe of the axe took one bandit's head from his shoulders and buried the axe head in the other's chest. Hot blood covered Brianna, but she hardly noticed. She was clambering to her feet to climb back into her wagon. She could hear Ingrid, Hilda and little Oslaf screaming.

Geoff's guards finally reached them, and soon the battle was over. Miraculously, everyone in Brianna's wagon was all right. Nolan and Jason had been able to keep the bandits from gaining the wagon until Geoff's men had reached them.

Ingrid saw Brianna covered in blood and almost fainted.

" 'Tis not mine," she assured the old woman. "I have to change."

Ingrid held up a blanket while Brianna changed behind it into what was now her only remaining dress. Then she gathered up Hilda and little Oslaf and quieted them. Outside, the commotion in the camp slowly died away.

"Brianna!" Stefan's voice called.

"Just a moment," she answered. After a while she was able to transfer Hilda and Oslaf back to Ingrid. The infant had fallen asleep, but Hilda was still wide awake and frightened. Brianna picked her up, and Hilda clung to her neck, sobbing.

"I'm proud of you," she whispered to Jason. "You stayed to protect your sister. That was very brave."

"I knew you'd kill me if I didn't," Jason explained, but she could tell that he was pleased by her words. She kissed his forehead before leaving the wagon.

"Are you all right?" Stefan asked when she climbed out of the wagon with Hilda.

"I am fine," Brianna said. "Hans?"

"Fine," Stefan replied. "Geoff lost a couple of his men, and a few are wounded."

"They were after me," Brianna said.

"Don't be ridiculous," Stefan said.

"Actually, she's right?" Geoff said.

"What do you mean?" Stefan asked.

"The bandits attacked because they saw that we had women," Geoff explained. "At least that's what the only one we captured had to say."

"We caught one?"

"He died," Geoff said. "My captain didn't like his tone."

"Ah," Stefan said.

"It appears that I'm going to have to hire more guards if I keep transporting you people," Geoff said. "Oh, well. I'll charge Wilhelm for them."

"I am sorry, Master Geoff," Brianna said.

"Pah!" Geoff replied. " 'Tis not *your* fault. Clean up

your area and then get some sleep. We're moving out of here at dawn.''

Construction on the barn had almost ground to a halt. Loud-mouth just couldn't keep up with the demand for stone. Between hauling the wagon from the rock bed further up-stream and plowing the fields, the poor mule was about to give out.

Ian was going to have to give him some rest. For that matter, the men had been working for over a fortnight without a break. They now had over three acres cleared and planted.

"Give him some extra feed," Ian said to the man tending Loudmouth, "if he'll eat it."

"Yes, lord," the man said.

Ian found Theodr by the cook fires. The old man looked tired. He had been working alongside the rest of them. Even though he was the oldest one here, there was still a lot of strength left in him. Ian wondered just how old Theodr really was.

"I'm thinking about proclaiming a rest day tomorrow," Ian said.

"That would be a popular decision," Theodr agreed.

"We've all been working hard," Ian said. "We need a rest. I'm afraid Loudmouth may have to take more than one day."

"Is the mule in bad shape?" Theodr asked.

"Yes," Ian replied. "I'm going to send one of the ox teams to get the next load of stone. That will give Loud-mouth a rest."

"Probably a good idea," Theodr said.

"We need more animals," Ian asked. "If we sent a mes-senger to Bjorn, do you think he would send us some more?"

"I doubt it," Theodr said. "Giving up ten oxen for the summer was not an easy thing for the lodge to do. Between that and taking half the men, I imagine they're working pretty hard back home, too."

"You are probably right," Ian said.

"We should have more help soon," Theodr said. "Fjalin will be bringing us people soon."

"We don't need more people," Ian said. "We need more animals."

"We shall have to settle for what we get," Theodr said. "That's why we are here—to give them a place to come."

"I know that," Ian said. "It would just be nice if they brought a few more oxen with them."

"It would be nice if they didn't have to come at all," Theodr pointed out. "But they do, and we have to do the best we can with what we have."

"I wonder when they'll start arriving," Ian wondered aloud.

Brianna rode beside Nolan on the driver's bench of the wagon. It had been eight days since the attack, and they had left Pine Grove behind them yesterday with no other problems. The spirits of the magi improved as the forest around them thinned.

Master Geoff had remained with his goods in Pine Grove, turning the refugees over to a gruff and short-winded guide name Johann. The man spoke as though each word cost him a measure of silver to utter. He never used two words where one would suffice.

Still, he had carried important news to all of them. Hunter's Glen was now only five days away. He knew nothing of their destination after that—only that Hunter's Glen was not their final stop.

Brianna wondered if they would ever stop travelling. Was there truly a new home for them, or would they simply travel forever?

That was just despair talking. Despair was all too easy to succumb to in hard times. They lived, they were well, and soon they would start a new life. Brianna had lived through despair before, and she and Klaus had beaten it to build a good life.

She would build a good life for her children again. She

had friends—friends who would stand by her against even the Hunt. Friends who were, even now, helping her to rebuild her life.

These were *good* people. Simple people nothing like the monsters the temple had taught her to believe. Brianna laid her head over onto Nolan's shoulder. The old man looked over and smiled at her, sadness and happiness mingled into one expression.

She was certain that her own smile was just as mixed as Nolan's.

Ivanel broke the wax seal bearing Gavin's signet and unfolded the parchment. The note was short and cryptic.

Uncle, come to Reykvid with all possible speed, Gavin had written. *I need your help on an urgent matter. Gavin Urqhart, King of Reykvid.*

There was no explanation of what the "matter" on which Gavin needed his help was. It must have been something he did not want to trust to paper.

"Guard!" Ivanel called.

"Yes, my lord?" the guard replied, opening the door to his chambers.

"Send for Arik," Ivanel said.

"Yes, my lord," the guard said. Ivanel picked Gavin's letter back up from the table, as if he could divine some further piece of information from it.

Nothing further could be produced from the message, however—no matter how many times Ivanel read it. What could have happened to inspire this cryptic message from the king? He was not certain he liked the feel of this.

"You sent for me, my lord?" Arik said as he walked into Ivanel's sitting room.

"What do you make of this?" Ivanel asked, handing Arik the letter. Arik read the short missive and handed it back to Ivanel.

"I don't know," Arik said. "It sounds urgent."

"Yes," Ivanel agreed.

"Are you going?" Arik said.

"I can't very well ignore such a summons," Ivanel replied.

"Do you want me to go with you?" Arik asked.

"No," Ivanel said. "You need to get our new guests to Star Lake. Take them tonight, and hurry back once you have delivered them."

"Yes, my lord," Arik replied.

"That's all, Arik," Ivanel said.

"My lord?" Arik asked.

"Yes?" Ivanel asked in return.

"Take care, my lord," Arik told him. "I do not like the feel of this."

"Nor do I, my friend," Ivanel agreed.

Arik rose and left the room. Once again, Ivanel read through Gavin's note.

What, he thought, *is going on in Reykvid?*

Baron William wondered that as well. He had been rousted from his bed in the middle of the night and handed a letter from Gavin. The letter began with two words that chilled William's heart to the core.

Valerian lives, Gavin had written. William considered himself a brave man, but those two words had made him want to climb back into his bed and hide under the blankets like a frightened child.

He still had nightmares about being flayed alive, memories of his days in Valerian's tower. It did not help that those events had been illusion, created by Valerian's foul sorcery. The pain had been as real as if he had lived through it.

And now Gavin told him that that monster still lived? That was impossible. William had seen the man's head himself.

But deep down inside, he knew that, with a MageLord, nothing was impossible. If Gavin said that Valerian still lived, he probably did. And that made the rest of Gavin's note, commanding him to leave at once and travel to Reykvid without delay, impossible to ignore.

So here he was, in the middle of the night, riding to Reykvid with a score of his castle guard. Gavin and Valerian be damned, he was going to make camp tomorrow night!

The towers of the palace finally came into view late in the afternoon of Ivanel's third day of travel. Ivanel breathed a sigh of relief. Now he would finally learn what emergency had commanded his presence at the palace.

The repairs were progressing well. The outer wall was almost intact once again. As Ivanel passed through the gatehouse, he saw that repairs on the palace itself were also going well.

Good. Perhaps he would be able to stay in the palace during this visit, instead of one of the barracks as he had had to do the last time.

Pages took the horses, and Ivanel walked into the palace itself. The garden was beginning to look pleasant again.

"My lord," a guardsman said to him, "his majesty is waiting for you in the throne room."

"Thank you," Ivanel said. The guards must have been watching for his arrival. Apparently Gavin wanted to know the moment he arrived.

Ivanel walked to the large double doors of the throne room. The guards held the door for him as Ivanel walked into the throne room.

"Greetings, uncle," Gavin said from the throne.

"Greetings, majesty," Ivanel said as he walked toward the throne. He stopped abruptly as two of the guards leveled their pikes at his throat. From the corner of his eye, he saw that two more pikes were facing him from behind.

"Remove your sword belt and let it fall to the floor," Gavin ordered coldly. Anger blazed in his eyes.

"What is the *meaning* of this?" Ivanel roared. "Gavin, have you gone mad?"

"You are charged with treason," Gavin said, "and with the practice of the Forbidden Arts."

Gods above! Ivanel thought. How had Gavin found him out?

"That's preposterous!" Ivanel said. And then he saw Mathen step out from behind one of the pillars. For a moment, he could not hide his surprise.

"That's right," Gavin said. "Remove your sword belt, uncle, before the guards are forced to fulfill their duty."

Ivanel unbuckled his sword belt and lowered the blade gently to the floor.

"You may thank whatever gods you hold dear that you are of royal blood," Gavin said. "You will live out the rest of your days in the palace dungeon. When you die, your body shall be burned and the ashes dumped in the sea."

"I see," Ivanel said. "You are going to believe the lies of this whore's bastard over the word of your father's brother."

"You mean over the lies of my father's brother," Gavin replied.

"My clansmen will not be happy with this," Ivanel said.

"I suspect they will be even less happy with your crimes," Gavin retorted. "Take him away."

Ivanel looked up to see William also watching as they led him away. The hatred that burned in his eyes was even more vicious than Gavin's. Even that was better than the smug, gloating look on Mathen's face. Ivanel privately swore that someday he would finish the task his son had started.

So, Ivanel thought, *the Hunt has finally caught up with me.* At least it had not been before he had saved many others from it. Then they half led him, half dragged him down the stairs to the dungeon, and he descended into darkness.

William walked with Gavin to where the army was gathered on the plains outside the palace. Five thousand men, mostly infantry, had been assembled to retake Smithton. Gavin did not expect any serious resistance. This force was primarily to make certain that none occurred.

"Who are you going to make chief of the Sword clan?" William asked.

"My father had a nephew a little younger than Ivanel," Gavin replied. "His name is Evan, and he is the captain of the guard at Northguard. His mother was sister to my father."

"He is loyal?" William asked.

"I have never had reason to doubt it," Gavin replied. Of course, he had never had reason to doubt Ivanel's loyalty, either.

"Mathen will tell me if he, too, is a mage," Gavin added. "Expect me back within a fortnight. If it appears that I will be gone longer, I shall send word."

"Take care, majesty," William said. "We do not know how far this has spread within Ivanel's hall."

"That is why I'm taking Mathen," Gavin said. "He can sniff out the mages for us. Smithton will be secured as quickly as possible. Guard the kingdom well in my absence."

"I shall, majesty," William assured him.

William made his way down the stairs to the dungeon. He stopped at the door to Ivanel's cell and waited while the guards opened the door.

The cell had been furnished with furniture from one of the chambers. A bed, two chairs and a small desk occupied the cell. A door had been set into the wall leading to the next cell, where a bathtub and privy had been placed. A shelf of books sat against one wall next to a wardrobe. An oil lamp on the desk lit the room.

"Not bad for a dungeon," Ivanel said as William entered the room.

" 'Tis more than you deserve," William said bitterly, taking the seat opposite Ivanel.

"Why are you so angry with me, William?" Ivanel asked.

"I *trusted* you!" William said.

"So far as I know, I have never violated your trust," Ivanel said. "Or Gavin's, for that matter."

"What?" William said. "How can you claim that? You've lied to me the whole time I've known you. And to Gavin for his entire life."

"What was I *supposed* to do?" Ivanel asked. "Admit that I was a mage? Perhaps I should have tied myself to the stake while I was at it? The only crime I have committed was not choosing different parents."

"Your parents?"

"That's right," Ivanel said. "Specifically, my mother. Magnus was a mage, too—although he did not know of it. For that matter, so is Gavin. Do you think he will place himself on the stake? I think not."

"Gavin and Magnus did not practice the Forbidden Arts!" William objected. "They did not *use* their Power."

"*I have no Power!*" Ivanel shouted. "I am as ungifted as a stone. Magnus had more of the Talent than I, and so does Gavin.

"Even if I did," Ivanel added, "what would be the harm? Do you remember Bjorn, William?"

"I do," William said coldly.

"Was he a monster?" Ivanel asked. "Was he so evil? Do you remember how outraged he became over someone firing at deer on the riverside?"

"I do," William admitted.

"Do you remember what you said to him on that day?" Ivanel asked.

"That you can tell a lot about a man by what makes him angry," William replied.

"Do you remember how he risked his life to save us from Valerian?" Ivanel asked. "Was Bjorn an evil man?"

"No," William said after a moment.

"Neither am I," Ivanel said. "The only crime I have willfully committed is saving innocent people from being burned alive. *That* makes me angry! Gavin is murdering his own people."

"He knows where you're sending them," William said.

"What?"

"Mathen followed Ian to Bjorn's lodge," William explained. "Gavin plans to lead an army to destroy them."

"Why?" Ivanel asked. "They are nowhere near his lands. They are *no danger* to him!"

"Mathen claims that Bjorn is a MageLord," William said. "That his aura glows like the sun. Gavin thinks that Valerian took Bjorn's form somehow. That we really killed Bjorn, not Valerian."

"That's preposterous!" Ivanel said. "Mathen is a fanatic. He will tell whatever lies suit his purpose to carry out his 'divine quest.' *There* is the man who should not be trusted. The man who cuts the throats of a woman's children while she watches him do it. *I* am not the monster, William. Mathen is—and he has the king's ear. Just like Valerian had Magnus's."

"Valerian controlled Magnus's mind!" William objected.

"Mathen controls Gavin's," Ivanel countered. "Instead of sorcery, Mathen uses fear to control his mind. And yours."

"He does *not* control my mind!" William objected.

"Truly?" Ivanel replied. "The William I know would never stand by and watch his friends be imprisoned over their lineage. It seems to me he controls you quite well."

"You are trying to confuse me!" William said.

"I am trying to make you *think*!" Ivanel replied. "You *know* this is wrong! You *know* the Hunt is wrong! You *know* these people are innocent! I would rather think that you are being controlled than think that you are the type of person who could *condone* these atrocities!"

"I must go," William said, rising to his feet.

"Is it that hard to face?" Ivanel asked.

"I would advise you to hold your tongue," William said.

"You came to speak with *me*, remember?" Ivanel pointed out.

"That was obviously a mistake," William replied. "Guard!"

The guards opened the door, and Ivanel watched the man who had once been his friend leave the cell. Then the door closed, and Ivanel heard the heavy bar slide into place.

William walked back up the stairs to the throne room. *Damn* Ivanel! The man had always been able to talk circles around him!

The worst part was that William couldn't find anything Ivanel had said that wasn't true.

CHAPTER

------- TWENTY-THREE ------------

ARIK CRAWLED CLOSER to the camp through the spring
corn. The banner of Reykvid flew in the center of the camp,
as it had outside the other gates of Smithton. *Gavin.*

This camp was roughly the same size as the other three.
That would bring the total to roughly five thousand men.
Five thousand of Gavin's soldiers camped outside Smith-
ton.

Arik crawled backwards away from the camp. He would
return to his own hidden camp and wait until nightfall.
Then he would make his way to Hervis's farm and see what
news his fellow Guardian had to give to him.

Arik was fairly certain he knew what was happening,
though. This smelled of the Hunt.

"Arik!" Hervis said in surprise when he opened the door.
"Thank Bairn you're here. Get inside, quickly, before
someone sees you!"

"What is going on?" Arik asked.

"Wait," Hervis said. "I will put the wagon in the barn.
Then we'll talk."

Arik waited while Hervis took the wagon to the barn.
The little farm was doing a lot better. If Hervis weren't
careful, he might actually turn into a farmer.

"*What* is going on?" Arik asked when Hervis returned.

"The Hunt has taken Ivanel," Hervis said. "Gavin lured
him to Reykvid and imprisoned him. They have seized control of the city and placed Ivanel's nephew Evan over the
clan."

"Evan is an honest man," Arik said. "He will take good care of the clan."

"Perhaps," Hervis said, "but he is burning everyone that Gavin's pet priest accuses of being Circle."

"Eva?" Arik asked.

"Eva is safe," Hervis said. "She was able to get away from the castle. She is here, in the cellar."

Arik nodded. How ironic that the place they had built for others was now saving their own lives.

"Who is this priest?" Arik asked.

"His name is Mathen," Hervis said. "The First Knight of the Hunt."

Arik closed his eyes and sighed. He had suspected as much. When next he saw Ian, Arik was going to explain to him that you always made *certain* that such men were dead before you left them.

"What are we going to do?" Hervis asked.

"You are now Guardian," Arik told him. "Pick your successor and have him meet us here tomorrow night. I will show him where to take others in Star Lake. Make certain he is a skilled woodsman."

"Must you go?" Hervis asked.

"I am too well known," Arik explained. "I will be suspect. This Mathen is a mage—he can see auras."

"A *mage*?" Hervis asked. "One of our own?"

"Yes," Arik replied. "Instruct everyone to take the appropriate precautions. Go. I will wait here until you return."

"Gavin has imposed a curfew," Hervis said. "None are allowed out after sunset."

"Then don't get caught," Arik replied.

"Is everyone ready?" Arik asked.

"We are," Eva answered back.

"Then let's go," Arik said. Because of Gavin's curfew, they were not going to be able to take the wagon. People on foot could avoid the soldiers.

The wagon waited for them outside of town. Mikhail,

the new Guardian of the South, had taken it to an abandoned barn about a day's travel to the north. Hopefully, he had not been found.

Arik helped Eva out of the shaft. She was followed by two of Ivanel's guards, still wearing their armor from the castle. Karl the stablehand was the last one out of the cellar.

A motley band, without family or children, thank the gods. Slipping out of Smithton with children would have been almost impossible. As it was, they stood a good chance of capture.

"Follow me," Arik told them. "Mikhail is waiting for us with the wagon. We should be there by dawn."

Silently they slipped out into the night as Arik led them, and now himself as well, into exile.

Ian waited on horseback south of the first cleared fields. He had felt Fjalin's touch on his mind this morning. Apparently Ian was about to receive the first of his subjects.

There wasn't much for them to see, unfortunately. Only a boy chieftain and one small, almost completed barn. They had cleared a little less than ten acres. The field was planted with wheat, nowhere above knee height.

Ian saw them. Three wagons of people. The wagons were covered with tents. They appeared to carry little more than people.

Ian's eyes were on the horses, however. Six strong wagon horses for the lodge! He could set two of them to hauling stone and use the other four to haul felled logs. That would free the oxen for the sole duty of removing stumps.

They could almost double the amount of land they were clearing a day! This was the best thing that could have happened for the lodge.

Ian felt a despair that he had not known existed lift from his heart. They could make this work after all!

With a new feeling of confidence, he rode forward to meet his new subjects. He just hoped that the welcoming speech he and Theodr had worked up was as good as Theodr seemed to think it was.

Two days later an ox-drawn wagon arrived from Bjornshall carrying another moon's food from the lodge. Ian promptly commandeered the ox team, replacing them with two of the new horses and the promise that when the oxen were returned at the end of the summer, Bjorn's people could keep the horses.

Ian was pleased—this gave him another team of oxen for stump removal. They would be able to clear even more land each day. If Fjalin were able to borrow another team from Hunter's Glen as he had asked, that would help as well.

The workers had started digging the foundations of the lodge today. With the new team of horses hauling stone from up north, they should have ample supplies of stone to keep the builders busy.

Ian stepped into the men's bath tent and shrugged out of his tunic, stiff with dried sweat from the day's work. He took the boiling pot off the firepit and poured it into the tepid water of the tub. He set the pot aside and climbed into the warm water.

For a moment, he just sat back, letting the warm water ease his tired muscles and dissolve away some of the grime that coated his body. The tub could really have used another pot of boiling water. Oh, well.

"Comfortable?" a familiar voice asked him. Ian jumped in surprise and then saw Bjorn standing next to the tub.

"Very," Ian replied, relaxing back into the tub. "The food supplies arrived today. Thank you."

"That was what I was here to check on," Bjorn said. "You will begin receiving a wagonload per sevennight, now that your first barn is finished. Has anyone arrived yet?"

"Yes," Ian said. "We got our first group three days ago. Six men, four women and eight children. By the way, I appropriated the ox team from the wagon. I hope you don't mind.''

"Ian, we need those animals," Bjorn said. "I can't lose a team of oxen every time I send you a wagon."

"I replaced them with two horses," Ian said. "And you're welcome to keep the horses permanently."

"Where did you get horses?"

"The refugees came in wagons," Ian explained. "We're having a great deal of difficulty clearing farmland. I'll send the oxen back with the next wagon if you don't want the horses."

"No, that sounds like a fair trade," Bjorn said. "One team of horses for one season's use of an ox team. Keep them until the first snow. Whatever possessed you to settle in such a heavily forested area?"

"*All* of the land out here is heavily forested," Ian said. "This site at least has a stream and good soil."

"That means we'll have to support your lodge for a while longer," Bjorn said. "Still, we've started expanding out in the manner you suggested. We've gotten another two score acres under crop with the outlying farms. Next year, we'll add another hundred. So, I suppose we'll be able to help feed you."

"That's good to hear," Ian said. What he wouldn't give right now to have a hundred acres under crop!

"I'm going to go speak with your father and let him know that the first victims of the Hunt have started to arrive," Bjorn said. "Would you like me to pass any word along for you?"

"Let him know how things are going here," Ian said. "And tell him I miss him."

"I shall," he promised, smiling. "You've done well, Ian. Especially considering the land you have to work with. I'm sure he'll be proud of you."

"Thank you," Ian said. And with that, Bjorn simply disappeared. Gods, Ian wished *he* could do that!

•   •   •

Bjorn looked around in surprise when he found Ivanel. This was not Ivanel's castle. He had arrived unseen so that he could determine if Ivanel was alone. He was—but these were *not* his chambers. This was a small, stone-walled room that had the appearance of having been hastily furnished. Two heavy oak doors were the only means of egress from the room.

Bjorn passed through one of the doors into a hallway lit by oil lamps. A guard in the colors of Reykvid stood at the doorway. The door was barred.

Bjorn *knew* this hallway. He himself had been a "guest" here for a short time. This was Gavin's dungeon.

What the hell *is going on?* Bjorn wondered. He passed back into the cell. Ivanel sat on the bed with a look of utter and abject boredom on his face. Careful to remain out of sight of the door, Bjorn allowed himself to become visible.

"Bjorn!" Ivanel said.

"Shh!" Bjorn admonished. "The guard."

"Sorry," Ivanel said. "You startled me."

"Ivanel," Bjorn said, "what in Frigga's hell is going on here?"

"We have a problem," Ivanel said. "Mathen still lives. And he knows about you."

Bjorn sat up and stretched. He was always stiff after projecting for a long time.

This was *not* good. Mathen, the First Knight of the Hunt, had survived to follow Ian and Fjalin here where he had seen Bjorn's aura. He had immediately headed back to Reykvid, where he reported all of this to Gavin.

Now Gavin had convinced himself that Valerian had taken Bjorn's form to escape after his battle with Arcalion. It was actually a reasonable explanation, given the facts as Gavin knew them. Unfortunately, it also meant that Gavin felt it worthwhile to respond with force even this far from his lands.

Still, it would take time to march an army this far into the Wastes. And Gavin had other concerns, as well, with the placement of a new chieftain over the Sword clan. Bjorn doubted that Gavin could move against them until next spring.

Even so, they could not relocate. There was nowhere else for them to go, and if they did try to move on, they would be facing the same challenges that now faced Ian. Trying to feed an entire lodge on a few acres of cropland would not work.

No, they would have to face Gavin here. *That* was not a pleasant prospect. Bjorn's people could not withstand an assault from just a few hundred troops, and Gavin was likely to bring more than that.

Bjorn took the Silver Book from its shelf. It was no longer silver, but that was still how he thought of it. Valerian had removed the protective spell that had preserved it through the centuries, only to find a beginner's tutorial. Useless to him—priceless to Bjorn. Its secrets had already made the people of his lodge the most powerful magi in the world, and Bjorn the most powerful among them.

He had promised the others that he would hold back—that he would wait as they learned along with him. But this development made it more important than ever that he unlock the secrets within this tome.

Bjorn sat down at his desk and opened the book.

William walked down the stairs leading to the dungeon. He had spent much time thinking about his conversation with Ivanel almost ten days ago. No matter how he tried to find his way around Ivanel's arguments, his conscience kept bringing him to one conclusion.

Ivanel was right, and Gavin was wrong. Wrong to imprison his own uncle, and wrong to be persecuting his own people in the name of the Hunt. Ivanel was right. Mathen was using the king's own fear to control him, just as Valerian had once used sorcery.

The only question now was what to do about it. William would have no more luck convincing Gavin of his error than Ivanel had had before he was imprisoned. He stopped outside the door to Ivanel's cell and waited as the guard unlocked the door. He stepped into the cell as the guard closed the door behind him.

"Greetings, William," Ivanel said. "To what do I owe the pleasure of your company?"

"I have something I must ask you," William said.

"Oh?"

"Yes," William said. "I know that there are many who serve in the palace from your clan."

"So?"

"Are there any among the guards?" William added. "Particularly any who share your . . . crime? Any that I should *not* place in guard over your cell?"

"Do you honestly expect me to answer that?" Ivanel asked.

"I do," William said.

"I am sorry," Ivanel replied. "I cannot help you."

"You would not be helping me," William said. "You would be helping yourself."

"I don't under . . ." Ivanel began. His words trailed off as he suddenly realized that he *did* understand what William was asking him.

"I have your *sworn* word," Ivanel said, "that this information will not be used against any such individual?"

"Except for my assignation of dungeon guards," William agreed. "I so swear."

"And you will not pass this information on," Ivanel added.

"I swear to that as well," William agreed.

"Very well," Ivanel said. "There is one young man— Finn Unferthson. He has no family, but he is of the Circle."

"Very well," William said. "I shall be certain *not* to post him outside your cell. Good day, old friend."

"Good day to you, William," Ivanel replied. William turned and left the room, and Ivanel heard the guard close the bolt.

If William was planning what Ivanel suspected, that might be the last time he heard that sound.

• • •

Finn Unferthson stopped outside the door to the chambers assigned to Baron William. The guard on duty knocked and opened the door for him.

"You sent for me, my lord?" Finn asked.

"Yes," William said. "I understand that you are from Smithton?"

"That is correct, my lord," Finn replied.

"I have been working up the guard schedules for to-night," William said. "And I have assigned you to stand guard over your former chieftain, Ivanel."

"My lord," Finn said, "I would feel more comfortable if you assigned that duty to someone else."

"I am sorry to say that I cannot do that," William said. "Don't worry, lad. I have the utmost trust in you."

"Thank you, my lord," Finn replied.

"I am certain you would not try to help your former chieftain escape," William added.

"N-no, my lord!"

"Good," William said, nodding. "And I am certain you would never even *dream* of taking the time you have before your watch, which begins at midnight, to have two horses from the stables waiting outside the south postern gate for you and your lord to take flight after such an attempt. I mean, the horses would almost certainly be seen. Unless, of course, they were blackened with soot first."

"My lord?"

"Because, if you were foolish enough to do such a thing," William added, "you would have to go into exile with him yourself. And what man, with a promising military career, would do such a thing?"

"I-I . . . do not know, my lord," Finn replied.

"So I am certain that I can count on you," William concluded. "I *can* count on you, can't I, Finn?"

"Yes, my lord!" Finn replied.

"Good man," William said. "You are dismissed."

"My lord!" Finn replied. He left William's chambers much more confused than when he had entered. If he did not know better, he would think that William had just *ordered* him to help Ivanel escape.

He had best hurry. He only had two hours before midnight.

Ivanel rose to his feet at the sound of the door being unlocked. Finn Unferthson stood in the doorway.

"My lord," he whispered.

"Finn?"

"My lord," Finn said, "we must hurry."

"Let me guess," Ivanel said. "William put you on guard duty in the dungeon?"

"Aye sir," Finn replied. "After explaining what a bad idea it would be to help you escape and exactly *which* method of escape would probably be a bad idea to try. Do you think 'tis a trap?"

"Somehow, I think not," Ivanel said. "Lead on."

"Yes, my lord," Finn said.

William was awakened early by a loud and insistent banging on his door.

"Come in, confound it!" he shouted, sitting up in the bed. A guard opened the door.

"My lord," the guard said, almost shouting in panic, "Baron Ivanel has escaped!"

"What!" William exclaimed, clambering out of the bed. "How? When?"

"We are not certain, my lord," the guard replied. "The guard found the dungeon empty this morning. There is no sign of his guard, and two horses are missing from the stables."

"Who was watching him last night?" William demanded.

"Finn Unferthson, lord," the guard replied. "He is originally from Smithton."

"Damn!" William shouted. "Find them! I want a dozen patrols out looking for them before I can get dressed. Find them, or the king is going to have my hide! And I shall have *yours*!''

''Yes, my lord!'' the guard replied, hastily leaving the room. William began to dress—leisurely.

I hope you have the good sense to ride hard, my friend, he thought.

CHAPTER

------- TWENTY-FOUR ------------

"MY LORD, WE'LL be recognized," Finn said, looking about nervously as he and Ivanel led their horses through the south gate.

"Oh?" Ivanel said. "Have you been to Star Lake before, Finn?"

"No, my lord," Finn replied.

"Neither have I," Ivanel said. "I doubt we'll be recognized. We'll take rooms here. A friend of mine knows the proprietor."

Ivanel had stopped under the sign of the Ship's Star Inn.

"We don't have much money, my lord," Finn objected. "This looks like a fine inn."

"We will correct that problem once we've gotten rooms," Ivanel assured him. "Come along."

Finn followed Ivanel into the inn. If Ivanel knew the innkeeper, he did not give any sign of it. He simply asked for a room for himself and his son, meaning Finn. Ivanel paid the innkeeper, and, after stabling the horses, they were back in the streets of the city.

"Where are we going, now?" Finn asked.

"To visit a moneychanger," Ivanel replied. "Stop asking questions, Finn! You're more nervous than a spring hare."

"My apologies, lord," Finn said. Ivanel stepped into another inn and asked the innkeeper for directions to the counting house of Feithel the moneychanger. For never having been to Star Lake, Ivanel seemed well acquainted with its businesses.

If Feithel's counting house were any indication, the moneychanger did quite a business. The counting house, and Feithel's home, occupied an entire three-floor building. Ivanel walked through the front door.

The man who looked up from behind the tall counter must have been Feithel. Finn noticed the two armed guards who stood crisply at attention to either side of the door. Ivanel removed his signet and handed it to the moneychanger.

"I believe you have a thousand gold measures on deposit for me," Ivanel said. Finn could not stop his mouth from falling open in surprise. A thousand measures!

"That is correct, m'lord," Feithel replied, handing Ivanel's signet back. "How may I help you?"

"I need to withdraw all but a hundred measures," Ivanel said.

"That will take a little time," Feithel told him.

"I understand," Ivanel said. "How much can you give me now?"

The gnomish little man consulted a ledger for a moment.

"A hundred measures now," Feithel replied.

"That will do for today," Ivanel agreed. "Can you have the rest for me by morning?"

"I believe so, m'lord," Feithel replied, scribbling in the ledger. "By tomorrow afternoon at the latest."

"That will do nicely," Ivanel said. Finn watched as the moneychanger counted out a hundred gold sovereigns. Ivanel scooped them into a bag, which disappeared into his cloak. Finn followed Ivanel out into the street.

"If you've never been to Star Lake," he said, "why do you have so much money here?"

"When this nonsense began with the Hunt, I thought it might be best to set aside some funds in a secure place," Ivanel replied. "They were deposited for me by Arik."

"Why are you leaving a hundred here?"

"Moneychangers don't like to give you back *all* of your money," Ivanel explained. "Especially when it is a large amount. I'll get the last hundred before we leave. 'Twill be less painful that way. Come, we have some purchases to make before we go back to our room.''

Arik waited in the underground cellar. He and the others from Smithton shared the crude earthen cellar with another dozen refugees from Star Hall, Ravenhall and even a few from the Boar clan. Sixteen, all in all. As far as Arik knew, this was the single largest group to wait on the ship.

And there was a good chance that even more would be arriving before the ship got here. Captain Oslaf would not be happy. More than likely the latest arrivals, including himself, would have to wait for the next ship.

That would not be pleasant. Now Arik knew how things felt from the victim's point of view. He had only been forced to remain here for three days, and the confinement was already grating on him.

The trap door above opened.

Oh, Bairn! Arik thought. *Please don't let it be more refugees. We're packed in here like cattle already.*

Chances were that more refugees would arrive before the ship did, however. According to their landlord, it would be at least another sevennight before the ship arrived.

The two men who climbed down the ladder wore armor and carried weapons. Arik rose to his feet. He had not heard any sounds of alarm from above. The first man, a boy really, looked familiar. The second man, older, was one he knew well.

''My lord!'' Arik said, stepping up to Ivanel.

''Arik!'' Ivanel said. ''I was hoping to find you here.''

''Greetings, my lord,'' Eva said, also stepping up to the ladder.

''Eva,'' Ivanel said, taking Eva's hands in his own. ''Thank the gods you made it out. Wiegel? Is that you?''

''Aye, my lord,'' Wiegel replied, rising to his feet. He was fully armored, as if he had just come off his shift. ''Me and Orlas.''

''My lord, how did you escape?'' Arik asked. ''The last

I heard, you were a prisoner in Gavin's dungeons.''

"William made the mistake of assigning Finn here to guard me," Ivanel explained. "We were out of the palace less than an hour after his shift started."

"Unferth's son?" Arik asked, turning to Finn.

"Yes, Guardian," Finn replied.

"Good work, lad!"

"How many did we lose?" Ivanel asked before Finn could stammer out a reply.

"Three before I left Smithton," Arik replied, turning back to Ivanel.

"It could have been worse," Ivanel said quietly.

"We have at least another sevennight before the ship returns from Nalur's Ridge," Arik said. "And I don't think that Captain Oslaf is going to agree to take this entire group."

"We won't be waiting for him," Ivanel said.

"My lord?"

"I have been to the docks," Ivanel explained. "There is a small longship we can purchase. We'll be leaving the morning after tomorrow. We might as well take these people with us."

"It is *good* to have you back, my lord," Arik said, smiling.

"It is good to *be* back, Arik," Ivanel replied.

"Escaped!" Gavin shouted. William dropped to his knees and bowed his head, avoiding Gavin's angry gaze.

" 'Tis my fault, majesty," William said. "I assigned a soldier named Finn Unferthson to guard him. The next morning both he and Ivanel were gone as were two of the horses from the stables."

"Who was this guard?" Gavin asked.

"After the escape, I learned that he was from Smithton," William said. "Majesty, I accept full responsibility for this disaster and throw myself at your mercy."

"Majesty," Mathen said, "it is obvious that this man Finn was one of your uncle's coconspirators. I don't think the blame for this tragedy lies with Baron William. His grace can not be faulted for not knowing the background of your guards.''

My thanks, you pompous toad, William thought.

''Do you have any idea where he went?'' Gavin asked.

''No majesty,'' William replied. ''Ivanel hid his trail well. Our men could not pick it up. I sent word to Northguard, but no one there reported seeing him.''

''He would not try to return to Smithton,'' Mathen said. ''Not knowing that your majesty was there in force. I would guess he went straight to Star Lake.''

''Of course!'' Gavin said. ''Mathen, I wish you to leave for Star Lake immediately. See if you can find word of my uncle there.''

''Yes, majesty,'' Mathen said. ''I shall depart as soon as I leave here.''

''You may rise, William,'' Gavin said. ''You had no way of knowing that Finn was a traitor. These people have always been good at slipping through the cracks.''

''They excel at it, majesty,'' Mathen agreed.

''Depart for Star Lake at once,'' Gavin said. Mathen bowed to the king and left the throne room. Gavin rose from the throne once the priest had left.

''William, come with me,'' Gavin ordered. ''We have to discuss the campaign against Valerian.''

''Yes, majesty,'' William replied.

Arik supervised the loading of the new longship. As Ivanel had warned, it was not large—only fifty feet from bow to stern. The cabin would only hold two, Ivanel and himself. Everyone else would have to sleep in the crew quarters below deck.

Of all of them, only Ivanel and Arik had any sailing experience. Fortunately, this was only a short river trip, and working the oars was not difficult to learn. With only the one mast, Ivanel and Arik could handle the sails.

The two horses had gone into the hold, and now supplies for their trip were being loaded aboard. Ivanel planned to buy wagons and additional horses in Nalur's Ridge. Arik went below with the refugees to supervise the securing of their cargo.

The hold was mostly empty. Two moons of food for eighteen adults and nine children did not take up a lot of room as far as a ship was concerned. Even with the horses, they still had room for a larger cargo.

"Is everything ready?" Ivanel asked as Arik returned to the main deck.

"Yes, my lord," Arik replied.

"Then man the oars and let's get out of here."

He turned and waved to the dockhands below, who removed the mooring ropes from the pilings of the dock and cast them onto the deck. Arik turned back to the crew.

The ship was severely undermanned. Six men manned the oars on each side of the longship—barely enough to man half the oars at two men to an oar. Arik climbed to the top of the cabin.

"Deploy starboard oars!" he shouted. "Portside, push off!"

The men on the starboard side of the ship lowered their oars into the water and began to row. Arik called out the cadence to the rowers as the men on the port side of the ship used long poles to keep the ship away from the dock.

With almost painful slowness, the longship backed away from the dock.

"Deploy stern portside oar!" Arik shouted once the stern of the longship had cleared the dock. Two of the men on the port side sat and manned their oar. This lessened the tendency of the ship to turn to port. Still, the men at the fore had to work hard to keep the longship away from the dock. Ivanel stood at the tiller, forcing the ship back to starboard.

"Deploy portside oars!" Arik shouted once they had cleared the dock. The last four men on the port side took their oars and began to row in time with Arik's cadence.

Ivanel brought the tiller back to center as the ship backed slowly, but smoothly, away from the dock and into the lake.

Arik turned to watch the dock retreat as he continued to call the cadence.

"Ship oars!" he commanded once they were more than far enough from the dock. Six oars lifted from the water and were hauled back onto the deck.

"Oarsmen, face stern!" Arik shouted and the rowers changed benches, placing their backs to the fore of the ship. They lacked the smoothness of some of the crews Arik had seen in the past, but at least they had all remembered what to do.

"Deploy oars!" Arik shouted. Six oars bit the water.

"Wheel to port!" Arik commanded. The crew lost it. Oarsmen pushed against each other's efforts, and the ship went nowhere.

"Rest oars!" Arik commanded. The crew lifted their oars from the water.

"All right, you oafs!" Arik shouted. "When I say 'wheel to port,' that means the oarsmen on the starboard side row normally." Facing the bow, Arik gestured to the men on starboard with his right hand.

"And the oarsmen on the port side *push* against the oars," he added, gesturing to his left. "Do you think you can manage to *do* that this time?"

A few muttered "ayes" reached him.

"Deploy oars!" Arik waited as the men got their oars back into the water.

"Wheel to port!" The ship began to slowly turn to port. The men on the starboard side were able to get more leverage, and the ship pulled forward a bit as it turned.

"Rest oars!" Arik commanded, once their turn was complete.

"All ahead!" Arik shouted before the oars had been fully lifted from the water. The ship moved forward as all of the oarsmen put their backs into the oars together. Arik continued to call the cadence as he descended from the cabin roof to the deck.

Arik glanced up at the banner flying from the mast. The wind was at their backs—good. He untied the mainsheet

and lowered the square sail, which immediately caught the
wind.

The ship lurched forward, breaking the oarsmen's
rhythm as Arik pulled the sail down and tied off the mainsheet.

"Secure oars!" Arik called. The men pulled up the oars
and laid them on the deck in front of the benches. They
started to rise from the benches.

"Tie those oars *down*, you idiots!" Arik shouted. Arik
watched as the men sat and tied down the oars. Again they
started to rise from the benches.

"Did I *say* you were dismissed?" Arik shouted. They
all sat back down on the benches. Arik walked between the
rows of rowing benches, slowly. The crew looked away
from his gaze except for the guardsmen from Smithton.
They patiently waited for their orders.

"Dismissed!" Arik finally shouted. "Finn, take the till."

"Yes, my lord," Finn replied.

Arik turned to the east as the sun broke over the horizon.
This was much better than waiting in that cellar for another
sevennight. Ivanel walked up beside him.

"They didn't do too badly," he noted.

"True," Arik agreed. "We may survive this trip yet."

Fjalin walked into Brand's store. There were no customers.

"Fjalin!" Brand said. "How was your trip?"

"Tiring," Fjalin said. "But otherwise uneventful."

"Good," Brand said. "Another group is waiting."

"*Another* one?" Fjalin replied. "Already?"

"I fear so," Brand said.

"Brand, we've got to get someone else to rotate this
chore out with," Fjalin said. "Maybe someone from Ian-
shall can come down once a moon or something. People
are going to wonder."

"I agree," Brand said. "Perhaps you can talk to Ian
about it and see if there's someone he can send down every
moon."

"I'll do that," Fjalin said. "There's one other thing."

"What?"

"Ian wants to know if we can loan him a team of oxen until first snow," Fjalin said. "He's having a hard time clearing all of that land."

"I'll see what I can manage," Brand replied. "Why don't you go home and get some rest?"

"You'll get no argument from me," Fjalin said. He left Brand's shop and headed for his father's farm. He could also ask his father about lending Ian an ox team.

Brianna stood over the fire cooking breakfast with Ingrid and Wilhelmina, Ohthere's oldest daughter.

"Good morning!" someone called from down the trail. Stefan and Ohthere were on their feet quickly to meet whoever was coming. Brand walked into the clearing with another man. Between them, they led four oxen, yoked into teams of two. Brianna wondered at this, because the oxen were not pulling anything.

"Is this our guide?" Stefan asked.

"Yes," Brand replied. "This is Fjalin. He will be leading you to your new home."

Home? Brianna thought. Could it be true?

"Is this our last journey?" she asked.

"Yes," their guide replied.

She looked at the others. Ingrid and Nolan looked relieved more than anything else. The others seemed to share her excitement, though.

"What's it like?" Brianna asked, turning back to the guide.

"Not much, yet," Fjalin said. "But 'tis growing. They should have started on the lodge by now."

"What's a lodge?" young Jason asked.

"A large house," Fjalin replied. "Where all of the people of the clan live. A hall."

"Oh, that's wonderful!" Brianna exclaimed.

"How long will it take to get there?" Stefan asked.

"Approximately three sevennights," Fjalin replied. "So we had best get started—after breakfast."

Brianna returned to the preparation of their meal. The camp, which had before been silent, was now filled with excited conversation.

They were going *home*!

Ian inspected the construction of the lodge. It was much more complex than the barn. The barn had been a simple shell. The stalls within it would eventually be fashioned of wood.

The lodge, on the other hand, had rooms to build in. Not many—a few storerooms, the chieftain's chambers, some private chambers for other high-ranking clansmen and a council chamber. They had decided to duplicate the design of Bjornshall for no better reason than that they knew it.

The stone foundations had finally been brought up level with the ground. The floor of the lodge would be thick planks cut from the numerous pine trees that had been felled. Save for the stone-lined firepits and the bed of the kiln, of course.

As a result of these additions, the lodge would take much longer to build than the barn. Ian had hoped to get another barn erected before winter. Now it did not look as though that would be possible.

Over all of this hung the shadow of his father's imprisonment by Gavin. Any hopes he might have nurtured of returning home had been dashed by the news of his father's capture.

Now he was indeed alone. On his shoulders rested the responsibility of protecting the magi and finding a way to deal with the arrival of Gavin's forces in the spring.

There was nowhere else for them to go. The magi had fled as far as they could. Ian looked around at the short stone walls that would become his lodge. Here they would have to make their stand. Right now he felt more like a little boy than a clan chief.

"Bairn protect us," he whispered.

EPILOGUE

THE APPRENTICE WALKED through the marble-columned halls to the throne room. The Call had woken him from his enchanted slumber. He wondered how long it had been *this* time. How long had he slept before the Lord had found need of him? Years? Decades? Perhaps even centuries.

He entered the throne room as the gilded doors swung open before him. Along the walls, massive murals were framed in gold. The first depicted a simple stone lodge in a winter forest. In another, massive armies marched while a town burned on the horizon. Above them all a man rode through the sky on a mighty dragon.

Another painting depicted the same massive dragon looming over a mighty castle, breathing fire. In yet another, a screaming woman was tied to a burning stake while the bodies of her children lay at her feet on the pyre.

Raoul knew that these were not merely paintings. They showed events that had been foretold and that either had come to pass or would soon come to pass. In another mural, a lone man rode on horseback across an endless plain of grass toward a peculiar domed city on the horizon. In the distance, another mounted figure followed him.

In the last mural before the throne, a great House rose from the desert. Portions of the House were whole and fresh, while others crumbled into ruin.

Behind the throne was the final mural of another great House rising from a winter forest. Raoul knelt before the radiant personage that sat on the throne above him.

"You Called, my Lord?" he asked.

"Yes, Raoul," the Lord replied. "It is almost time. Rouse the House and prepare the Circle for battle."